GW00458662

IMPULSUM

Megan Daisy

ISBN: 9798720477769

Chapter 1

Last night had been the start of it all. Most people were tucked up in bed for a restful night's sleep, blissfully unaware of how much their lives would change in the next few months. Out in the Meru National Park, Jaylen knew something was off the second Rocco started acting up. It wasn't like him, the German Shepherd was usually calm and obedient, helping shield him from the potential dangers out here in the open, but in the crisp evening air he had stood to attention, ears pricked and staring over the empty field ahead. When Jaylen moved towards him, Rocco's gaze snapped back, and he was once again the happy two-year-old that had accompanied him on many of these late-night perimeter checks. He crouched down to stroke the dog and could still feel the tension in his small body. Something was out there. Something wasn't right. Rocco growled at the small lake to the left, but Jaylen couldn't see anything. His growling intensified into aggressive barking but eventually calmed again, as if it had vanished. Probably a bird, he thought to himself. Pushing it to the back of his mind, Jaylen walked back to the house, Rocco taking up his usual position, sniffing anything and everything, tail wagging in contentment.

Once morning came, nothing seemed out of the ordinary. After his walk, Jaylen had joined a group of returning British tourists for drinks and inevitably, that was all he could remember. He woke to the sound of little Nia Mwangi reading his Uncle's papers again, reminded of why his Aunt had told him to burn them before curious children believed what had been written in them. The same phrases he had heard over and over again caught his attention and he groaned. One day that girl would find a hobby.

"Did he say you could read that?" Aluna's voice rand out from the back door. Having the usual impact, her presence caused Nia to slam the laptop lid shut and go to leave the room, most likely heading back to whatever duties her scientific curiosity had distracted her from. That was typical for Nia, always getting distracted. But the two friends owed her family a favour, so continued letting her help while her parents were working and begrudgingly cooked her dinner three nights a week.

"Rise and shine, *Kaka*, you're supposed to be giving tours," sang Aluna, throwing a handwoven pillow at the hungover man. Despite their long-term friendship, he would have happily strangled her if it meant just a few more hours with his eyes shut on the sofa. His plans were foiled, however by the realisation that, if anything happened to her, it would leave him to deal with Nia alone. He'd also have to give up his precious nights of partying in order to get anything done.

The resulting groan let Aluna know Jaylen was really not in the mood. The effects of last night's events were fully hitting him now, and he was not nearly drunk enough to deal with the next influx of over-excitable children who thought wild animals were the same as their household pets. One day he would probably end up letting one of them lose an arm, or maybe just a finger, so the others would stop asking him to let them cuddle a lion cub.

"You're not going away, are you, *Dada*?" he mumbled, and Aluna grinned cheekily, knowing that her task of human alarm clock was complete. When she turned around, Nia was back at the laptop again, her thirst for knowledge overtaking her nerves. Her reading caught his ear again and his Uncle's crazed words filled the room. Mass extinction. Human ignorance. Silver spirals. Denial. International crisis. It would take an absolute moron to believe any of it.

"Jaylen, what are these silver spirals?" Nia looked confused for a second and silently, Aluna wanted to knock some sense into her. There was nothing but nonsense in this research, Zaiden Hatfield was a raging lunatic. It was a miracle that, despite his passion for drinking, Jaylen seemed to have avoided inheriting any of the family's crazy gene.

"It's just gibberish, Nia. *Upuuzi*. He's probably just ranting about some piece of art or other rubbish. He used to collect rare paintings. Stupid habit for a supposedly respectable scientist, collecting junk like that."

"Junk. You remember that, *Mtoto*? The junk I asked you to move from the front entrance to the warehouse. Yesterday? We'll need the free space to get the plane ready. Etana hasn't had power in over a week, we're going to help her fix it."

Etana ran a small bed-and-breakfast outside the park, and without power she would have no opportunities to filter water or to store food for the guests. It had been a week since she had sent out a distress signal via radio, and it had taken all of that time to find the tools and hire a plane to go out and fix the problem. Aluna hoped that there had been a temporary solution put in place to hold them out until this afternoon when they couldn't fix the power. Otherwise, it could have serious implications on her business, the family's only source of income.

It was an effort and the result of multiple strong coffees, but Jaylen brought himself round enough to get a car full of tourists, as predicted mostly consisting of families with children who were seeing this environment for the first time, out into the park. It was eerily quiet. Normally, there would have been at least one other vehicle out, especially with it being the peak season. Not that he was complaining. The other unusual thing to note was that, despite the perfect weather and the lack of human activity, there was almost no movement coming from the surrounding grasses. Not even the familiar buzz from the insects or occasional glimpse of a bird up in the bright blue sky. There were no signs of animals lurking in the bushes or locals going about their day. With an unfamiliar sense of unease setting in, Jaylen was glad to have Aluna there with him. He would trust that girl with his life. She had saved it on multiple previous occasions.

Chapter 2

Caroline and Lyla were walking home. They'd been out in their local nightclub until closing time, and now the cold air was dulling the effects of the four rounds of shots they'd taken. No one could blame them for that. Pamela had just come into her inheritance and decided it was her duty to treat them. The discussion had turned to the absolute failure that was their current dating lives and their pathetic attempts to find men that evening. Of course, Pamela had left early with a tall, muscular man on her arm. It wasn't their fault; the two younger girls tried to reassure themselves with little luck. Surely, they'd just picked the wrong night, the wrong group to hang out with or were just simply in a long run of bad luck. The wind rushed down the street and Caroline cursed herself for not thinking to take a jacket with her. She half contemplated calling her father, but knew he'd be furious at her for not taking one in the first place and for walking home drunk in the dark dressed, as he would say, like a stripper. He was paranoid; they were only a five-minute walk from their apartment building thanks to the shortcut Lyla had found.

A little orange tabby cat darted out from the shadows and across their path and Lyla grinned, evidently forgetting that, when sober, cats scared the living daylights out of her. She suddenly went pale and stepped behind a nearby dumpster, most likely to throw up the contents of an evening she probably wouldn't even remember. Caroline walked further ahead and stopped to wait for her friend, scrolling through her Instagram waiting for Lyla to catch up. Pamela had posted a cute picture of the three of them and Caroline liked it, leaving three fire emojis in the comment section. Kaleb had liked it too, and she wished then that he'd been with her in the club. She'd ask him to go with them next time. Lyla was taking ages, Caroline noticed, and she glared at her watch.

But Lyla was no longer following her. She had stood up, wiping her mouth on the tiny blue lace top she had worn to the club and was no face to face with an actual, live, crocodile. Her first through was that she had already passed out, and this was some alcohol induced nightmare. Her second was that crocodiles were a lot larger in real life than on television. Then she felt the reptile's warm breath right on her face. She turned around to see that another had Caroline cornered. That was when she screamed. And the crocodile struck.

It was all over the news by morning, Annabelle noticed. Crocodiles breaking out of sanctuary and killing two girls in an alley. It was miracle they hadn't hurt anyone else. Not the sort of thing anyone expects to hear while they're forcing themselves to get up for class. It almost distracted her from the fact that she'd once again completely forgotten her assignment was due and she was already on thin ice with the academic board. Fighting personal injustices, however, necessary, apparently wasn't an excuse for her horrific performances this term, and if she was being honest, Annabelle wouldn't blame them if they kicked her out this time. But she'd held on before, and her incredible ability to ace exams without putting in nearly as much work as she'd have liked, kept her average grade twelve percentage points above failing. Although that was unlikely to be good enough at Oxford.

She took a seat at the back of the lecture theatre, needing to at least finish the morning's investigation before the man at the front realised, she was there and interrogated her about a missing essay or two. Maybe more than that. No. She had to find answers. It was too much of a coincidence, all the interviews seemed too much like hastily constructed cover stories to be the truth. Animals don't just figure out how to escape a secure compound where they had everything they could want, and then go on a killing spree. This was exactly like before, strange events occurring in nature with no logical reason, which in Annabelle's mind was concrete proof that she was right. Someone knew more than they were letting on. She had pages and pages of documents there on her computer, on one side the official report of yesterday's tragedy, on the other, a list of expenditure reports. Spotting patterns was one of her strengths.

She'd emailed as many people as she could think of as soon as she'd first heard the story, and the responses were as vague as she had been expecting. If they really believed what they were spouting, they'd sound more confident, they'd be able to expand on details but there were no details, not really. All anyone had to say was some variation of 'we don't know what happened, just leave us alone'. Annabelle suspected she was gaining a less than stellar reputation amongst potentially dodgy business owners, but she'd rather that than believe the ridiculousness that had the rest of the country fooled. Somehow, she had to get justice for her father.

It was a surprise when, despite her distractions, she was able to continue her frantic perusal for the rest of the lecture without being noticed, called upon or even spoken to by a fellow student. Annabelle supposed that after a term of being the 'weird library girl' the rest of the cohort had gotten used to her not wanting any attention. Her very public breakup with Madison had done nothing to boost her popularity.

She had planned out an entire day of research, people to find and talk to in desperation for some sort of concrete proof. This could be the big break she needed. All that suddenly came to a halt when Julius called her name out from the front of the hall.

"Annabelle Summers, I need to see you in my office." All eyes turned to her, and she felt her face redden.

Well, that couldn't be good. She had never heard a lecturer summon someone like that before. Usually, they sent messages out via email.

The office was larger than she had expected and somewhat comfortable, although despite three patterned armchairs she was not permitted to take a seat. That was definitely the second clue things were not working in her favour. The third was the angry expression on Julius' face.

"Miss Summers, are you aware that of the four assignments I have given you this term, not a single one is here on my desk?" His eyes were boring into her and she wished he would look away or even blink.

Annabelle didn't have an answer, at least not one that would be appropriate for this situation. Instead, she opted for just staring blankly at him. In response, Julius pulled up a spreadsheet.

"Miss Summers, here are your marks for this term. As far as I can tell, none of your other lecturers have logged a grade for you from any of your six modules. Yet you sit in every lecture typing notes at breakneck speed. Or can I assume that these are not notes you are typing?"

"They are notes." Technically Annabelle wasn't lying, the pages of detailed summaries she had in her bag proved that, but they weren't exactly on the topic of law.

"This, Miss Summers, is the university server your laptop uses to access the internet," he paused for a second to take a sheet of paper out from a folder sat in front of him. "Read this for me, the underlined section."

Annabelle gulped silently and took the printout from his hands. It was a scan she'd made of her handwritten notes in the library last night, covered in scribbles, highlighted words and annotations, her overtired brain desperate to make the connection between the Northmoor deaths and these. "Prime Minister behind mass cover up. Potential US deal. Contaminated water supplies causing animals to target vulnerable humans. Sir, why am I here? This is nothing to do with my schoolwork."

"Evidently. Miss Summers, are you aware that it is the very government you insult that run this institution? This ridiculousness is against almost all of our policies, and you posted it on a server everyone at the university has access to.

It is the decision of the board they will be suspending you until you can submit some genuine work. Then they will decide if you have learnt your lesson. Get out of my office."

Chapter 3

They had finally gathered their supplies onto the plane and depart to help Etana. Aluna was flying, being the only trained pilot in the area, a skill that had so far proven to be invaluable. Jaylen wasn't sure exactly what skills he brought to the table, but the camp managers didn't need to know that. His Aunt had brought him to Kenya as a child, after his Uncle's actions had led her to fear for their safety. It had been a big change and until he had found Aluna, Jaylen had been extremely lonely. So, when she started working at the same camp his Aunt worked at, Jaylen made the decision and went with her. Some days he wondered what his life would be like if he still lived in Michigan. Would he have a regular office job? Would he be working in science like his Uncle had pushed him towards? Would he have even considered having a brilliant young woman like Aluna as his best friend? Probably not.

"Jaylen, we really need to do something about Nia. She has so much potential that is just wasted with busywork and childish fantasies. I've not seen a child that curious in a long time."

That was typical. Aluna always saw the good in people. Jaylen couldn't do that. His life experience had taught him that people couldn't just be good, they usually had some ulterior motive.

"Do we really need to go over this again? If she really wants to get somewhere in life, she needs to get her nose out of those old papers and start learning real facts. Things that are actually valuable. Everything on that laptop is less than useful, nothing more than complete and utter nonsense. It's the journal of my Uncle's descent into insanity."

"Your Uncle was brilliant, absolutely off his rocker, but brilliant. There must be some glimmer of truth buried in those papers and if anyone can find it, Nia can." As usual, Aluna was probably right and as they began their descent onto the small grass covered airfield Jaylen pondered what that might mean for them all. There was no chance his Uncle's theories were completely right, every academic he'd ever shown them to had dismissed them outright. It went against everything they already knew about life on this planet, everything that humanity used to survive another day. He couldn't contemplate the possibility of death on two cups of coffee and minimal sleep.

Etana's bed-and-breakfast was on the outskirts of Kinna and consisted of ten naturally styled cabins and a main reception building. Less popular with tourists than your standard fancy hotels with floodlit pools and built-in spa facilities,

Etana relied on the current season, and the generosity of her friends to feed and clothe her three children. It was the way things worked around here, local people pitching in and helping each other when things were hard.

All looked normal as the two friends walked up the dirt track. Unlike this morning's venture, the chirping of birds and the faint sound of crickets filled the air, relieving the earlier tension. What was less normal, however, was the complete and utter lack of people. On every other visit to the area Etana had greeted Jaylen and Aluna with iced cocktails and fruit platters, the older woman always grateful for the company. Assuming she was dealing with a dramatic guest or two, the friends continued on to the main entrance, not yet spotting any sign of human activity.

Jaylen halted when he caught his foot on something. Looking down, a dusty blue rucksack lay forgotten, and a sense of unease set in. It was small, as if it belonged to a visiting child. There were signs up everywhere reminding people not to leave their belongings lying around. Mainly to avoid losing things but also to protect the large volume of wildlife that visited the camp. To see someone's bag lying like this, as if thrown aside in panic, was unsettling.

It only became more suspicious when they opened the door and inhaled the horrific stench of rotting food. What appeared to be a breakfast buffet had obviously been left out for days. Half-eaten plates covered the tables and spilled juices stained the white tablecloths. Jaylen could see hundreds of flies buzzing around everything, and it became a challenge just to open his mouth without accidently swallowing one. The smell was causing his eyes to water and bile rose in his throat.

The latest iPhone lay on a nearby table, and he picked it up. Thankfully, the owner had not seen the sense to put a password on it, and the image of a happy couple with their two children faded into the background. Bringing up the photos, Jaylen found evidence of a seemingly uneventful work trip. The owner of this phone appeared to be your average business executive staying at Etana's for a few nights to avoid paying the higher prices associated with staying in the more well-known hotels. He let out a hiss of pain as his finger caught on a shard of broken glass. Turning the phone over, he noticed cracks stemming from the lower left corner where there was an almost circular hole.

Acting on a hunch, Aluna walked towards the office. The smell of rotting food lessened the further she went down the hallway and there was a slightly hopeful voice in her mind that Etana would still be in there, that she could explain the scene they had just witnessed. Maybe some kind of infestation had caused the guests to eat in their cabins. The door was already open, the wood splintering around large dents. It appeared as though something or someone had been slammed into it. She couldn't see Etana anywhere. A faint humming noise caught her attention, and a thought came to the front of her mind. Ready to test her theory, Aluna pulled the string just inside the doorframe and the lights came on. The power was working as normal. There was something else going on here. Etana's phone call had described a total blackout, failed backup generators and a lack of air conditioning in the guest cabins.

Jaylen suddenly appeared in the doorway looking determined and went to switch on the computer system. It started up instantly, showing footage from the security cameras that surrounded the buildings. Someone had paused the feed, capturing the seven-thirty breakfast slot the morning after Etana had phoned for help. Rewinding it a few minutes, the two friends watched what appeared to be the outdoor eating area, lightly populated with guests. Suddenly, a wooden structure on the right of the screen fell over, and then people were screaming and running fast in the other direction. Etana was among them, shepherding the younger guests to safety. But whatever had caused the terror was not visible from the cameras, and there were no others for this area. Jaylen turned to look at Aluna, whose face had gone pale.

"We need to go get a car. Maybe we can find some guests or the staff, see if they can tell us what happened. There might still be people out there who need help." He agreed with her and together they walked back out of the building. There were seven cars on the property, and they loaded their things into the back. As they pulled out of the covered parking, Aluna could see huge dents like the ones in the office door covering other surfaces. What had happened here?

Chapter 4

After the disaster of that morning, Annabelle put her personal issues out of her mind for now and continued digging into the crocodile attacks. At some point she would have to deal with her academic situation, but this was more pressing. Her first stop was the village of Alvescot, where the sanctuary manager lived. He had made a Facebook post earlier that day, containing details of the party he was throwing. She wondered what sort of person he was if his response to teenage girls being torn apart by the creatures he looked after was to throw a party. At least when this had happened in other places the people involved had just covered it up, not started celebrating.

Securing a parking spot that hopefully wouldn't lead her to a fine she seriously couldn't afford right now; Annabelle took in the picturesque cottage. Sanctuary managers evidently made more money than she had predicted. There were balloons surrounding the front garden and guests were piling in. Wow. The number of apparently insensitive people in this neighbourhood was astounding. Back home, people had some sort of compassion.

Everything about this situation was ringing alarm bells in her head. Why had nobody else noticed what she had? The police should be everywhere right now, trying to stop more people, more innocent teenagers, from being eaten alive. Even the thought of being outside in the dark was beginning to scare her and she made a quick resolution to stay in her flat after sunset for the foreseeable future.

It didn't take her long to find her way into the back garden. Someone had set two tables up and piled both high with various foods. Had her reasons for being there been different, she would have sampled a few. A small group of giggling children were picking shamelessly at the plate of orange frosted cupcakes. Mr. Travis McKnight was currently standing in the far corner talking to a small group of official looking adults, most likely concocting another abysmal cover-up story. The least they could do was make their attempts believable.

All social niceties out the window, Annabelle strode quickly towards them. He knew who she was. The number of email and phone conversations they'd engaged in made sure of that. As soon as he spotted her, his face contorted in anger.

Annabelle didn't have an answer to that. She had a friend who was rather adept at finding well-hidden documents and hacking into private servers. Without Alessandra, she wouldn't have half of this information.

"You don't deny it, Mr. McKnight."

"The animal protection laws dictate ever decision made at the sanctuary Summers. If we broke those laws, the board would shut us down for good. This wasn't our fault, sometimes these things just happen." He paused for a second, looking over her shoulder at a little boy crying. "If you're so into finding conspiracy theories, then maybe you want to investigate that."

"And what is that exactly?" Annabelle replied, trying to at least act civil.

"Every pet in the local area has mysteriously vanished. And not just cats and dogs either, rabbits, guinea pigs, even some farm animals. The police think there's a serial animal abductor, but nobody's been spotted. It has devastated all our children and we decided to throw a party to cheer them up. Now if you don't mind, get out and stop ruining it!"

Begrudgingly Annabelle left the garden, having learned nothing new. She would have been better off getting more documents from Alessandra and analysing data than trying to get any information out of the people involved. As for the pets, unless they started attacking their owners while they slept, they were of little interest to the cause.

Luckily for her, no parking official had been around to issue a fine, and as she slammed the door shut, she rested her head on the steering wheel in despair. What was she going to do now? This had bene her biggest lead in seven months, and Annabelle wasn't sure she could wait that long again. The situation was getting increasingly dangerous, more and more people were dying, and no-one was doing anything to stop it. What would happen if it got worse? Crocodiles were easy to spot in the daylight and it had only been two of them. If venomous spiders started killing people, then things would escalate to a level Annabelle wasn't even sure she could imagine. She had to make someone listen to her, find someone who knew deep down that these events were in no way normal.

Chapter 5

After half an hour of searching, the two friends had found nothing. There was no evidence of anyone lost or stranded, and the two locals they had asked knew nothing about what had occurred. They were ready to turn back and fly over with the plane for a better view when Jaylen noticed a crumbling building on their left. The grass appeared trampled down slightly, and whoever had been there last had left the door ajar.

"Aluna, what exactly is that?" he asked, having never been this far out before.

"I think it's one of the old school buildings, let's have a look in case anyone made it this far and took refuge." Jaylen had to remind himself that was unlikely. Making it all the way with the heat and no water was almost impossible.

They didn't leave the safety of the car without some protection. Aluna had pulled the gun out from under the front seat and kept her body between Jaylen and the school. Out of the two, she was the better shot. Once he had armed himself and prepared to leave the two set off through the grass, eyes peeled for any potential threats. Having grown up in a small village near Etana's, Aluna knew all too well how unpredictable and dangerous the environment away from settlements could be. There was also the minor detail that whatever had caused terror at the cabins could still be out there.

It was her who noticed it first. A boot lying in the grass, wet drips of blood smearing the once shiny surface. Someone, and something had been here recently, judging by the blood. She checked their surroundings carefully, pausing on the trees in the distance, and then looked back.

"I'm going in. This is fresh blood, there's nowhere else out here for an injured person to go. Cover me."

He wanted to stop her; remind her she'd be better off than him out here with a potential predator. But once Aluna had made her mind up, there was no changing it. Jaylen nodded, watching her cross the field, moving urgently towards the wooden building. The yellow grass was tall and thick, making it difficult to keep an eye out for potential dangers. It would be easy for a predator to be merely feet away, putting them both in danger. He kept his hand over the trigger as Aluna pushed the front door fully open and stepped over the threshold. It was a fairly small building with two large windows that were currently open, a door and a tiny storeroom to the back where the staff had kept supplies. Once more families moved closer to town, the school had closed, but tourists and so-called celebrities still used the building when they paid exuberant amounts of money to have photoshoots and weddings out in the 'natural world'.

A cry of pain sounded from the building, revealing that the injured had indeed manged to find shelter. But that was not the only sound that alerted Jaylen. Something was moving through the surrounding grass, and judging by what they had seen today, it was unlikely to be friendly. Another rustle in the grass from behind caused him to turn around and end up face to face with a cheetah.

Jaylen stayed as still as physically possible. With so many humans driving backwards and forwards, the animals around here were unlikely to just attack. If he kept still and silent, it would likely lose interest, turn round and go back to wherever it came from. There was no point running, its instincts would kick in and you couldn't exactly outrun the fastest land animal, even with the car being such a short distance away. And, he reasoned, if he did somehow get to the car and escape, he would have to leave Aluna stranded.

A younger woman caught his eye. She was running towards him from the other side of the building. Her eyes were wide, clothes soaked through with sweat, and congealed blood had built up around a large incision on her forehead. It had matted into what seemed to be blonde waves and dripped onto the corner of her peach sundress.

"Run" she yelled at him, grabbing his hand and trying to drag him towards the car. She was incredibly strong for her small stature, although that might have been the adrenaline, and he almost gave in. Then, all at once, seven cheetahs sprang out from the grass around them and sprinted towards the school. Two leapt through the open windows, one through the door and the others froze as if to keep watch.

"ALUNA! ALUNA!" Jaylen screamed in terror, begging the young woman to escape out the back but knowing realistically it was impossible. A loud chirp from the cheetahs cut him off before he could call again. Someone in the building fired two gunshots in quick succession, followed by more chirps. The waiting animals slipped inside.

"Please, we need to get out of here," begged the blonde girl as the cheetahs exited the school. Despite his own panic, Jaylen noticed an unusual calmness in her voice. Either she was a psychopath, or someone trained her to keep her head in a crisis.

One of the animals had visible bloodstains on the fur under its chin and was staring directly at them. Jaylen fired his own gun, his hands shaking in anger caused him to miss his target. It was almost mocking him now, sat there unafraid of the weapon.

The sound of more movement finally allowed him to give in to the girl's demands and follow her back to the car. The cheetahs followed. They weren't running, just walking in the car's direction, but Jaylen wasn't taking any chances, especially when he had an unarmed woman to think about. Although something about her suggested she was more than capable of handling herself, he couldn't take the risk.

He quickly locked the doors and went to start the engine when suddenly one cat was on the windscreen. Cracks like those in the phone he'd found formed as the animal lunged at the glass. There was something unusual about this cheetah. From this close up, Jaylen could see a large patch of discoloured fur around its ears and paws. The others appeared to have the same condition. Something else concerned him. He knew these cats well, and the two females closest to the car, Diva and Cali, belonged to completely distinct family groups and normally stayed miles away from each other. Somehow the cheetahs, and he couldn't believe what he was thinking, had organised the attack. The cheetahs had found a way of planning and carrying out the murders of all these people over a distance so great they shouldn't even be able to hear each other.

Another cheetah jumping up onto the roof brought him out of his thoughts while the rest of the group scratched and pawed at the doors and wing mirrors. The girl was screaming, pressed as far back in her seat as physically possible, and the fear froze Jaylen in place. Never in his time out here had the animals targeted him. He had seen his fair share of animal attacks, sure, but not like this. Usually the animals ignored the cars, sometimes sniffing them and occasionally climbing onto the roof, but one at a time, calmly and not with the apparent intent of killing the people inside. With a sinking realisation he realised that this must have been what happened back at Etana's. Had a group of hyper-aggressive cheetahs stormed the guests, they wouldn't have stood a chance. Evidently, at least two had escaped, one killed later, and the other sat next to him, surrounded.

He heard gunshots from the school, and the bodies of two dead cats fell from the roof of the car. Someone was coming to help. He looked out of the window, expecting to see another car, a rescue team, but the actual cause made his jaw drop. Somehow, Aluna was running towards them, white tee stained with what Jaylen hoped was another person's blood. He leaned into the backseat and threw the door open, letting her leap into the vehicle. With all her remaining strength, she slammed it closed, breathing heavily and dropping her weapon to the floor.

Finally, starting the engine as the cats became more persistent, Jaylen drove as fast as the car would go back to Etana's. Thankfully, the cheetahs didn't bother to give chase and in relief he finally addressed the petite woman sat, trembling, in the passenger seat.

"Jaylen," he said by way of an introduction. It seemed a little too late for introductions given what they'd just witnessed, but it didn't hurt to be polite. "I live in the area, giving tours at a park. This is Aluna."

"Akari," she replied.

He handed her a bottle of water and she downed it in seconds, having spent days out here in the blistering heat. It was a relief she found shelter.

"Don't worry, Akari. We're going to go somewhere safe and get help."

Chapter 6

Annabelle was thankful for the summer sun and gentle breeze as she stepped out of her car. She had intended to go straight to Travis' house, get the information she needed, and return to her flat. Instead, she was now about to go trapesing round a crocodile sanctuary where they kept seemingly murderous reptiles. It had surprised her to see it was open, but after the party she'd just seen, people's apparent insensitivity wasn't too much of a shock. It would be now that her cousins would pull her aside to remind her to stop being so cynical, but they hadn't seen what she had.

The sign at the front of the building was showing all the different exhibits, no warning signs anywhere. She had expected something along the lines of 'enter at your own risk' to prevent any further tragedy or at the very least protect the sanctuary from a lawsuit. Families with small children were happily wandering around with no concern for their safety. Staff were selling ice creams, handing out maps and taking photographs of various guests. Annabelle navigated her way towards the freshwater exhibit where the two culprits had escaped from. She had done some digging in the carpark and found as much information about the centre as possible, hoping that she would at least appear to know what she was doing. It was there that she had found the phone number of one of the research teams investigating the escaped crocodiles. The only person to have bothered to pick up the phone was a neurobiologist by the name of Dr Christopher Pearson who seemed like he had better things to do than answer the questions of an 18-year-old girl. At least, unlike the management, he actually appeared to care about the situation at hand. Although, she reasoned, the management had bothered to employ a research team so they couldn't be completely oblivious.

There was a lab at the end of the building, and she recognised the man through the window. He had a significantly smaller reptile on a table, hopefully incapacitated, and was looking at something on a screen. Despite the crocodile's small size, the sight of large teeth still sent a shiver through Annabelle's body. She knocked cautiously on the door, not wanting to annoy the one person who seemed willing to give her information. This was the only legal lead she'd had in a while, and although she was grateful for the information Alessandra could get her, if she ever wanted to make this public knowledge her sources had to be something other than the efforts of a teenage hacker.

"Dr Pearson? I'm…" He stopped her.

"Annabelle Summers. The person who all of my colleagues warned me against speaking to. It appears you've been pestering them with absurd conspiracies."

"I just wanted to ask you some questions, really. There are some things that even the most internet savvy people can't find via google."

"You have a theory?"

"It's more than a theory, actually. There's evidence to suggest the water sources around here have been contaminated with dextro-rinoifane."

"Ignoring the fact that it isn't even legal to produce that drug over here, it wouldn't cause these sorts of behavioural changes, this is some sort of neurological defect, a genetic change. You see April over here" he pointed towards the crocodile on the table. "If it was a chemically induced change, you'd expect to see evidence of the same changes in her brain, but they aren't here."

Science had never been Annabelle's strong suit, but she nodded anyway. It was better than appearing completely clueless.

"April is unrelated to either of the two escaped males, but Archie and Scooby were father and son. That shows me she has inherited the defect. Or there's something in her genes that makes them more susceptible to a virus."

"So, what exactly are they doing to stop it happening again?"

"Well, there isn't much they can do to fix the problem, but upper management stopped all breeding until we can screen all the animals for the defect. We might end up having to import some new animals though, but that's just how the business works."

"Look, can you just ring me if anything occurs to you? Please, it's important."

He nodded in response, and Annabelle took that as her cue to leave.

As she made her way through the crowds of families on her way out of the sanctuary, she wondered how many of them had come out just because of the attacks. All the research she had done in the past few years had shown her that this sort of tragic event attracted more attention than calm did. The man on the gate thanked her for visiting with an over-the-top smile as she crossed the grass, more questions in her head than she had when she arrived.

Annabelle had snagged a parking space right at the front of the car park, just behind the disabled bays. Her phone rang as she was sliding into the driver's seat, and she answered without checking the number. Most likely it was Madison. She'd seemed to realise yesterday that sleeping with Jaycee was a bad idea and that Annabelle was suddenly expected to forgive her and take her back without a second thought.

"Annabelle Summers."

"Miss Summers, it's Chris. Dr Pearson. From the lab?" she could hear him cringing on the other end of the phone as he spoke.

"Yeah," she answered.

"Right, well…" he let out a long breath. "You said to call you if something occurred to me."

"Okay," she responded, willing him to get to the point. She didn't have time for this. She needed to get her act together and find out what the hell was going on here. Where was the next tragedy going to occur? How would anyone prevent it from happening if they didn't know it was happening in the first place?

"Well, something occurred to me."

This conversation was really testing Annabelle's patience, but she was pretty convinced that this was just some personality quirk rather than a conscious attempt to annoy her. That, she could put up with. She'd met people with worse.

"What is it?"

"I haven't eaten lunch yet," he rushed on, clearly relieved that she hadn't snapped at him. "And judging by the time and how quickly you drove over here, you haven't either." He was right, and anything would beat the small meal she'd end up putting together with what was left on her shelf in the communal fridge.

"What did you have in mind?"

"There's a little burger place that's still somewhat unknown in this area."

"What's the address?"

He was already there when she pulled up, and he lifted his hand in greeting as Annabelle stepped through the glass door into the tiny space. There were maybe fifteen tables with a couple of small booths at the back. The walls comprised dark wooden panels and a variety of framed photographs had been hung seemingly at random. Despite the worn floor and chips in the paintwork, the place looked clean, and the smell of bacon made her stomach growl.

"Hey," Chris rose halfway from his chair as she sat down in an echo of chivalrous manners. He looked as uncomfortable with this whole thing as she was, and Annabelle smiled at him. Things couldn't go wrong if at least one of them remained professional.

"Hi." She wondered what exactly had been going through her head when she had agreed to this. The last lunch date she'd had was with Madison. To say it ended badly would probably be the understatement of the year. Before she could make some excuse to leave or even to turn this into some sort of interrogation, he leaned back in his chair and tapped the table with two fingers.

"I don't normally do this sort of thing."

"Eat lunch?" She was being purposefully vague but told herself that he'd kind of asked for it. The voice in the back of her head was telling her to back off, but she ignored it.

He chuckled. "No, I mean ask someone I just met out to lunch. I don't even ask people I've known for years out to lunch."

"Then why did you?" the curiosity that had prompted her decision to go to law school was slipping through the professional attitude she'd been sticking to. Why couldn't she just stick to her resolutions for one night?

"I don't know," he answered. "Call it a feeling, I guess." He paused as the woman from the counter came over and took their drink orders, a Pepsi and a beer. "Why did you say yes?"

"A feeling." She responded instantly. "So why neurobiology?

"It's methodical. Something happens, we study it then we find out why. Logical."

That was probably the reason he was so reluctant to believe her about the dextro-rinoifane. Not enough logic. The server deposited their drinks and took their orders, a cheeseburger for him and a pasta salad for her. Annabelle took a sip from her plastic cup. "There's a story there."

"Not one I'm willing to share," he retorted. "At least not yet. Trust me, nothing about my life is interesting enough for conversation over lunch. Maybe over drinks. Lots and lots of drinks."

It sounded a lot like an invitation, and Annabelle gulped the last bit of water in her mouth a little too fast, coughing suddenly. His face flushed slightly as he realised how she had interpreted his words. She smiled at him. "Maybe some other time then?"

Chris seemed relieved by her olive branch and seized it with both hands. "What about you? Anything happen in your life that's interesting enough for a lunch chat?" The beer he'd ordered was an off-brand Annabelle didn't recognise, and his fingers picked at the label between sips.

Truthfully, her past was a complete mess of events that strung together to create the beautiful disaster that was her life. Deciding that topic was best saved for another time as well, she shook her head. "Not really," she told him. "I grew up in near Derby, moved to Carterton to study law." She left off the part where she got suspended.

"Is your family still in Derby?"

"Yep," she nodded. She didn't elaborate; didn't tell him that her father had died tragically, and her mother had disappeared soon after when she couldn't handle the stress of their life anymore. That was too much to dump on him hours after they'd just met. No one in this town, not even Madison, had heard that story. The arrival of their food saved her from any further explanation. As they ate, their conversation turned to more mundane things. She found out more about his research, and he asked about her degree.

"What's this I hear about you emailing everyone in upper management? You've got quite the reputation in this business."

"I have a natural talent for solving mysteries. Maybe I should refocus that away from chemical contamination theories and try to find the pet burglars of Alvescot."

"Pet burglars?"

"I went to Travis McKnight's house to talk to him about the crocodiles and he told me someone had been stealing the neighbourhood pets, but the police couldn't find any evidence."

"You went to Travis' house?" This was usually the point where people made the decision that she was insane. Or a stalker. Or both.

"Mystery-solver. I had to find answers somewhere, and he seemed like the person who could give them to me." He laughed then, a rich sound that filled the surrounding space. She wondered absently if it was supposed to be this way. Their conversations came easily, and she didn't feel as awkward as she had with Madison during those first few dates.

Slow down, Annabelle. She told herself. Get it together.

Her phone buzzed in her pocket, loud enough for him to hear it. She was going to ignore it, but he nodded toward her resignedly. "I'm guessing your lunch break is over?"

It seemed as good a stopping point as any, and it would save them the embarrassing departure that would inevitably follow. She pulled her phone out and tried to keep her face from showing anything as she read Madison's text. Apparently, she was unsuccessful.

"That bad?"

"It's nothing. Thank you for lunch, Chris."

"Listen, if anything else occurs to me…" he began. He took a breath to calm himself, and it reminded Annabelle that she probably wasn't the only one feeling weird about all of this. "Can I call?"

She knew very well what he was asking, and it had nothing to do with their earlier interview. She thought about Madison and the other girl who had probably shared her bed last night. They were done, that much she was sure about, but starting something new right now would be foolish. Still, she looked down at his hopeful smile and she knew her answer.

"Sure."

Chapter 7

Chris watched her slip into the back of the conference room without missing a beat in his presentation. Thankfully, the group of trainees didn't seem to notice, and he continued his explanation of the importance of proper reptile nutrition. She waited as he finished speaking, but the moment he dismissed the group, Annabelle was dashing forward eagerly. Never had Chris witnessed so much passion and enthusiasm over the behaviour of crocodiles. There must be a reason this mattered so much to the young redhead. He'd never tell her but seeing her sent a thrum of energy through him. He shook it off, berating himself for acting like a schoolboy, and began packing his things away. Making sure none of his colleagues were within earshot, for fear of ever-increasing ridicule, he gave her a cursory glance as she stopped on the other side of the table.

"You know, thanks to you, everyone here now officially thinks of me as insane."

Annabelle was already riffling through pages and pages of notes in a thick folder, and he was only half paying attention as she explained the data. Their lunch yesterday had been pleasant enough, and it had been a long time since he'd felt interested enough in anyone to socialise with them. Despite his nerves, he thought it had gone well, but it looked like her interest was purely professional. She saw him as nothing more than a source she could exploit for her research, and he cursed mentally for thinking she'd felt anything more.

She was coming to the end of her rant about dextro-rinoifane leaks from waste products, and the sour thoughts swirling in his head leaked into his tone.

"As interesting as this is, I have quarantined crocodiles to deal with." He shouldered his bag and walked away, but she dropped the other proverbial shoe.

"Wait, there's more!" She seemed almost excited about the information she'd gathered, and he couldn't help but think she was even more attractive when she was riled up. "Last month, people spotted unmarked vehicles dumping waste products into natural water sources. Any guesses where?"

"Seeing as we're already down this rabbit hole, I'm going to guess Alvescot." He could see where she was going with this train of thought and he wasn't particularly sure he liked it.

She lit up happily "Yes! Alvescot!"

The mystery of the pet burglar in Alvescot had piqued his interest. Despite needing to deal with work and prepare presentations for tomorrow and at some point, actually sleep, he'd spent the night browsing articles and reading desperate Facebook posts from concerned pet owners. There had been no evidence anyone had taken any of the animals, no suspicious cars, no break-ins, no barking, and yet every pet in the neighbourhood had vanished. He couldn't deny the puzzling mystery that was unfolding here. His scientific brain was already firing out potential questions and theories. And even though she had shown little interest in him other than as a sounding board, he couldn't help but relish the idea of spending more time with her.

"Fine," he responded, leading her down the shallow steps away from the conference room. "Let's just say for a second – for a second – that you're right and that illegal drugs are being deposited in the water supply. We could find out for sure by going and examining the enclosures." He had really hoped she wouldn't be right, but the more involved he became, the harder it was to cling to his beliefs.

"Great!" she seized his office. "Then there will finally be proof." It wasn't the first time he'd noticed the desperation in her eyes.

"You are thoroughly obsessed with this, aren't you?" he noticed her shift slightly under his scrutiny. "I mean in ways that go beyond your typical environmental activism." That had been his first thought. That Annabelle was another teenager fuelled by internet politics who thought her actions alone could change the world.

There was that pause again. He'd noticed it yesterday when he'd asked where she was from. But he shouldn't have noticed. Chris Pearson was not the sort of person who took any interest in other people's problems, and normally he would have ignored her hesitation, taken it as an opportunity to stay away. There was something about Annabelle Summers, something that begged him to forge a deeper connection. He had to know, had to understand why she was so hellbent on proving this, for all intents and purposes, conspiracy theory.

Her eyes darted down a bit, and he realised she knew she was being a bit too overbearing.

"Yeah, I am." It was a simple answer to his question, and he knew she didn't want to talk about it. But he was inquisitive by nature.

"May I ask why?"

She seemed to find a well of strength, because she answered faster and more assuredly. There was a hint of sadness in her eyes, and Chris almost wished he hadn't pushed the issue.

"Because of what happened in Derby."

It was a vague answer that failed to satisfy.

"What happened in Derby?" He had an inkling, of course, and her next words confirmed his suspicious.

"People dumped it in the river, people died, and the police covered it up." She looked so desperate there, everything thing in her brain most likely telling her he would take this opportunity to run, to run away from the girl with this insane theory. To brush it off as her just being over-dramatic. But he couldn't. He could see in her eyes that she was being genuine, that even if there was more to it, she knew exactly what she was talking about and knew the ramifications.

He blew a breath out through his nose and took another deep one before he spoke. "That sounds like a story that needs drinks."

"Lots and lots of drinks," her lips twitched in the imitation of a smile and he counted it as a win."

"I know a great bar that's not very crowded on a Thursday night if you've got time." He angled his body back toward the door, realising that at some point he'd turned to face her at the bottom of the stairs. She chewed her bottom lip thoughtfully, and suddenly all of those voices that told him she wasn't interested in him fell silent.

"Why not? I've got nowhere to be right now." She shrugged and stepped past him toward the door.

Relief flooded him, and he fought the nerves off with a joke.

"Just the thing a guy likes to hear after he asks a girl out."

"Technically, you didn't ask me anything." She pushed through the door with a triumphant smile, and Chris felt his estimation of her rise ever so slightly. Annabelle was proving to be a rather intriguing companion, and as he followed her to the parking garage, he looked forward to learning more about her. It was the first time he'd felt this way since Gina.

He shook those thoughts from his head quickly. Going down that road only led to disaster. Besides, he would spend tonight listening to Annabelle's story and seeing what he could do about seeing that smile again. Rationally, he was probably setting himself up to get his heart broken, but he pushed the thought aside, deciding to deal with that if it happened.

"Where are you parked?" he asked, glancing around at the smattering of vehicles in the guest car park.

"Uh," she shook her head, "I didn't bring my car."

Drinks and a ride home, he thought as he directed her toward his vehicle. This was shaping up to be a good night. "I'm over here."

They pulled up outside the bar thirty minutes later. During the day it was a great lunch spot, but at night they reopened as the best pub in town for a quiet drink. The wooden bar sat in the centre and warmed by the light of hanging sconces. True to his word, the place was nearly empty when they walked in and the bartender lifted an arm in greeting as they slid into a booth along the sidewall. A young blonde woman hurried over with a smile and two napkins.

"Hi! My name's Skyler. What can I get you?"

"Guinness," Chris ordered right away, changing from his usual whisky double. Annabelle ordered a lager and water, and Skyler dashed away to the bar with barely a nod. Chris settled back and watched her take in the scene. This was one of his favourite places, though no one here would know his name. He was always sure to come on random days and sit as far out of the way as he could manage. He recognised the bartender, Isai, but not the server. That wasn't surprising though, students were constantly picking up shifts here.

"You come here often?" Annabelle interrupted his thoughts, and he realised she was staring at him.

"Often enough," he nodded.

"This is on your way home?" He recognised an attempt to deflect the conversation away from herself – it was a technique he'd mastered years ago. She didn't want to talk about Derby, or what had happened there. He was happy to go along with her until she felt more comfortable.

"No," he chuckled, "opposite direction, actually. I live in Worsham. You?"

"Carterton," she told him, leaning back when Skyler deposited their drinks on the table, completely ignoring Annabelle.

"Can I get you anything else?" she asked brightly.

Chris raised his brow at Annabelle in question. "You hungry?"

"No," she shook her head quickly.

"Onion rings," he looked up at Skyler with the politest smile he could muster. She winked at him and turned on her heel, leaving him shaking his head at her eagerness. "Must be slow tonight." He waited a few beats, but when she said nothing, he pushed forward. "So," he took a sip from his bottle, encouraged when Annabelle did the same. "Derby?"

"Yeah," she looked down at the table. She didn't give him anything else, and he wondered how many people had heard her story and dismissed it out of hand. She confirmed it with her next words. "I don't really like to talk about it with everyone."

"Hey," he leaned forward, "if you can't tell a practical stranger whom you just met yesterday, who can you tell?"

Her breath of amusement eased the tension from her shoulders, and she relaxed. "It was ten years ago. I grew up in a tiny farming village near Derby and one morning, in the middle of a heatwave, all the kids ran down to the river only to find it completely blocked off. Water testing, they said, completely routine. That night, the people whose windows looked over and saw military, US military, trucks driving backwards and forwards with water tanks and biohazard warnings. It didn't make any sense." She took a deep breath. "A little over two weeks later we were let out of school early because the air conditioning failed, and it was the hottest day on record and most of the village went to go swimming. Every single person who went in the water died by the end of the month. There were investigations and police found dextro-rinoifane traces in their systems, decided that someone had been experimenting with making the drug and wrote the entire thing off as a wild party gone tragically wrong. They sent teams of specialist's round, giving the children who were left assemblies about how taking illegal drugs is, well, illegal. And that was it. No further investigation, no anything." She took a long sip from her glass and slammed it back down on the table. "Everyone seemed to forget that it isn't even possible to get dextro-rinoifane in this country. It's made in one specialist facility in the US, and nobody outside the research team knows how to produce it. They brought it here, killed people and no-one outside our village cares."

Skyler chose that moment to come back with his onion rings, and Annabelle turned away from him to wipe her eyes as Chris thanked the young girl. He pushed the dish aside for the moment and concentrated on Annabelle, who was gathering herself again.

"Listen. I'll do whatever I can to help. Tomorrow, we'll go run some tests on the water and the crocodiles. If there're any signs of that drug, we can start building a case."

The transformation was immediate. Chris wondered if he was the first person to ever actually believe her, to offer to help. She'd been carrying this burden for ten years, and for just a moment that burden was a little lighter. She smiled at him gratefully and reached across the table to grip his hand.

"Thank you."

She pulled away for a second, embarrassment written on her features. She tucked an errant strand of hair behind her ear and finished her drink.

"Do you have any family?" I never asked."

He winced and drained his own beer. "Yeah, we're not close." He caught Skyler's eye and lifted two fingers to indicate another round. She nodded and busied herself as he turned back to Annabelle. "As you can imagine, I'm an acquired taste."

"In the beginning," she agreed lightly. "In the end, though, you come through." Emma dropped two full beers on their table and collected the empties. Chris lifted his is salute and Annabelle tapped hers against it. They finished the second round, and she helped him with the onion rings as they planned the next day's investigations.

Chapter 8

Today's lunch turned out to be a takeaway from a Thai place a few miles from the sanctuary. Chris met Annabelle outside the staff gate and let her in, walking the short distance to the lab. His office inside the building was little more than a square closet tucked at the end of a long hallway. He didn't use it much, preferring to spend his time at the sanctuary working with the animals or going over data pattern in the exam rooms. Management had reserved most of the space in the building for exam rooms designed to fit large animals. A thin corner desk and two chairs were the only pieces of furniture in the room, and he had to clear a pile of old spreadsheets and reports from one chair to make room for her.

"Cosy," Annabelle glanced around curiously. It wasn't the tidiest of offices, but Chris knew there were other staff members who were worse. His finicky nature kept his space more organised, but there was chaos among the order. He had recently tossed his navy wellington boots in the corner in case he needed to trudge through the water in an enclosure. A black jacket with the sanctuary's logo emblazoned on the front was hung from one shoulder on the back of the door. The files on his desk were neat, but there were more than a few water bottles and crisp packets littering the space. He cleared them embarrassingly as Annabelle sat in the newly vacated chair.

"I'm honestly not in here a lot," he told her. "Most of the time I'm at home working on research or in one of the exam rooms." He unpacked their lunch, humming in approval at her selection. Neither of them said anything as they ate, both eager to get on with their plan.

After finishing their meal in comfortable silence, Chris walked her down to the room he'd been using the other morning.

"You're going to have to wear the…." He stopped mid-sentence and stared dumbfounded at the empty room. "Where the hell are my animals?"

Now confused, and more than a little frustrated, he grabbed the nearest phone and called the security office. No one answered, and he slammed the receiver down harder than necessary.

"Come on." Annabelle followed him out of the building and through a small gate that opened into the visitor area. Chris stormed into the freshwater exhibit and found the current guide, Briana Thornton. She looked up from her clipboard and smiled brightly.

"Christopher, hi!"

Chris sighed internally and steeled himself for her bubbly personality. Briana was too much to deal with most days, but especially when he had important things to be getting on with. "Briana, this is Anabelle Summers. I needed to show here some data from Archie and Scooby, but they're both gone."

Briana frowned slightly and dusted off her uniform issued cargo shorts before turning to walk away. Chris fell into step beside her with Annabelle just a pace behind as they passed an enclosure with a Siamese Crocodile sunbathing lazily.

"I'm sorry," Briana said finally, "but they aren't here. They've been destroyed."

"They were in room 3 yesterday! When did that happen?" Chris knew that management would want this situation under control as soon as possible, and with official sources not ruling out the possibility of a virus, it made sense to destroy the bodies to prevent contamination. He just thought that, seeing as both Archie and Scooby were under his care, they'd at least take the time to notify him first.

"Yeah, last night," Briana kept her voice quiet to avoid startling any visitors passing by.

Next to him, he felt Annabelle stiffen.

"On whose orders?" Chris knew she was probably already spinning a theory in her head, but if Briana noticed her tone, she was unlikely to bring it up.

"Borough Council? Or maybe the board of directors, I'm not sure."

Chris turned to give Annabelle his best not now look. She looked like she wanted to say something more, but wisely kept her thoughts to herself as Briana continued unaware. Now was not the time to induct another person into this, especially one as trusting as Briana. One word from the authorities and they would convince her to spill their secrets. There wasn't enough proof, let alone legally gathered evidence, to make their case public.

"Are you still living in Worsham, Christopher?"

"Uh, yes," he ignored Annabelle's enquiring eyes. "It's convenient."

"I love it there."

"Tell me, Christopher," Annabelle interjected, "could we not just run the same tests on a different animal, from the same enclosure?"

He knew where she was going, and he had already promised to help. But helping her meant asking a favour from Briana. Annabelle was going to owe him a lot more than lunch after this.

"There are certain tests I could run that wouldn't be harmful."

"What's this about?" Briana had her eyebrows raised and Chris realised it might not be as easy to get something past her as he had first thought.

"Just don't want it to happen again," he said hurriedly.

"Of course."

"Christo," Annabelle cut in again, mimicking Briana's use of his full name. "I don't suppose it's possible for Briana to arrange for us to borrow a crocodile?" Chris had been secretly hoping she would ask. Even so, he shot a teasing glare in her direction and she smirked back.

"Sure, anything to help." Briana agreed almost instantly.

It was dark by the time she dropped off one of the younger animals. "This is Timmy, the night guard knows you have him, but they think you're doing his check-up so you might want to get that done while you have him."

"Thanks," Chris accepted the plastic carrier gently. "See you tomorrow." Briana waved and got back into the white van, leaving him holding a rather docile Timmy. "Come on, buddy."

Annabelle was waiting in the exam room like he'd asked, holding two beakers of old enclosure water, but she perked up when he entered with the carrier. She moved to help him, but he shook his head.

"Stay back until I have him sedated. You're not covered under out insurance." She stopped but didn't retreat, clearly eager to see the young animal up close. Chris had already prepared a syringe of the sedative, and he carefully injected Timmy through the holes in the carrier's side.

"How long will that take to knock him out?" Annabelle asked.

"Not long," Chris told her. He checked on Timmy every few seconds as he tested the water sample. As he worked, he brought up something that had been on his mind ever since their meeting with Briana. "Christopher?"

Annabelle's face scrunched up in confusion. "What?"

He chuckled under his breath.

"Earlier, you called me Christopher the entire time we were talking to Briana."

"Oh," she huffed, "I did that because of her.

"Uh huh," he was smiling now, and she scoffed.

"She's obviously into you. If I called, you by a more familiar name, she might have got defensive. In my experience, defensive people are less cooperative."

"Oh," he deflated a little as he entered the data into a spreadsheet. He tried not to let her know how delighted he'd been at what he'd thought was jealousy. Her amused smile told him he'd failed. "What?"

"Nothing," she shook her head. "Is he out?"

Slowly opening the carrier, Chris got a good look at the hatchling within. Timmy was currently completely under the effects of the sedative, and his chest showed the steady rise and fall associated with deep breathing. Underneath him was a blue towel and, to be on the safe side, Chris used that to pull him out gently.

Once he had confirmed that, yes, Timmy was fully sedated, Chris lifted him up, motioning for Annabelle to grab the towel. She laid it out on the table, and he set the hatchling on it, never taking her eyes off the sleeping crocodile.

"This your first time seeing one up close?"

"Yeah," she breathed. Her hand lifted to touch the hatchling almost automatically, but she halted her movement halfway and glanced at Chris in question.

"Go ahead," he nodded, and she slid her fingers along Timmy's thick skin. He watched her for a moment and tried to remember if he'd been that fascinated the first time, he'd encountered an animal other than the traditional household pets.

Her lips curved up slightly as she became bolder, running her finger down the hatchling's nose softly.

"Okay, we might have a match." He was cautious, not wanting to make a direct leap without more proof.

"So, does that mean…"

"Not necessarily. Technically, all this proves is that Timmy drank some contaminated water and now he has dextro-rinoifane in his system. It doesn't prove that it is what caused the older two to kill the girls, though. Or that the water was contaminated when they drank it, but it is now." She looked slightly defeated at that statement, and Chris rushed on. "It's a start Annabelle, it's more evidence than we had this morning."

Chris began clearing up his equipment and a sharp knock on the door caused his head to snap up. Deciding it was probably the night guard coming to check on Timmy, he went to open it. Across the threshold were three tall men in suits.

"Are you Dr Pearson?" Annabelle moved slowly behind him, and it reminded Chris that she didn't even have permission to be on the property after closing time.

"Who's asking?"

"We work for Miss Zielińska. You have been conducting some research that is of interest to her organisation. Seeing as you have evidently shared your findings with the young woman trying and failing to not draw attention to herself, Miss Summers over there may accompany you."

Chapter 9

"You know that we just got on a plane a flew to Poland because some guys told us to, right?" Annabelle had never been much of a fan of air travel. The two of them were sitting in an office conference room. The worn blue carpeting was peeling slightly in the corner, and there was a questionable stain on the corner of the wooden table. From the way the men had acted on their way here, she had expected something a little more official.

It was at that moment the black painted door slid open, and one of the hotel workers escorted another man and woman inside the room. The man was slightly shorter than Chris, with lightly tanned skin and light curls on top of his head. The woman was taller, her dark brown hair styled in springy coils framing her round features.

"Jaylen Hudson, Aluna Otiengo." The worker introduced the two strangers, and Annabelle was ever more confused why they were here. Clearly this wasn't just someone about to chastise them for the illegal documents she had on the water contamination.

"And this is Dr Christopher Pearson and Annabelle Summers." Bold as ever, Annabelle was the first person to step forward and shake their hands. Both Jaylen and Aluna seemed as confused as she was, which was slightly reassuring.

"If you would all take a seat, Miss Zielińska will be along in a moment." There was that name again. Miss Zielińska. If she had more time to prepare, Annabelle would have spent hours researching to give her some idea of what to expect.

She did as she was told, pulling out a chair next to Chris, as Jaylen and Aluna claimed the other side of the table. Annabelle didn't know who Miss Zielińska was, although based on the secrecy she had a hunch that this woman would be someone very important. She glanced to her left at Chris, who appeared to be trying to figure out what on earth was going on.

The doors slid open again, and a woman in her thirties walked through it, hair scraped back into a bun and wearing a navy-blue suit.

"Good afternoon. My name is Alicja Zielińska. Welcome to Warsaw. You are all probably wondering why I have brought you here. We are still waiting on some guests and then things will become clear."

Ten minutes passed before anyone dared to speak. Predictably, it was Chris who went first.

"I think we can all agree this is not your average Friday afternoon."

"Yeah, what exactly is going on?" Jaylen agreed, and the tension broke slightly. Miss Zielińska just shook her head slightly, remaining stood at the head of the table. Annabelle had taken to counting the tiles on the ceiling while she listened to the tap tapping of Chris' shoes on the floor. She caught Aluna smiling across the table and sent a smile back.

The door opened once again, and another woman entered. Her hair was drawn off her face in a tight ponytail and she was sporting a panicked expression.

"Ah! Zofia!" The new woman walked straight over to Miss Zielińska without uttering a word.

"Thank you all for agreeing to meet with us here. I have selected this group based on events that you have witnessed over the last few days, camp raids by cheetahs in Kinna and alleyway murders by crocodiles in Oxford. They reported just last night, cows attacking babies in Venezuela and sheep pushing over cars in Hungary." Annabelle turned back to Chris as Miss Zielińska turned on the projector screen. He looked just as concerned as she felt, realising that this had to be way bigger than a contaminated water source at the sanctuary.

The screen showed a theme park crowded with people. Two huge rollercoasters dominated the image, and it reminded Annabelle of a park her grandparents had taken her to years ago.

"In Malaysia, a colony of wild rabbits swarmed a control room, causing an electrical failure at this park. Guests were stranded, upside down, on rollercoasters for over twelve hours. Seventeen people fell to their deaths before rescue teams could arrive. In Paris, rats invaded a day-care facility, causing injury to six children and later death to three. No one has made any link between these incidents. Officials have reported them as tragic accidents. We do not believe these are accidents of any kind. Mr Hudson, your uncle wrote multiple research papers on the potential for nature to cause a global crisis. We believe he was correct."

"Wait a minute." Chris was trying to process all this information, and he turned to Jaylen. "Who's your uncle?".

"Kelvin Hudson, ecologist." Despite the two being related, Jaylen didn't look too pleased at the mention of his family member.

"Kelvin Hudson? The same Kelvin Hudson that chained himself to a jet engine because he was convinced the trees told him to. You seriously expect us to believe the theories of a complete and utter lunatic?" Aluna glared at him, and Chris shifted uncomfortably in his seat.

"The five of you will help us figure out if Dr Hudson's theories were true."

"Five?" Annabelle questioned, looking at the three other people sat around the table. "But there's four of us."

Whoever had been waiting outside chose that moment to open the door. A petite woman walked in; her blonde hair secured in a braid over her left shoulder. With the level of confidence she projected, Annabelle guessed she had more information about their mission that the rest of the team. Zofia smiled at her.

"This is Agent Akari Tanaka. She is currently on loan from MI6 and will lead your team, reporting directly to me." Annabelle was beginning to seriously question what she was doing here. Everyone else in the room appeared to be qualified for this mission. She was 18 years old and had just been suspended from the law school she had only barely got into. Unless the people behind this team knew of her theories. Although, she reasoned, if the government knew what was currently on her laptop, she'd probably be in prison, sharing a cell with Alessandra.

Zofia and Alicja left the room, and Akari took her position at the front.

"Okay, so our first task is to fly to Beijing. I've already booked the tickets for tomorrow morning so it will be an early night for everyone. There is a group of people waiting for us there. They all work at a riding school and have three horses in quarantine that they think we should take a look at."

"We're not just dropping everything and going to Beijing on your orders." Chris was evidently not pleased with this latest development.

"Whether you like it or not, we have to get this done. You can all be replaced, you know."

She packed up the equipment the older women had left behind and Annabelle stood up, followed by Chris. Before today, Annabelle had never even left

England and now she was flying from Poland to Beijing to run tests on psychotic horses. What on earth had her life become?

Chapter 10

Chris ran through the last 24hours in his head, trying to figure out how he'd gone from being an anti-social neurobiologist and part-time exotic reptile specialist to a member of a five-person team trying to solve what seemed to be a global crisis. The team had sat down in a café at Chopin International Airport waiting for their flight to Beijing for the first of many stops on this insane quest. His stylus tapped the tablet beneath it thoughtfully. He's always found writing his thoughts down helped him figure things out, and this mystery was no exception. He'd created a table that morning, one column for 'Events' and another for 'Causes'. The second column was woefully blank, and he scribbled a question mark childishly. Next to him, Annabelle glanced over from her screen as he dropped his stylus in frustration. Wordlessly, she reached over, erased his question mark, and wrote something in the empty space. Dextro-rinoifane.

She dropped the stylus triumphantly and raised her eyebrows.

"Can we go home now?" he looked at her for a moment.

"Unfortunately, we need proof that's not just unofficial tests from a baby crocodile and whatever illegal and unofficial documents you have on that laptop of yours."

It was then that Aluna and Jaylen arrived at their table.

"Tea?" the dark-skinned woman laid four mugs down on the table. Jaylen walked over, carrying his own, and sat in the seat across from Chris. Hearing Kelvin Hudson's name in yesterday's meeting had instantly set the scientist on edge. That man was a warning to all scientists in his class, don't get too involved or you'll end up going completely off the deep end. He had taken his theories too far, and now Chris was part of the team jetting around the world to see if those theories were right.

"Thank you," Annabelle smiled at Aluna. "You read my mind."

Chris returned to his notes to ignore his two teammates, but Jaylen had other ideas. He reached over and set a mug in front of him.

"There you go." Chris glanced up begrudgingly.

"Thank you." And then, because he could see Annabelle staring at him pointedly, he picked up the drink and blew softly before taking a sip. He dropped his eyes back to his tablet for a moment but looked back up when Jaylen produced his own and lay it down on the table. Chris was not a people person, and that Jaylen was pushing his insane Uncle's agenda did nothing to help his current mood.

"Does any of this make sense to you?" His tone was even and polite but not at all friendly as he handed over a scrap of paper, and Chris knew it was because of their first meeting. First impressions were never really his strong suit. Add to that finding out the entire reason for creating this team was the research of one of the most delusional scientists in the world, and it was a wonder either of them was keeping a civil tone.

"And who wrote this?"

"My uncle, I found it in with some of his research papers" Jaylen answered in that barely civil tone.

"Right," Chris should have guessed. "Well, Ursus Maritiumus, that's the Latin name for polar bears. The rest of this seems to link to brown bear hybrids."

"Polar bears?" Aluna questioned, then turned to Jaylen. "You have any idea why polar bears would be so important to your uncle?"

"No." Jaylen shook his head and Chris went back to staring at his tablet. Annabelle had almost finished with her tea, and she'd procured a packet of biscuits from her bag. She offered him one, and he took it gratefully. They still had twenty minutes until they needed to leave the café, and it was looking likely that they would spend those twenty minutes in an awkward silence.

Thankfully, Akari came up behind them, oblivious to the tension in the air. "Guys, there's been a change in the schedule, we're being sent to Washington."

Jaylen spoke up before anyone else could. "Washington? What happened to Beijing?"

"There's been an attack at a school. Thousands of snakes attacking students and teachers." Akari answered.

Snakes. Attacking a school. Washington. This situation was getting more and more insane. When Annabelle had first come to him with her theories, he had genuinely expected this to be a one-off situation, not a worldwide disaster.

The flight to Washington was worse than the flight to Warsaw. With 14 hours in the air, the team ended up losing almost an entire day in transit. It was afternoon by the time they landed at the Washing Dulles airport, and Chris' mind and body were exhausted. Annabelle had managed a few hours in the seat next to him, though she hadn't leaned on his shoulder like she had on the flight from London. As they grabbed their bags and trudged up the bridge towards the terminal, he noticed the dark circles under her eyes.

"Hey," he leaned in close on the escalator that would take them to the car park. Zofia had already procured two vehicles for them, and the rental manager had handed Akari the keys upon arrival. Annabelle turned her head slightly, and he cleared his throat. "You okay?"

"Yeah," she nodded and turned her head back to watch her step as she left the moving stairs. He followed her a second later and made room for Aluna behind him. "You?" she returned.

"Peachy," he grumbled. "I've spent more time in the air this week than the rest of my life combined."

"I know what you mean," Annabelle laughed as Akari searched for their cars. "Did you get any sleep?"

"A little," he lied. Truthfully, he didn't sleep much anyway, but he didn't want her to worry. "I'll be happy for the bed this evening, though." Zofia had already got them rooms at a local hotel. They would be in town for as long as it took to figure out what happened at the school.

Akari gestured for them to gather around as she delegated the day's responsibilities.

"So, Jaylen, we'll take the Toyota. Aluna you'll take the Buick." She threw them the keys.

"Why do we need two cars?" Jaylen questioned, apparently uncomfortable about splitting up the team so early in the mission. But Akari appeared to know exactly what she was doing.

"You, Annabelle, and I are going to investigate the school. Chris and Aluna are going down in the sewers to catch a snake. Apparently, they came up through the plumbing."

"Sorry, what" Chris stammered. He hadn't been paying too much attention to the conversation until that point.

"Yes," Akari affirmed. "I expect studying one of them up close might give us some needed answers and…"

Chris' brain had finally caught up with the conversation, and he didn't like the fact that Annabelle would go off with virtual strangers. He'd never say that, though, so he went with the next best thing.

"No," he interrupted, "I don't know the first thing about catching a wild snake."

"Which is why Aluna will go with you. Assuming she isn't too scared." Akari fired back.

Jaylen seemed as reluctant to separate from Aluna as Chris was from Annabelle.

"Wait, why don't I just go with Aluna?"

"That's fine with me," Chris jumped on the younger man's suggestion.

"But I need someone who knows a thing or two about snakes with us at the school." It was a well-reasoned argument that Chris would have appreciated at any other time. With no more objections that didn't make him sound overbearing and insecure, he gave in.

"Are you coming?" Akari called from across the garage.

Jaylen was the first to move, following her with barely a glance at Aluna. "Yeah."

Chris turned back to Annabelle, offering her a small wave as she shrugged and stepped around him. "Be careful," he whispered loud enough for her to hear, but not too loud as to carry across the concrete structure to where Akari was standing, a disapproving look on her face. She half-turned as she walked away, giving him a reassuring smile before turning back and sliding into the back of the Toyota.

As they pulled up outside the school, Annabelle was amazed at just how many people were crowded outside. Police officers and journalists surrounded a series of metal barriers, and two officers were keeping members of the public at a safe distance from the building. Apparently the press' appetite for tragedy was even greater here than it was back in England.

"Are you sure we'll even get in?" Annabelle asked, realising that she had no official reason to be here right now. Zofia had made it very clear in the briefings she had given them that this mission of theirs that it was to be kept a complete secret – if the public found out that this was a widespread issue, it could cause a mass panic. Privately, she wasn't too sure of that logic. But if snakes were using the plumbing to attack places and crocodiles could break out of locked enclosures, then she wasn't sure how much the officials could do to keep people safe even if they knew.

Akari drove to the carpark entrance and showed the officer on duty her badge. He lifted the barrier, and they found a space. That had been easy than Annabelle expected, and it restored some of her shaky confidence in the team and their mission.

They exited the car and walked over to the front doors where another officer was standing.

"Agent Tanaka, MI6." The officer took her ID and examined it carefully before handing it back.

"Who are these two?" he asked.

"They're here to assist me with my investigation." Annabelle tried to keep her face professional, and the officer accepted their cover story. It wasn't a lie; they had just left out the reason they were investigating in the first place.

"Alright then. The investigative team is in the courtyard, straight down the main corridor and through the door on your left. Next to the cafeteria. Whatever you do, don't use any of the facilities, the pipelines are still being checked.

Akari nodded in understanding and lead Annabelle and Jaylen through the door. It was eerily quiet inside and had there not been evidence of a crisis Annabelle would have thought it was just the middle of exam season.

Lockers had been left half open, piles of textbooks falling out onto the floor. Someone had evidently triggered the fire alarm, and pools of water coated the cream-coloured floor. A patch of dried blood was visible next to the girl's bathroom door, and the door itself was tipped slightly in response to the top broken hinge. Annabelle peered inside one classroom and saw more chaos. Chairs had been tipped over and displays knocked onto the ground. Someone had smashed a window in an attempt by someone to make a quick escape. The floor around the teacher's desk was covered in wet sheets of paper, which from a closer inspection appeared to have been a test the students were due back. One minute everyone had been going about their normal day and then suddenly it had been plunged into one of terror. For most of these students, Annabelle suspected that every day they had to spend in a school building after this one would be nerve-wracking. They would sit watching the crack under the door, flinching if something brushed their leg under the desk. After what she'd seen at eight years old, it had taken five years for her to even sit and watch someone swim. She still wouldn't get in the water, the image of her father gasping for air still fresh in her memory.

They kept walking, picking up the pace towards the courtyard. The cafeteria was blocked off with yellow police tape and from what Annabelle could tell; it appeared to be the most affected room they had seen so far. The courtyard door was propped open, and the authorities had erected a tent outside where a group of officers were talking. Akari led them up to the group and introduced herself.

"Hello, I'm Agent Akari Tanaka, I believe I spoke to a Mr Proctor on the phone?"

A young man in a suit and tie stepped forward, a folder of documents in his arms. He placed it down on a table and shook her hand.

"Agent Tanaka, Dustin Proctor. I have the files here you requested. Is there anything more we can do for you?" there was a slight edge to his voice and Annabelle wasn't entirely sure they could trust him. Although, she reasoned with herself, that could just be the unease at their current situation. After all, it couldn't be an everyday occurrence that you had to investigate snakes attacking school children.

"Actually, I have a question." It was Jaylen who spoke up, and Dustin nodded for him to go ahead.

"How did you get rid of the snakes? There aren't any bodies in there, so unless the clean-up of over a thousand of them took less than twenty-four hours, they must have left on their own."

"We killed a large number, the bathrooms are full of them, but when the police arrived at the scene, they were all fleeing back down the pipes. No one knows why or what suddenly caused it, but it's almost like they knew we were coming." Jaylen nodded in thanks for Dustin's answer as Akari took the files and they left the school.

Annabelle took her tablet back out as they drove back to the hotel. Pictures of the attack were plastered on the front page of news sites. She realised suddenly that, while most of the pictures and video footage showed terrified students, the same girl appeared calm. She looked around fifteen years old and was wearing a pink coat with a fur-lined hood.

"Jaylen. Look at this? That's weird right?"

"Definitely. Any ideas who she is?"

"No, but I think I know how to find out." He nodded and, in the mirror, Akari looked pleased that they were making progress. Annabelle grabbed her phone and sent a quick message to Alessandra. If anyone could find out who this girl was without leaving a trace, it was her.

Chapter 11

The group had just finished eating dinner, Zofia's promise to pay for all their expenses was going to become difficult to keep if they kept ordering this much via room service. With their bellies full, exhaustion wasn't too far behind. Aluna and Akari excused themselves first, the former promising to meet Chris down in the lobby bright and early for their sewer adventure. Jaylen was next, standing with a brief stretch.

"I'm going upstairs to see if they have anything other than alcohol at the bar. Any of you want something?"

"Chamomile tea?" Annabelle requested.

"Sure," and he exited Chris's room with a small wave. Annabelle used her fork to push the last few bites of food around on her plate as Chris rifled through his bag for the paperback he'd brought before their flight to Warsaw. He expected her to excuse herself to her room and was content to spend the rest of the evening reading until his brain tired enough to fall asleep. Instead, she set her plate on the cart and leaned back in her chair as if to stay a while longer.

"Crazy day," she started, as though she was unsure if he wanted her company.

"Yeah," he tossed his bag onto the spare bed and sat down on the other. "Tomorrow's probably going to be crazier."

Annabelle laughed lightly. "I have a feeling crazy is about to become the new norm."

Chris grunted in agreement as he flipped through the book absently. "Crazy and impossible," he intoned. "I have to say, my life was a lot less interesting last week."

She didn't laugh, and he glanced up nervously at her intense stare. Not for the first time he wished he knew what to say instead of the snarky comments he usually made. She stood up and made her way to the door, and Chris cursed inwardly. She paused with her hand on the doorknob, half turning to catch his eyes as he watched her leave.

"For what it's worth, I'm glad you're here." She left him to his solitude then, letting the door fall behind her with a soft click. Chris stared after her for a few moments, trying to remember if anyone had ever paid him a better compliment. He wanted to go after her, to tell her it was worth quite a lot to him, but his feet wouldn't cooperate. Instead, he flopped back on the mountain of pillows that seemed to be a staple of higher end hotels, all thoughts of his book forgotten.

Annabelle made her way back to the room she was sharing with Akari. The older girl was growing on her and the tea she had asked for was already sitting on the dressing table, right next to her tablet. Arianna had sent her research through during dinner and she was itching to go through it.

"Akari, look at this." Arianna's research was huge. "This girl, Naomi Stevenson, she was the one to pull the alarm."

"Okay, so,"

"Here's the thing, she told everyone about the snakes before they started coming into the school. They expelled her from five schools already for bringing in weapons and attempting to hurt students."

"So, you think she lured the snakes in? But how?"

"I don't know, but we need to find her."

The Sewers

Chris's prediction about the next day had actually fallen short of the mark. Crazy had compounded on top of impossible to give him something resembling the most frustratingly chaotic day he'd had in recent memory. They'd captured a live snake and discovered multiple bodies floating in the water. He and Aluna were just about to head back to the Buick when Akari and Jaylen appeared.

Chris glanced around expectantly, but when a third person didn't materialise, he turned to a rather dishevelled looking Akari. "Where's Annabelle?"

"She found important information about this student, Naomi Stevenson. It's looking like she brought the snakes into the school. I told her to go over to this girl's house, see if the parents can offer anything useful," she explained.

"On her own?" A gnawing worry in his gut began and wouldn't let up as he thought about all the ways this was a bad idea.

"She'll be fine," Akari reassured him. "I see you've found a snake." Chris nodded, and the four of them walked back to the car. For a moment Chris suddenly realised that it would be rather difficult to explain the stench of the sewer they'd waded through when they returned the car to the airport.

Worry for Annabelle and a series of increasingly persistent texts from Gina made him irritable on the ride back to the hotel. Aluna wisely didn't peruse any small talk with him, choosing instead to scan the radio for an acceptable soundtrack for their drive. She settled on a classic rock station, singing along with a few songs as Chris stared out the window. He'd sent Annabelle a text the moment he'd got back to the car, but she hadn't replied yet. He was toying with the idea of calling her when they pulled into the hotel car park.

By unspoken agreement, they used the car for their experiments. They had moved the snake from its bag on to the back seats, and they all winced as the sewer water began staining the leather. Akari had gathered as many supplies they could find from the hotel room.

"Zofia is going to have one hell of a bill," Chris quipped. "Okay, I still need distilled water, tap water, a knife, teaspoons, disinfectant, and second kettle," Jaylen help up his hands.

"I'll go ask housekeeping about the kettle and cutlery, there's disinfectant in the cupboard under the sink in the rooms, I can grab that on the way out."

"And I will go ask the bar about the water," Akari added. They left quickly, and Aluna chuckled at the expression on Chris's face.

"She is fine, Chris. As I understand it, Annabelle is quite formidable. Surely a teenage schoolgirl and her parents aren't much of threat."

Chris grabbed the kettle they had previously on top of the mini-fridge and scowled at the stains on the glass. "Do me a favour, Aluna. Clean that." He handed it to her without looking. While she was busy was busy with the bowl of warm soapy water in the boot, Chris checked his phone once again. Still nothing. He was about to press the call button when Akari came across the car park.

"They didn't have distilled water, but they said they'd track some down for you. Here is the tap water, and I brought up some glasses in case you needed them."

"Thanks," Chris nodded, inspecting them appreciatively. They were almost like the beakers he had back at the sanctuary. "Can one of you get some extra towels?"

"I will go, Aluna interjected. "That way they will not be getting so many requests from just one person."

"Whatever," Chris waved at him absently. He rummaged through his bad and produced four latex gloves, then turned to Akari. "Guess that makes you my assistant for the day."

By the time Aluna and Jaylen had returned, Chris had figured out a way of knocking the snake out with sleeping medication left by his room's previous inhabitants. Akari's phone rang as they were working, and she stepped away to take it as Chris moved back to the snake. It was a tight fit inside the car. This was not a space designed to perform surgery on a live animal.

"Alright," he gestured to Jaylen, who was ready with a sterilised knife and every towel they had procured. Chris handed him a torch and traded it for the knife as they set to work. Aluna slipped on a pair of gloves and used two teaspoons to place samples of blood into the glasses." Akari had come back into the car now and was watching with a look of minor disgust on her face.

Chris's phone chimed on the table across the room, and he glanced up from his work to Akari. "Grab that, will you? It's probably Annabelle."

Akari smiled knowingly and pressed the green button. "Hello?"

Chris divided his attention between the surgery and the phone call. Akari was being unhelpfully quiet as Annabelle spoke, and Chris clenched his jaw as he forced himself to do his job. After securing enough blood from the snake, he closed the wound with a needle and thread he had found in Akari's bag.

"Okay, be careful," Akari said before hanging up. Chris looked up sharply as the petite woman set his phone back on the dashboard. "Annabelle is heading back to the school to go through Naomi's locker. She believes there might be something in there to explain the snake attack."

"How the hell is she going to get inside there without you?" Chris wondered aloud.

"She is resourceful," Akari answered. "She is confident that she will get access to the locker. I did not ask how."

"Of course, you didn't," Chris mumbled snidely. If Jaylen heard him, he said nothing, but he saw Aluna trying to hide a smile behind her hand as she faked a cough.

"Alright," Chris snapped off his gloves and inspected his handy work. It would scar something horrible, but given his limited supplies, he felt he'd done fairly well. "Now to test this blood. Can you guys keep stirring this, so it doesn't congeal"

He grabbed a notepad and began writing furiously. At a strange look from Akari, he spoke. "If this proves anything, we're going to need to repeat it, and for that, we need exact notes." She seemed to accept his answer and continued stirring the blood, silently hoping that these glasses were deep cleaned before the next guest drank from them. It wasn't as though they could tell the staff what they had been doing with them.

"Okay, now I'm going to add the distilled water to this glass, Akari, keep mixing the other sample. It the blood congeals, I'll have to open the snake back up again and I don't have any more of this makeshift sedative" There didn't appear to be any reaction, which was what Chris had expected. The distilled water would be free from any kind of contamination. Currently, Annabelle's theory about the water was the only guess they had and with the snakes coming up through the toilets it was making more and more sense.

"Let's try this sample." As predicted, the second he added the tap water from the hotel bathroom, the snake's blood fizzed and steam dramatically. Small clots appeared and the remaining fluid lightened in colour to a greyish pink.

"What the hell." Aluna was the first to speak. Akari's phone rang again, and she left the car once more.

"This." Chris responded, "is proof that something in the water is causing chemical changes to the animals. Although what we can't currently prove is what that something is or why it's causing a reaction. But this is a start, an excellent start."

"Guys we have to go, the officers thought Annabelle was acting suspicious and they're sending a team over here to ask us questions. I've messaged her, told her not to come here." Akari looked scared and with her words, the same expression was mirrored on Jaylen and Aluna's faces.

As they were packing up their things and leaving the snake in the bag behind a bin, Chris called animal control and reported the injured snake before hightailing it out of the carpark with the others. Safe to say, they likely wouldn't be welcome at that establishment – or maybe even in Washington – ever again.

The team were silent on their way to meet Annabelle, and Chris tried to keep his leg from bouncing in anticipation. Get a grip, he scolded himself. It hadn't even been a full day, and Annabelle was more than capable of taking care of herself. Still, they'd spent the last week or so in each other's company and he was growing accustomed to seeing her face. Knowing she was out there on her own made his stomach ache.

"This is ridiculous," he muttered to himself.

"I'm sorry?" Akari asked from the seat next to him. Chris shook his head and kept his eyes out the window. As Aluna pulled into the garage, he breathed a sigh of relief at the sight of Annabelle's slight frame standing off to the side.

"What happened?" she asked as they piled out of the car. Her eyes sought Chris's immediately, and he gave her a reassuring smile as he noticed her giving him a once over.

"It turns out when we go in there asking questions and then you rummage through a girl's locker and she then goes missing, the local police decide to pin the blame on us."

"I found something in her locker," Annabelle held up a notebook and spoke in a rapid pace that meant she was keyed up about something she thought was important. Akari took it from her and began flipping through the pages. "It's full of information on drug laws. Stuff that isn't even public knowledge."

Seeing her had quieted the restlessness he'd been feeling all day, but rather than voice his relief, he fell back on his time-tested snark. "Well, she is a student. Maybe this is just some research project she picked up for extra credit."

She dug into her back pocket and produced a small piece of paper. "I also found this." Chris craned his neck as she passed it to Akari, surprised to see a family photo in front of a research facility, an unknown man standing next to what appeared to be Naomi's father.

"That's Naomi," Akari pointed out. Next to her, Jaylen had stiffened and reached for the picture with trembling fingers. "What is it, Jaylen? Do you recognise the other guy?"

"That. That is my uncle." Jaylen glanced up at them in shock.

Chris groaned inwardly and ran a hand over his face. "Alright, question and answer time is over. We need to get out of here before Animal Control gets to the hotel and even more people start looking for us."

"What happened at the hotel?" Annabelle couldn't resist asking a question, even as they piled into the Buick. Aluna took the driver's seat again, leaving Annabelle in the middle seat between Chris and Akari. Jaylen sat silently in the passenger seat, his fingers still clutching the photograph.

As they drove, Chris tried to explain the events of the day to Annabelle, and at one point he saw her try to stifle a smile. "What?" he asked.

"I can't believe you managed all that with literally no scientific equipment." He thought he'd heard a touch of awe in her voice, though that could have been wishful thinking on his part. "So, we know that the city water supply was causing the snake's behaviour. Do we know what specifically was in the water?"

He knew where she was going with this, but as far as they knew, it could literally be anything. "I don't know," Chris admitted. "But I know where we can find out. Akari, can we take this car to Massachusetts?"

"Yes, I believe so," she answered. "If I may ask, what is in Massachusetts?"

For a moment he thought about telling them the truth. Then he remembered all the reasons that was a bad idea. "A lab we can use, or at least a better makeshift one." He didn't want to tell them about the small they'd moved to after his parents had divorced, about how his mother had lived in near poverty after his dad had left, or how Chris left them behind as soon as possible for a new life in England. He guessed the kitchen of the town hall where he used to run experiments hadn't changed too much, and provided they did what they had to do quickly, they could be in and out before anyone knew they were there.

Akari called Zofia from the car after programming in directions to Salem, and in the front Aluna was concentrating on the road as Jaylen stared at the photo.

With the other occupied, Annabelle leaned in close to him and whispered. "You alright?"

She must have picked up on his mood change, but he really didn't want to dredge up ancient history. On top of it, the texts he'd been receiving all day from Gina had gnawed at him. Kendall was begging to see him. Of course, he hadn't actually told Annabelle about Kendall, or Gina, and he didn't want to bring it up now.

So instead, he clenched his teeth and exhaled sharply through his nose. "Fine," he told her, her head turned to glare out the window. He felt her eyes on him for a moment longer before she sensed he didn't want to talk about it and pulled out her phone.

As her right hand thumbed through the day's news, her left fell to her lap and slid over to where their legs pressed against each other in the cramped back seat. Chris tried not to think of what had been on that seat less than an hour ago. He felt the heat from her hand through his jeans and barely resisted the urge to let his fingers slide over hers. Still, the contact on his leg was sure and comforting, and he took a few steadying breaths before letting his head fall back against the headrest wearily. Before his eyes slipped closed, he felt her fingers curl ever so slightly against the rough fabric of his jeans in a light caress, and he fell asleep with a sigh.

Chapter 12

They'd picked up the equipment they needed on the way to Salem.

"The website says the senior's aerobics class starts at 9:30 tomorrow morning," Annabelle looked up at Chris. "You sure you can get in and out in time?"

"Yeah," Chris had limited himself to one-word answers ever since they'd arrived in Salem, Massachusetts. They'd driven in near silence, save for Jaylen's musings on why Naomi Stevenson was in a photo with his uncle. Akari and Aluna had tried to get more information out of Chris, but he had adamantly avoided every question. Annabelle's senses were telling her there was a story here – one he didn't want to see the light of day. Shoving her curiosity to the side for the moment, she gave him some breathing room.

"Alright," she turned to Akari, "we are running woefully short on clean clothes and food. Chris and I can handle the town hall. Why don't the three of you gather supplies and find somewhere to do laundry?" It was unlike Annabelle to take charge so suddenly, and Akari raised one delicate eyebrow. Her eyes shifted between the two of them, her mouth opening to make some comment.

"I can do laundry," Jaylen offered quickly. "I dislike shopping."

"Okay," Akari finally agreed, "Aluna and I will resupply while the two of you test the water and Jaylen washes the clothes." She shot the man a teasing smile which he returned easily. "We will pick two of you up at the town hall at 9:30 and meet Jaylen at the restaurant on the corner by 10 to go over the results?" Everyone nodded in agreement, or at least didn't argue, and Akari bid them goodnight and retreated to the room across the hall. Chris stood as well, having once again snagged a solo room. Annabelle followed him into the hall and shut the door to Jaylen and Aluna's room before reaching for his sleeve.

"Hey, you alright?" He stopped and tuned, his eyes darting around to keep from looking her in the eye. Annabelle guessed he really didn't want to talk about it. "I just thought, maybe…"

"It's alright," Chris ran a hand down his face then back up through his hair. "I just didn't think I'd come back here."

Annabelle had guessed Chris had some sort of history with the town. "You grew up here?"

"No," Chris shook his head. "After my parents divorced, my mum and I flew out here. She knew a guy who knew a guy who got her a job at the local school."

Annabelle smiled at this piece of the puzzle that made up Chris Stuart. "Your mum was a teacher," she didn't sound surprised.

He relaxed a little, his stance a little more defensive as he answered her non-question. "Biology."

"Is that where you got the science bug from?"

His entire demeanour shifted then, and his eyes clouded over. "I'm exhausted. I'll see you in the morning." He turned to escape to his room, and Annabelle felt guilty for bringing up what was obviously a bad memory.

"I'm sorry." She blurted out. He paused at his door and Annabelle saw his shoulders rise and fall with a sigh.

"Me too," he glanced at her. "Do you, uh, want a drink?" He nodded his head sideways in invitation, and Annabelle jumped at it.

"Yeah," she propelled herself forward and through the door as he held it open for her. He had previously tossed his messenger bag onto the single bed, and he cleared it out of the way and gestured for her to sit. This hotel wasn't nearly as fancy as the one in Washington, and the small room barely had space for the bed, the chest of draws, and the tiny mini fridge. Chris opened it and pulled out two beers from the six-pack he'd bought earlier when they'd stopped to refuel the car. He twisted the top off of the first and handed it to Annabelle before opening his own. He turned and leaned back against the dresser, taking long drinks as they sat in a heavy silence.

"Is your mum still alive?" Annabelle asked finally. "I didn't think before…"

"What?" Chris's brow wrinkled in confusion, then flattened as he shook his head. "Yeah, she's still alive. She's back in the UK now, Northampton."

"That's nice," Annabelle smiled. Then, because she couldn't handle the tension that had settled between them, she continued. "I was afraid. I mean, because of the way you reacted. I thought maybe she wasn't, and I had brought it up…"

"No, she's good," Chris interrupted her rambling. "My father is a biologist, of sorts," he added under his breath. "I used to want to be just like him until I found out he had been cheating on my mum with just about every woman he could get his hands on." He took another drink. "Including her best friend."

Charlotte grimaced. "Ouch. I'm sorry."

"Yeah, he's a peach." Chris finished his beer and went for another. Annabelle shook her head as he offered her a second; she was only halfway through her first. "I've pretty much cut off all contact with him. Haven't spoken to him in… eleven years?"

There were a few minutes of silence.

"This is fun," Chris drawled. "Here I have a beautiful woman in my hotel room and I'm depressing the both of us by digging up ancient history."

Annabelle blushed at his compliment. "You're not depressing me," she told him. "It's nice to know there's more to you than science and snark."

His self-deprecating laugh filled the space, and he toasted her with his drink. "I hate to disappoint you, but that is pretty much all there is."

She stood then, hitching her hip against the dresser next to him as he turned toward her. "No, it isn't." His eyes followed her movement as she set her bottle down on the cheap wood top. She'd promised herself on the flight to Warsaw that she wouldn't actively pursue anything more between them, but if things progressed naturally, she wouldn't try to shy away. Seeing his current expression and hearing his obviously low opinion of himself ignited something inside her. Could he honestly not see how wonderful he'd been since the day they'd met? He'd pretty much but his life on hold to help a stranger, and then with very little convincing he'd flown halfway across the country and stood beside her as her world had come crashing down. Deciding she'd had quiet enough of his self-doubt, she forged ahead with her thoughts. "And you couldn't disappoint me."

His eyes snapped up to hers, hesitant and searching. She let him look, resisting the urge to drop her gaze or step away. He shifted his weight from one foot to the other as he shuffled a step closer, and she pushed away from the dresser to meet him halfway. His hand was cool on her arm, damp from the condensation of the bottle he'd abandoned.

Annabelle inhaled deeply as he kissed her, feeling his fingers slide through her hair to cradle her head. Her own hands settled on his waist, and just as he started to pull away, she began kissing him back. Time fell away from them as they stood in the tiny hotel room, moulding their bodies together.

Only the late hour and the realisation that Jaylen and Aluna were literally feet away through a very thin wall allowed Annabelle to keep her head. She pulled away first, letting her head fall against his jaw as she leaned into him. His arms banded over her shoulders to pull her flush against him.

"I should get back to my room," she muttered, making no genuine attempt to let him go. She had to admit – at least to herself – that it felt good to let him hold her.

He hummed in response and tightened his hold, causing them both to laugh quietly. She pushed back and slid her hands from his waist to his chest, letting one travel further to press against his cheek. His eyes looked brighter than they had before, and Annabelle felt giddy at the prospect of being responsible for it.

"I'll see you tomorrow." Her hand fell away as she stepped back. He followed her to the door and opened it for her, standing in the doorway as she walked across the hallway to her own room. She slid the plastic key card into the slot and waited for the beep. As she turned the handle, Annabelle glanced back over her shoulder and smiled at Chris. He answered it with one of his own and waved as she stepped into her room and closed the door.

Chapter 13

Akari dropped Annabelle and Chris off on the corner of Congress Street with a promise to return at 9:30 to collect them.

"We'll be here," Annabelle promised. She closed the door and turned to Chris, who was staring at the surrounding buildings with a grimace on his face. He wasn't happy to be back. "Let's go," she urged him forward with a nod of her head, leading him across the street and through the open fence line to a back entrance. Just as Chris had said, the doors were open.

"They always come around to turn the heating on before class starts so the doors should be open." Annabelle checked her watch. It was twenty minutes to nine.

"Where to?"

He led her to a small kitchen space at the back of the hall. It was cleaner than working in the hotel room. Annabelle pulled her rucksack off her back and retrieved the equipment inside. They'd had to stop at four different shops to obtain the necessary tools, but after what had happened in Washington, they didn't want to cause any more suspicion.

"Ok, so essentially we're going to set this beaker of water up with the indicator in these beakers. Add heat and the water should separate and tell us what we're working with."

It seemed way too simple. "Is that it?"

"Yeah, we just have to hope that whatever is contaminating this water isn't flammable." Annabelle suspected that an explosion in the kitchen of the location for senior aerobics was going to be a lot harder to explain than an injured snake in a hotel room.

Following his hastily drawn diagram, Annabelle placed the candle underneath the cooling rack. Chris was busy cleaning the beaker and filling it with a sample he'd brought with them from Washington. This was nothing like the chemistry experiments she remembered doing in school. Covering the other two beakers with clingfilm and poking holes in them with nail scissors, she set to work taping down the tubes they'd found in a model rollercoaster kit. Once Chris returned with a sealed beaker of water and a bowl of ice, she lit the candle and they waited in a comfortable silence.

It felt like forever before the water bubbled, and the other beakers filled. Once all the liquid had vanished, Chris turned to her.

"This one's just steam you can take it out and rinse it while I look at these." Annabelle nodded and took the warm beaker to the sink. The other two beakers contained a pale-yellow powder and another clear liquid.

She sat and watched him work for half an hour and then, at 9:15, he turned to her.

"Ok, we have results." He said, showing her the contents of both beakers and his accompanying notes. "This powder is something we didn't see in the water we tested with Timmy. It's called enolprilat, and it's a by-product of some pretty intense chemical reactions that don't happen in nature. It means that the contamination was man-made – engineered in a lab." He paused for a moment to let her take in the information. "This liquid is about 90% dextro-rinoifane, what I can't figure out is what makes up the other 10%."

So, despite the progress they'd made today, they still had more work to do. Gathering up the equipment they ran out of the hall where the Buick was waiting for them.

"What did you find?" Akari asked, turning in her seat to look at Chris.

"Someone manufactured a chemical compound and put it in the water. It's a mixture of dextro-rinoifane and an unknown substance."

"What does that mean?" Aluna glanced in the mirror.

"Perhaps we should wait until we meet with Jaylen," Akari said before Chris could launch into a lecture. Annabelle laughed and patted his knee sympathetically as he sank back into his seat with a frown.

Jaylen was already waiting at a table when they arrived at the restaurant. And Chris talked through the experiment and what the results showed, while Akari made a phone call to Zofia to update her on their progress.

"So, we still need to find this missing 10%. Any ideas?" Jaylen responded, and the group fell silent.

Off to the side, Akari finished her conversation and came striding over purposefully. "Aluna, Chris, we need to leave now. Zofia's booked us a flight back to New Delhi, they have a dog situation that apparently we will be very interested in." Annabelle was about to protest when Akari put her hand up and continued. "I need you and Jaylen to stay here, there's a government list of who can legally manufacture dextro-rinoifane in the US, and the only person even remotely willing to talk about it is Kelsey Shelton. You will both be going to meet with her."

Chapter 14

Annabelle packed her things quickly, thankful that Akari was downstairs arranging everything and not present to hear her complaining about her assignment. A knock on the door interrupted her grumbling, and she yanked open the door a bit more forcefully than she intended. Chris stood on the other side with a startled expression. She turned away and continued packing as he stepped inside and closed the door.

"You okay?"

"Great," she snapped. "I get to babysit Jaylen while the three of you get to go to India."

"Jaylen needs someone to help him track down Kelsey Shelton. You're really the best person for the job."

She whirled around with her hairbrush in hand, jabbing it at him accusingly.

"Don't you dare try to make me feel better with flattery and logical rationalizations. I'm ranting." He held up his hands in defeat and said nothing else as she finished throwing her things into her rolling suitcase. She struggled to zip it, growling in frustration as she could only close it halfway.

"You know," Chris said as he came up behind her, "this would zip a lot easier if you folded everything." He reached around her and pushed the top down, allowing her to finish pulling the zipper all the way around the case. She glared at him, but he just smiled back at her and took her hand when she finished. "Listen, I know you want to come. I don't much like the idea of being a continent away while you and Jaylen search for a phantom. But finding people that don't want to be found is something you're good at. Your skills are more useful here."

She slid the luggage from the bed to the floor, wincing at the loud thud that seemed to echo into the room beneath them. "I don't even know where to start."

"Start with the military." Chris answered easily. "You said it yourself. The trucks that were carrying dextro-rinoifane were US military trucks. See if there's any evidence of a Kelsey Shelton working for the military." She knew all of this already – she even had several ideas for documents she could get Arianna to send through. But pretending she didn't stop her from blurting out the one thing that had been on her mind since Akari had announced they would split the team again. She didn't want to sound too… needy? Clingy? Whatever had come over her last night and pushed her to kiss him had settled firmly in her gut and refused to leave. In the restaurant she had been overcome with an urge to demand she go to New Delhi and let Akari stay with Jaylen, but prudence and embarrassment at the way that demand could be received had kept her quiet.

She'd been quiet too long, she realised as Chris shifted his weight to take a step back. "When does your flight leave?" she asked suddenly.

"Uh," Chris glanced at the bedside clock, "Akari said something about leaving for the airport at three." It was just a little before eleven now, leaving them with almost three full hours with nothing to do. Thoughts of ways to fill that time entered Annabelle's head, and she coughed to hide the hitch in her chest those mental images gave her. She waved off his look of concern and fished her water bottle from the bedside table. After a few sips, she screwed the top back on and shook off the last of the flustering thoughts.

"Wanna watch some TV?" Annabelle offered lamely. She turned and reached for the remote, aiming it around his body, jumping as a rather boisterous advert blared from the speaker. She jammed the volume down button and winced apologetically, but Chris just laughed.

"Whoever was in here before you must have been a deaf spinster." He reached down and moved her suitcase to the far wall before coming back and settling on the bed. He adjusted the pillows to rest comfortably against the headboard, charmingly bolted into the wall to prevent theft – or possibly ruining the paint job from any vigorous activities. With that thought once more planted in her head, Annabelle kicked off her shoes and sat next to him. Their shoulders brushed as he made room, and she felt his eyes on her as she flipped through the channels for anything to watch.

She settled on an old black and white – a favourite of her Aunt's – and tried not to think about the warmth he radiated or the smell of his sandalwood deodorant that mingled with the soap from the hotel bathroom. She tried to focus on her upcoming task, to plan her moves and be ready when Jaylen inevitably turned to her to find Kelsey. But she couldn't seem to focus on anything but Chris's steady, even breaths next to her or the rustle of his clothing as he shifted to a more comfortable position.

His fingers trailed up and down her arm lazily, lulling her into a sleepy haze as the movie droned on in the background. When her eyes snapped open again, he was shifting to reach for the remote, and she glanced at the clock with a groan. She had fallen asleep, and their three hours were up.

"Time to go," she slurred, pushing up to sit as he slid off the other side of the bed. She followed him to the door and tugged on his sleeve just as he reached for the knob. When he turned around, she surprised them both by surging up on her toes and kissing him soundly. He hummed in approval against her lips, responding eagerly to her for a moment. When he broke the kiss, they were breathing a little more heavily.

"Call me when you land," she breathed.

Chapter 15

Salem

The next morning had been hectic. Dustin Proctor had somehow followed them from the school in Washington to their Massachusetts hotel and had a serious obsession with finding out what they were up to. Apparently, their new location was easier to find than they expected. It was situations like these, Annabelle thought, where it would have been useful for Akari to have stayed instead of her. Skilled agents had trained the woman to deal with these sorts of situations. Without her, Jaylen and Annabelle had decided they were better off co-operating with Dustin and letting him in on the mission. Initially, he'd been extremely helpful, helping to spot patterns that even Annabelle hadn't been able to find and agreeing to take the case to the authorities once they'd finalised everything. Then they'd made a breakthrough. Records of human trials Kelsey had discovered before she'd gone missing.

The case was almost finished when Dustin intercepted an email from Arianna. She had flown to a nearby hotel and had documents she needed Annabelle to see in person. Illegal documents. Initially, he had agreed to continue helping them, but still had to arrest Arianna. Jaylen had made the quick and smart decision to switch hotels in the middle of the night while they finished their search and had flipped the Buick on the drive over. So now, she had windscreen glass in her hair, blood on her favourite outfit, a police officer arresting her best friend, and Chris was a seventeen-hour flight away.

Annabelle sighed as the hot spray hit her aching muscles. She hadn't been in a car accident since college, and that hadn't nearly been as bad as this one. Every part of her ached, and it didn't matter how many stretches she did. She winced as the cuts on her face were exposed to the water, washing away the last of the dirt and grime left over from the crash. Jaylen had retreated downstairs to get drinks and to plan their next move. They needed to reunite with the others and discuss where to go from here. The little information she had received had shown them that dextro-rinoifane was being mass produced by the government as part of mind-control experiments.

Annabelle smiled as she thought about the information that would finally bring her family justice. The producers of this drug would answer for everything, and Annabelle felt a thrum of vindication course through her. It wasn't unlike the moment Chris had discovered the water contamination in Brize Norton.

Thoughts of Chris led her easily to the night before he'd left for New Delhi. Memory of the kisses they'd shared sent a different tendril of energy through her, and she closed her eyes as she remembered the softness of his lips on hers and the warmth of him as he'd held her. Her shower lasted a little longer than she'd planned, and as she stepped out onto the mustard-coloured bathmat, she heard someone knocking at her door.

Thinking it was Jaylen, she wrapped a towel around her body quickly and answered. She faltered for a moment as Dustin Proctor's gaze took her in.

"Oh," she managed. "Hey."

"Hey," he returned, making at least an effort to keep his eyes on hers. "Where's Jaylen?" he asked, glancing over her shoulder as though expecting to see the other man inside.

"Oh, uh, he's just getting us coffee," she told him.

"What, no celebrating?" Dustin's tone was cocky now.

"Well," she shrugged, "there are still more things we need to figure out." She felt more than a little vulnerable standing there in only a towel, but she refused to let him see it. It was true, they still had to prove that the dextro-rinoifane from Brize Norton and the Meru National Park was from these trials. Now they knew what they were looking for, the task was a lot simpler.

"Oh, come on," Dustin smiled easily. "You have all that evidence, right?"

"I guess so?" She wasn't entirely sure where he was going with this. She wished he would leave her alone so she could at least dress before they continued.

"So," he continued, either unaware of unsympathetic to her discomfort, "unless I'm missing something, it seems like your day turned out great." His eyes dropped again but darted up just as quickly. The suggestion was not lost on Annabelle. "So, if you ask me, you should be doing something about that."

He was flirting with her. If she wasn't standing almost naked in the hallway of a hotel, she might have laughed. Her earlier conversations with Chris came back to her, and she stifled a smile. "You're just saying that because I'm wearing a towel." It was a dismissal, a subtle hint to let him know she needed to put some clothes on. He didn't get it.

"I'm not going to lie; you are an excellent towel wearer." His smile turned into a leer as he leaned in slightly. "Among your other fine qualities." He leaned further and Annabelle realised he was going to kiss her. Her hand came up between them and pressed against his chest. He stopped and frowned. "What's wrong?"

"Nothing," she shook her head, "I'm just… sort of with someone."

"Jaylen?" Dustin guessed, and Annabelle laughed.

"No," she shook her head. "Listen, I am flattered. But…"

"Not going to happen," he shrugged. "I get it." There was something there, though, just on the periphery. Annabelle couldn't identify it, but she guessed it was something like disappointment.

Suddenly the tension between them evaporated, and she laughed. "Come on in," she stepped back. "I'll get dressed and we'll go find Jaylen."

"Sure." She left him standing in the small space between the door and the rest of the room as she retreated into the bathroom to dress. Once finished, she stepped back out. He was still there, and she slipped by him to find her shoes and bag. Her phone rang as she was checking the time, and she answered with a smile as she saw the name on the screen.

"Jaylen, hey."

"Annabelle, listen to me," he was frantic, and Annabelle's smile faded. "Dustin killed your friend. I just got access to her home security cameras. He didn't arrest her, he killed her" Her heart began pounding hard at his words. The officer's presence became looming and dangerous, even though he remained on the other side of the room.

"Okay?" she tried not to sound fearful. She knew Dustin could hear every word, and if what Jaylen was saying was true, she couldn't let on that she knew.

Knowing he would likely take too long to catch onto her clues, she decided for something that sounded nonchalant. "I'm actually with Dustin now, if you're still waiting, could you grab him a coffee too that way, we can all…" her phone was snatched from her hand and she gasped.

"You are a terrible liar," he whispered menacingly. She turned toward him and tried to back up, but there was nowhere to go. "Look, Annabelle, I don't want to hurt you. Just promise me you won't share that information." He pressed forward and Annabelle's fear ratcheted up to terror. "Now."

His arm shot out and gripped her fiercely, turning her toward the bed. For a moment a stab of cold read hit here, and she couldn't help the soft sob that escaped as he pushed her backwards on the bed. His body was heavy and oppressive over her as he leaned over.

"I will not hurt you," he confirmed, "just promise me." She pressed her lips together, unwilling to give him the one thing that would finally lay her demons to rest. He sighed heavily and reached for the lamp on the nightstand. He used the cord to tie her wrists to the bedframe, and she screamed as he finally stepped back, not wanting her voice to alert the guests in the surrounding rooms and purposefully placed his hand on his gun. She silenced instantly and then heard Jaylen's voice from outside the room. Dustin grabbed her laptop from the dresser and fled the room.

Annabelle heard the race of footsteps as he chased Dustin, and Annabelle silently cheered. Jaylen wouldn't let Dustin escape with their only hope of figuring out what his Uncle had been up to. She just hoped Dustin wasn't dumb enough to draw his gun in the hotel or use it to hurt Jaylen. He was still a police officer, even if he was a crooked one. The muffled sound of a gunshot told her she'd been wrong; Dustin didn't care about the consequences anymore.

With some difficulty she managed to get free and dashed out of her room, praying that Jaylen was still alive. The only thing at the end of this corridor was the spa, which was currently closed. She crashed through the door as she heard the sounds of a scuffle a few flights down. By the pool she found Jaylen lying underneath Dustin, his face bloodied from a beating.

"Someone paid you off, didn't they?" Jaylen growled.

"Get off him, you son of a bitch." Annabelle froze as Dustin looked up at her and laughed. Annabelle felt her blood boil at it, fury filling her at the simple way he dismissed her. Her eyes darted around frantically, finding his gun discarded over by the loungers.

Annabelle lunged a split second before Dustin did, but it was enough and when Annabelle lifted the gun and fired, Dustin stumbled back onto the steps of the pool. Anger and sting at his betrayal kept her finger on the trigger, squeezing off five shots in quick succession before the bile rose in the back of her throat. Her ears rang from the deafening sound of gunfire in a tiled room, and through the haze of anger she found Jaylen's eyes.

He rose slowly, as though it hurt him to do so, and walked over to stand at her side. He reached out and took the gun from her, and Annabelle let him. Panic replaced the anger as she realised, she'd just killed a police officer.

"Oh my god," she breathed. Jaylen's hand was warm on her back, and she slammed her eyes closed as the nausea swept over her.

"We have to do," he whispered, ushering her back into the changing rooms. He tucked the gun into his waistband and quickly pulled her through the door into the hallway. "Get your things together; we need to leave now."

Annabelle nodded mutely and dashed for her hotel room. Once inside, she lurched for the bathroom and emptied her stomach. Jaylen's rapid knock came just a few moments later, and she let him in as she zipped her suitcase closed. Curious guests had emerged from their various rooms, and Annabelle could hear the insistent shouting coming from the spa. Jaylen, at least, seemed to have most of his wits about him. He craned his neck above the crowd and tried his best to sound unaware.

"What's going on?" he asked.

An older lady with dyed hair and far too much make-up turned around with a wide-eyed expression.

"They said someone's dead," she whispered. "They won't let anyone in the spa. There were gunshots earlier, didn't you hear?"

"My girlfriend and I were in our room," he gestured back where Annabelle was trying her best not to catch anyone's eye. "Someone's dead?"

"That's what they said," the woman confirmed. She turned about around in the spa's direction and Jaylen quietly stepped away.

"Come on," he jabbed the down button on the wall and pushed Annabelle into the lift when the doors opened. "We'll go to a coffee shop or something. Hopefully Akari will call soon."

Soon turned out to be a few hours later, and by that time a full manhunt had shut the hotel down. It would take the police a while to piece things together, but Annabelle knew it would only be a matter of time before they identified Dustin's killer. Jaylen and Annabelle caught a bus to New Bedford, where Akari had arranged a car to meet them and drive to the airport. From there they'd be getting a plane back to London. The team would reunite there and then head for their next destination, wherever that may be. Her panic lessened only slightly as the jet lifted off the runway, and Jaylen put his larger hand over hers when he caught them shaking.

"You okay?" he leaned over from the aisle seat with a worried frown. She cut her eyes over to him for a second, then returned them to the shrinking landscape. Unable to find her voice, she merely nodded. He let her go and straightened, obviously responding to her body language. She felt bad for ignoring him, but there were too many thoughts swirling around in her head for her to deal with any sort of personal interaction.

She dozed against the hard plastic of the plane's wall. Her head bounced hard against it as they jolted on the runway, and Annabelle winced at the lingering soreness. She felt a little better for the rest, and she managed a ghost of a smile when Jaylen asked his question again.

"I'm alright," she told him. "Just… ready to get this whole thing over with."

He nodded in agreement and shuffled down the narrow aisle as the passengers disembarked. She followed him up the jetway and into the main airport. Akari had texted Jaylen and told them she, Aluna and Chris had already landed and were waiting in the lounge. Chris hadn't texted her since he'd landed in New Delhi four days ago, but she really didn't blame him. They had probably had their hands full with the dogs., and she had been preoccupied with her own piece of the puzzle. By the time things had slowed down enough she'd been in a car crash, they'd found the purpose of the dextro-rinoifane solution and Dustin was dead by her hand. None of it was appropriate to talk about over text.

Her steps carried her ahead of Jaylen as they neared the lounge. Her jitters at the events of the day had morphed into an inexplicable need to see Chris again, to listen to his steady drawl reassure her it was all going to be okay. She rounded the corner to the lounge and breathed a sigh of relief at the familiar outline of him against the grey chair. Her feet carrier her around him and to the empty seat next to his.

Chapter 16

Chris sat up straighter as Annabelle dropped onto the metal airport seat, his eyes cataloguing the tiny fresh cuts on her face and the slight bruising that coloured her cheek. Aluna had risen to meet Jaylen and voiced the question that had stuck in Chris's throat.

"Who did this to you?"

Chris tore his eyes from Annabelle's injuries long enough to notice that Jaylen actually looked worse. A healing cut on his lip and purple bruising around his eye spoke of a fight. Jaylen glanced at Annabelle for just a spit second, but it was enough to set Chris's hackles up. Clearly, something bad had happened to the two of them.

"It's a long story, and definitely not one we should discuss here," Jaylen dismissed his friend's concern. "I'll tell you guys later."

"Akari," Charlotte whispered. The name caught in throat slightly, and Chris tried to keep his worry from showing on his face.

The team turned their attention to her as she reached into her bag. She lifted a small envelope into her hand, keeping it hidden within the fabric of the bag. "What is it?" Akari questioned.

"Kelsey Shelton left this in her safe-deposit box. It's a record of hundreds of children that an unspecified branch of the US government tested the dextro-rinoifane solution on. They expected the drug to prove the possibility of total mind control, but according to initial reports it was a complete failure." The magnitude of this information fought for dominance in his brain.

"So, the same drug we've found in all these animals was developed to control the brains of children?" he summarised.

"Yeah," Jaylen nodded. "Kelsey Shelton claims that they're currently working on an alternative."

"Wait," Akari held up her hand to stop him and glanced around furtively. "Zofia has secured us rooms at a hotel just a few blocks from here," she said, reading the recent text from her phone.

"Then we should get some rest," Aluna stood and grabbed her small duffel. The others followed, though only Chris noticed the wince Annabelle tried to hide as she got to her feet. He reached out and took her bag, shouldering it along with his own. She shot him a grateful look and fell into step beside him as Akari led the way out of the airport and found a taxi.

It took an hour for the group to settle in Jaylen and Aluna's hotel room. It was a lot colder here in London than the hotels they'd stayed in during their trip, but a sense of being this much closer to home was comforting to Chris. The envelope holding Kelsey's findings sat in the centre of the bed as Jaylen read through the pages of data and explained what had happened leading up to their last day at Hotel Salem. Annabelle kept quiet the entire time; her eyes focused on a ball of lint that she continually nudged with her shoe. When Jaylen mentioned the crash and the few minutes he was convinced Annabelle had been unconscious, the entire team turned to look at her.

"I'm fine," she told them. She shrugged her shoulders, grimacing as her muscles protested her movement. Chris studied her face for a little longer as Jaylen returned to the list of tests performed on these children, but she wouldn't meet his gaze, There was something else neither her nor Jaylen seemed willing to mention. Something more than a car crash had stolen the fiery spirit from her eyes.

"There's more," Jaylen continued. "Dustin Proctor…'

That was as far as he got before Annabelle shot out of her chair and made her way to the door. She wrenched it open and dashed across the room she and Akari were sharing. Jaylen sighed and met his friend's curious stares.

"He's dead."

"Dead?" Aluna questioned. "Were he and Annabelle… close?" She asked the second with a nervous glance at Chris. Jaylen seemed to miss it., but Akari didn't. The scientist game nothing away, but inside his heart was hammering. The thought that she might have grown closer to the police officer snarled something in him. He didn't want to peer too closely at the reasons, though he was suspecting what he was feeling for the girl went beyond casual interest and attraction.

"No," Jaylen frowned and closed his eyes. When he opened them again there was a depth of sadness that hadn't been there before. "She killed him."

A chorus of incredulity met the confession, and Chris actually came. To his feet. "What the hell are you talking about?"

"He tried to get her to delete the data files," Jaylen explained. "He tied her up in her hotel room and stole her laptop. I caught up with him in the spa. We fought and Annabelle must have got herself free because I look up and she's there. Dustin's the one who gave me this," Jaylen indicated the bruise on his cheek. "In the fight he lost hold of his gun, and he and Annabelle lunged for it at the same time. She got there first, but he didn't stop coming at her. It was self-defence."

Akari breathed a curse under her breath, and Aluna stared stoically at her oldest friend. Almost as one, the three of them turned to Chris expectantly. He had planned on visiting her after their meeting broke up anyway; that they all clearly wanted him to do it now just got him out of there faster. He sighed and stood, stopping just as he reached the door to turn as Akari called his name softly. She padded over to him and slipped her key card into his hand. Chris stared at it for a moment, then nodded his thanks.

He came to a stop just outside Annabelle's door. He leaned in to listen for any clue as to what he might find on the other side, but there was only silence. It took a few tries for the key card to work, and finally it buzzed green and let him in. The room was dark, almost pitch black thanks to the heavy curtains that hung on the window. The light from the hall disappeared as the door closed behind him, and he shuffled forward, calling Annabelle's name softly.

She didn't answer, but the sniffles coming from the direction of the closest bed told him where she was. He stepped out of his shoes and sat on the edge, letting his eyes adjust to the darkness. She was curled in on herself; her back to the door and him. Chris was suddenly at a loss, unsure what to say that could make her feel better. So, he said nothing, choosing instead to let his actions speak. He laid down on the bed, stretching out on his side behind her to let her know she wasn't alone. Her sniffles became strangled sobs, and when he settled a hand on her waist, she rolled over and buried her head into his chest. He kept holding her until her breathing evened out, and he chanced a few lingering kisses into her hair.

"Did he hurt you?" he asked finally, unable to keep the question from spilling out in curiosity. She shook her head softly but said nothing. Her left arm snaked around his waist and pulled him closer, and he felt her shudder against him. "It was self-defence, Annabelle."

"Doesn't change the fact that I killed him," she returned. "And it will not take them long to figure out it was me. Hotels have cameras everywhere." She'd pulled back a little and laid her head on the pillow, though her arm remained resting over his hip. She breathed a sigh that drifted across his skin. "Maybe I should just turn myself in."

He couldn't put a name to it, but something in him told him that was wrong. He frowned and tried to catch her eyes, but she was staring at his shirt.

"No," he shook his head. "Look, Dustin was obviously either directly involved in producing this drug or someone who is, paid him to steal that laptop. I'm willing to bet he wasn't even an actual officer." She pushed away from him to sit on the side of the bed. Her hair was curtained around her face as she stared at the floor, and he knew without hearing her she was crying again.

Not knowing what else to do, he slid off the end of the bed and found his shoes. Maybe Akari could talk to her. She didn't move as he shuffled towards the door, but something made him stop before grabbing the handle. A conversation he'd had with Akari in New Delhi replayed in his head.

"You know, Chris, nothing weighs more than a secret."

He glanced back at her, finding her silhouette easily in the darkened room. She had hunched herself over her knees, burdened and broken, and Chris couldn't leave.

His approach was slow and careful. She didn't flinch when he stopped next to her, nor when he crouched down in front of her. His hands sought hers, squeezing her fingers as he spoke.

"Tell me."

She shook her head, pulling one hand away to wipe her eyes. Deciding that she might feel comfortable if he shared first, he rose to his feet and moved to sit next to her. He kept a hold of one hand, interlacing their fingers before setting them on top of his thigh.

"I have a daughter," he told her. "Kendall. She's eight. Her mum and I, well, we both thought it best if we didn't stay together just for her. Honestly," he told her with a wince, "I haven't spoken to her in two years, not since she lost her sight, not until today anyway." He took a shuddering breath and Annabelle shifted next to him, her leg pressed against his and her thumb stroked the back of his hand.

"Where does she live?"

"New Zealand," he answered. "Gina took her there when she was three. Then she remarried. Wade's a good guy. And he loves Kendall." The conversation fell flat then, neither knowing what else to say. The silence stretched on for several long minutes, and Chris had almost resolved to leave her alone and let her rest when she began speaking.

"I shot him," she admitted quietly. She wasn't looking at him now but staring down at her free hand twiddling in her lap. "Jaylen probably made it sound like there was this spilt second where it was either him or me, but it wasn't like that." She breathed a sound that reminded Chris of one of his own derisive scoffs. He didn't like it one on her. "I had the higher ground. I could have shot him in the leg, but I didn't. and then – her breath hitched once then twice as she fought to regain control of his emotions. He held on to her hand like a vice, anchoring her through whatever turbulent storm was raging in her. She looked anywhere but him, lifting her head to cast her eyes at the curtained window. "I kept shooting. He was down, and I just kept pulling the trigger. I was so angry at him. He'd used us – used me – to get those documents back." Then, in the smallest of whispers, she finished her thought. "I wanted him dead."

"We're going to figure this out, Annabelle. You, me, the others… it's coming together now. We have some actual proof. That's a big step to figuring out what's going on." He stood up and pulled her with him, releasing her hand in favour of wrapping his arms around her shoulders. "As for the rest of it, you can always come talk to me if you need to." Her shoulders shook with silent amusement as she turned her head to lay her cheek against his chest.

"You know, for someone who reportedly doesn't like people, you have a knack for knowing exactly what to say to make me feel better."

"You're the exception." He held her for a moment longer then relaxed his hold. She stepped back and wiped her eyes again. "You should get some rest," he told her. "We'll work it out tomorrow." He took a step back, clearly intending to leave her alone to sort through her thoughts, but her hand shot out and gripped his arm.

"Stay," she whispered. Her face was uncertain, but her hold on his arm was firm. She was at war with herself, and he found he didn't really want to leave her alone after all. Slowly he stepped around her, peeling back the covers on the bed so she could crawl in. Her shoes had been previously kicked off and forgotten in the corner. The slacks and blouse she wore weren't as comfortable as pyjamas, but they would service for the time being. Once she had buried herself under blankets, Chris moved quickly to swing the latch on the door. He set the alarm on his phone for six and shot a quick text to Akari that they would meet the rest downstairs for dinner. Her reply was simple, and Chris silently thanked her for not prying further.

Annabelle was already dozing when he returned, and he quickly toed his shoes off and laid on top of the covers. His body fit snugly around hers as he spooned up behind her, tucking her against him with one arm as the other propped his head up. Unable to resist, he leaned down and brushed a kiss against her cheek, smiling at the contented hum she emitted at his touch.

Jet lag and emotional exhaustion finally caught up to him, and he laid his head against the pillow to nap with her. A million thoughts raged in him, but as Annabelle's body relaxed against his, they quieted to nothing. Everything else could wait.

Chapter 17

Zofia had made another phone call to Akari, summoning the entire team to Tokyo. Crows had attacked a woman in her own back garden. Thankfully, they wouldn't have to risk staying in another hotel. Akari had an apartment just outside the city centre.

Charlotte Roberson fidgeted in her seat, wedged between Chris and the inner wall of the airplane. Beyond the window was darkness, but she could almost feel the vast expanse of water stretched out beneath them as they travelled towards Tokyo. Next to her, Chris was snoozing comfortably, his head laid back and his mouth slightly open as he breathed deeply. She thought about the million things that were flying through her mind, to let him help her sort it all out

It had been Akari who'd suggested changing her name. A few phone calls and some hastily signed documents and then Zofia had pulled some strings and Annabelle Summers was no more. There would be nothing left of the trail that led from Dustin Proctor to this team. Now, all of her achievements and accolades meant nothing. All the work she'd done, the hardships she'd endured in the name of her research. She knew this was safer, but it felt so much like a surrender.

Chris sucked in a sharp breath and shifted next to her. He didn't wake, but he hummed something unintelligible, and Charlotte stifled a giggle. Before she'd talked herself out of it, she pulled out her new phone and snapped a picture of him. At the very least, it was good blackmail material later (and if she used it as her contact photo for him, well, he would never know).

Charlotte checked her watch and groaned as she realised they were only about halfway through the flight. The flight was scheduled to land in Tokyo at 1pm local time. Charlotte glanced across the aisle where Akari was sleeping across both seats, having been lucky enough not to have a seatmate. Jaylen and Aluna were in the row ahead of her, both of them relaxed in sleep and unavailable for Charlotte's entertainment. Resigning herself to her solitude, she pulled a book from her bag and angled the overhead light so it wouldn't hit her companion as she read.

Chris offered to carry her bag for her as they deplaned. When he'd woken up, she'd joked that he hadn't been nice enough to share his melatonin. He'd obviously taken it more seriously, and the contrite expression his face almost made her laugh. Still, she took him up on his offer and let him fight with both her bag and his down the narrow aisle between seats as she followed him off the plane. When they reached the ramp, she tried to take it from him, but he insisted on being a proper gentleman and shouldered his duffel and gripped the handle of her rolling case firmly.

A dark Corolla was waiting for them out front, and Akari took the font seat to speak with the driver in their native tongue. Charlotte slipped into the back as Jaylen and Chris stowed all the bags in the back. Aluna took the passenger seat just in front of her, and when the others finally sat down, it was Jaylen who climbed into the seat beside her. Charlotte had never been to Tokyo before, but the weight of their task and the shadow of the life she'd taken smothered any excitement she might have felt at being here. Her mind wondered aimlessly even as Jaylen poked her as they passed various buildings and sights. The sound of gunshots echoing and the looked of pained surprise on Dustin's face filled her thoughts.

"Jaylen and I will go talk to the authorities and see what we can do about getting in on the investigation," Akari said from the front. She turned to address Chris. "They're keeping some crows sedated at a university lab. I've already told them you're coming, so we'll drop you on the way. Charlotte and Aluna can stay with you to help."

Charlotte didn't particularly feel like helping, but she didn't say so. It was only another ten minutes before they were deposited at the doors of a nondescript looking building. Akari went with them to find the leader of the research team, who thankfully spoke English. She seemed a little out of her depth and was visibly relieved when Akari told her that Dr Stuart would take over for a while.

The woman led them down a long corridor until they reached a back room. Someone had placed the crows on a table, various tubes monitoring each breath and heartbeat.

Chris turned to Charlotte and gestured to a table near her. "Grab that tray of test tubes over there, will you?" He grabbed a kit from the cabinet and pulled out a syringe. "I'm going to take a blood panel and hope that some foreign elements show up. If they do, I'll compare the results with the data we have from Kelsey Shelton. And if they match, we've got our answer."

Long forgotten chemistry classes sprang into Charlotte's mind, and she grasped at them in a desperate attempt to distract herself. "So basically, you're looking for a fingerprint, chemically speaking."

Chris looked up as he extracted the needle and gave her a teasing smile. "Look at you getting all science-y." She returned his smile with a mocking glare, accepting the syringe from him as he held it out. "Ten drops each, in each of those test tubes. And as a backup, we'll take a DNA sample."

Charlotte zoned out Chris's conversation with Aluna as she concentrated on the task he'd given her. She'd never been good at science, often relying on partners for most of her work. She'd helped them with other subjects. Now she wished she'd paid just a little more attention.

"Huh," Chris breathed, and Charlotte looked up from her test tubes.

 "Huh, what?" she asked.

"There's nothing here. No reports of any other unusual behaviour"

"That doesn't make any sense." Charlotte frowned and stood up. "Isn't the whole point of this that the solution is causing their strange behaviour? Shouldn't every animal that drank contaminated water be showing symptoms?"

"Yeah. They should be."

He began muttering to himself, going over hypotheses and theories as Charlotte returned to her task. When she was finished with the test tubes, Chris walked her through the procedure for recording the results. At her hesitation, he gave her an encouraging pat on the shoulder.

"I'll be right here," he told her. "Ask as many questions as you want. You can do it." He left her to it and grabbed Aluna for a complete beak to tail physical exam of the crows. It took her almost half an hour to work through all the data, and by the time she was done, so was Chris. He surveyed her work and snapped his gloves off with a flourish.

 "We'll make a passable vet tech of you yet, Miss Roberson. Outstanding work." He flagged down the research leader that had greeted them earlier and sent her off with the tests. While he was gone, Akari called Charlotte and told them about their meeting with the city board members.

 "So, they're just going to scour nests and steal eggs from potentially murderous crows?" Charlotte repeated sceptically. "How long with that take?"

"Hopefully not long," Akari answered." They're going to coordinate everything and start egg collection tomorrow. We will join them when they get a lead."

Charlotte heard Jaylen's voice faintly through the connection, but she couldn't make out what he was saying. "Yes," Akari agreed with whatever he'd said. "Jaylen and I will come and get the three of you. There's little more we can do today."

"Okay," Charlotte agreed. She was more than ready to just be somewhere she could sit down and process everything that had happened in the last twenty-four hours. "I'll let the others know."

Chris lamented not being able to stay and examine the crows more, but Aluna pointed out that they'd probably done all they could for now. Charlotte only half-listened to their light-hearted banter as she sank down in the desk chair.

A hand on her shoulder jostled her awake, and she blinked blearily as Chris's worried eyes found hers.

"You alright?"

"Yeah," she sat up and ran a hand down her face to make sure she hadn't been drooling. At Chris's soft laugh, she glared at him. "What?"

"Nothing," he shook his head and held out a hand to help her up. "Akari and Jaylen are here. You ready to go?"

 She slipped her hand in his and didn't let go as they walked through the lab door. He tugged on her hand and pulled her through the door and out into the Japanese afternoon. She climbed into the back of the Corolla with Jaylen as Akari gave the driver directions to her house.

They stopped at a store on a corner so they could buy ingredients for dinner. Akari and Aluna disappeared inside, emerging about ten minutes later with bags of food. Charlotte kept her gaze out the window the entire time, only half-listening as Chris and Jaylen discussed their different careers.

Once Akari and Aluna were back, they continued towards Akari's apartment. They pulled up outside a building on the bank of the Sumida river. Akari stepped out with a soft smile on her face. For a split-second Charlotte envied her. She was home. Charlotte no longer had one.

Akari's apartment was larger than the house Charlotte had grown up in, but she wouldn't say so. Judging from Chris's shocked expression, she wasn't alone. Aluna gave a low, appreciative whistle as Akari took them on a quick tour. The walls bore a gorgeous marble pattern, and the open layout of the kitchen and dining room made the space seem even larger.

"I have two guest rooms, a pull-out bed and a sofa that's comfortable enough if you don't mind firm cushions." She stopped in the middle of the room and spun around. "Make yourselves at home. I'm going to grab a change of clothes." She disappeared down a side hall, leaving the others in a mildly uncomfortable silence.

Predictably, it was Chris who broke it.

"Okay, how the hell do I get myself an apartment this fancy?"

"I think speaking Japanese might be a first step," Aluna joked with him, shifting her hold on the bags of food she carried.

"The only Japanese I know would get me slapped," Chris returned cheekily.

Aluna chuckled and turned to Charlotte. "You can have one of the guest rooms," she told her warmly. "And if you boys don't mind, I would really like to take the other." Jaylen just shrugged.

"Hey, I've slept in a hammock for the last few years. I'm not picky." He shared a knowing smile with Aluna, then reached for the food. "Why don't you and Charlotte get settled in the rooms. Chris and I can put this stuff away." He transferred one bag to Chris's hands, not bothering to acknowledge the look of surprised protest on the man's face as he took the other. Charlotte stifled a smile, but Chris caught it and glared at her. That made her smile more and Aluna laughed at both of them as Jaylen pushed Chris toward the kitchen.

Aluna and Charlotte made their way down the hall towards what they presumed were the guest rooms. Charlotte stopped outside the first open door, peering into the small room. There was a smaller-than-average double bed pushed against the far wall in front of the curtained window. On the near wall was a standing closet, and a small chest of drawers next to the bed.

"Cosy," Aluna commented. But Charlotte couldn't hear her. Her thoughts had begun to spiral, and she felt herself struggling to breathe deeply. Was this her life now? Moving from place to place? Never having a home to call hers. She couldn't live like this, never knowing if she was just one step away from going to prison for murder. It was too much. She pushed past Aluna and bolted back into the main area. Her eyes found an outside door, and just beyond it she could see the railings of a balcony. She yanked it open and pulled it closed behind her, gulping in huge breaths of the cool night air as she fought to calm her racing heart.

Charlotte half-expected Aluna to follow her, to placate her with meaningless words and false promises, but no one came. She didn't know whether to be grateful or disappointed. She looked to the nightlife, listening to the sound of the bustling city. It was comforting, reminding her of home. She closed her eyes and tried to imagine she was back in her apartment sitting in front of the open window, her only worries a looming deadline and what to wear for the dates Madison had planned. She had almost convinced herself that she was there, that none of the past few weeks had been real and that when she opened her eyes, she would be back on her worn sofa listening to the soft strains of whatever her downstairs neighbours had on blast.

"Annabelle, wine?" Aluna's quiet voice pierced the veil of her almost-fantasy, and she startled. He didn't seem to notice as he handed her a glass filled a little less than halfway with a dark red liquid.

"Thanks," she took it from him and sipped politely, trying not to cry as she realised her fantasy would never again be a reality. She was homeless. Jobless. Family-less.

"And it's Charlotte. We all need to get used to it."

"I'm going to take a wild guess that you're feeling guilty about dragging us into this. You didn't force anyone to protect you. I've spent my entire life trying to protect my family. And now, Charlotte Roberson, you are a part of that family."

She opened her arms and stepped towards her. For a moment she didn't react, but eventually she let her arms snake around her middle.

A sharp knock pulled their attention to the door. Chris stood on the other side with a smile and his own glass of wine. Aluna released Charlotte and moved to open the door.

'I'm not interrupting?" Chris asked, earning a soft chuckle from the larger woman.

"We were just talking." Chris stepped out onto the balcony. Aluna looked between him and Charlotte, then saluted her with her wineglass. "Anyway, I am in desperate need of a comfortable bed. Goodnight."

"Goodnight, Aluna," Charlotte smiled.

"You alright?" Chris's voice was warm and rich from wine, and Charlotte's grateful smile from Aluna's company morphed into something a little different.

"I am," she told him honestly. She turned and leaned sideways against the rail, her stance open and inviting. Chris took the cue and stepped up to her, reaching out his free hand to take hers. She sipped her wine for lack of something to say, turning her eyes to the city. He mirrored her, taking a long pull from his own glass. When the silence stretched longer than she thought it would, she turned her head to study him. His jaw was clenched, and he creased his brow in thought. Anyone else might think he was working through the global puzzle that had been forced upon them.

But Charlotte wasn't anyone else. With a start, she realised she was probably the person who understood Chris the best.

"Something's eating at you," she began gently. His frown deepened, but he said nothing. Charlotte pressed. "Is it your daughter?"

"No," he twitched his head to the side, "she's... she's fine." He took a deep breath and pulled his hand from hers. "Charlotte, I..." She saw his throat lift and drop and swallow, and a dozen things flitted through her mind at once. She shoved the most juvenile of them away and tried to let him know he could talk about whatever was on his mind. She squeezed his fingers between hers and his eyes dropped to their joined hands briefly before returning to the horizon.

"I, I contacted Warren Pittman, he's the man who sent Dustin. I told him we have Kelsey's data."

Chapter 18

He had blurted it out so fast she almost didn't catch it. Almost. Her stomach wrenched painfully as she gasped and released his hand.

"What? Why would you? When?" her mind couldn't seem to focus on one thing and as he turned toward her, she stuttered backwards one step, then another. Her back hit the rail, and she felt a coldness seep through her skin that had nothing to do with the cold metal behind her.

"Charlotte, let me explain."

"Explain?" she cried. "Yes, please explain to me why you would call the very person who's been trying to stop us. Who sent Dustin to spy on us! Explain why you would betray us?"

He moved to close the distance between them, then thought better of it. He ran his now free hand through his already dishevelled hair before taking a breath. "The department has plans to open a testing facility near where Gina moved to with Kendall," he started. "If they go through with it and there's any fallout, then Kendall might end up…" He didn't say it, but he didn't have to. It hung in the air between them, heavy and oppressive. Dead. His daughter would likely be dead before anyone knew the consequences of dextro-rinoifane production. He'd never forgive himself if that happened. Charlotte watched him jerk, as though the word itself had struck a physical blow. "There isn't much time," he amended. His eyes met hers and she could see how much his next words pained him. "They will move production somewhere else if I turn in the data."

"Bastard," Charlotte hissed, whirling away from him in anger. At least, that's what she told herself – that she was too angry to even look at him – when the truth was so much worse. She closed her eyes against the sting of tears and tried to ignore the way her heart pounded against her chest. Anger would be preferable to the agony she was experiencing now. She couldn't let him see how badly his betrayal had hit her. he couldn't know how close she had been to falling in love with him.

"Charlotte, I'm not-" She heard his shoes scuff the concrete floor of the balcony as he shifted closed. "I haven't done anything it's been one phone call. And this could work for you as well," he went on hurriedly. "They would clear your name in a heartbeat if we agreed to -"

"To what?" she turned back hotly, all thoughts of hiding her feelings a distant memory. "To give up our only change at finally making them pay for what they've done? Forget my father, look at what they've done to the animals, to the entire world!"

"We don't have to give them all of it," Chris argued. "Kelsey Shelton hid the information away for years. They have no idea how much of it we got hold of. We could keep enough for tests, for evidence, and give them what they want to keep Kendall safe. And you."

His logic was enough to cool her righteous anger, though barely. Charlotte took several long breaths through her nose as she thought about his plan. She had to admit it had merit, and it was simpler than the infiltrations she'd planned in her head. Still, her anger and hurt kept her from agreeing.

"Look, Charlotte," he took a small step closer, "I -"

"Don't," she cut off his apology with a shake of her head and an upheld hand. "Save it. I can't... I can't do this right now."

She pushed past him and escaped into the house, rushing through the dining room and ignoring Aluna's concerned glances. She found the room that she'd claimed and closed the door before throwing herself on the bed. Her own thoughts were a battleground as she warred between the heartbreak of his betrayal and the logic that the life of his daughter was worth more to him than anything. She vacillated between 'how could he' and 'you would have done the same for Dad' so often that her head ached. Quiet tears ran down her cheeks as she curled around a pillow, but she refused to wipe them away.

The minutes stretched on, and Charlotte heard the muted sound of the others talking. Even through the walls, Charlotte could pick out Chris's voice as he explained what had happened and told them about his plan. Then there was nothing, and Charlotte strained for any clue what was happening beyond her room. She jumped slightly when a knock came at her door and Aluna's voice floated through.

"Charlotte, are you alright? Are you awake?" She was quiet enough that, had Charlotte been asleep, it was likely she wouldn't have heard her.

"Yeah," she croaked, wincing at the obvious evidence that she wasn't alright. The door opened then closed again, and in the dark Charlotte felt Aluna's presence as she stopped a few feet from the bed.

"Chris told us everything," she said quietly, "and while I don't agree with him keeping secrets from us, his plan is good." Charlotte had nothing to say to that, so she kept quiet. Aluna sighed. "Charlotte, he did not have to tell you. He could have taken that envelope, arranged a deal, and disappeared. But he told you because he cares about you."

Charlotte couldn't help the soft snort of derision that escaped through her nose. She turned over and stared at where she assumed Aluna's face was. It was hard to tell in the dark. "If you care about someone, you don't go plotting to betray them."

"He saw an opportunity to save someone he loves," Aluna corrected gently as Charlotte pushed herself into a sitting position and switched on the bedside lamp. They both blinked against the light as Aluna continued. "And beneath that gruff exterior he likes to put up, Chris is not a man who can idly sit by and let someone he loves suffer. Not when he can do something about it."

Charlotte unzipped her bag forcefully and tried to hold on to the righteous anger that had consumed her on the balcony. It was cooling faster than she liked in the face of Aluna's steady rationalisations. Rather stubbornly, she refused to let it go completely.

"He lied to me, Aluna. How am I supposed to trust him?" There it was. The crux of the problem, she had refused to admit out loud. How could she trust him now? And if she couldn't trust him, then anything more…

She shook her head and grabbed her laptop, eager to occupy her brain with anything except Chris Stuart. Aluna sighed heavily as she sat down on the bed, effectively ending the conversation.

"What are you doing?"

"Looking for a way into this Warren Pittman's computer system. Thankfully, Arianna taught me a few tricks before Dustin murdered her. If we can access some sort of financial database, we can track down the money he paid Dustin to steal the envelope."

"If Chris's plan works…"

"Look, I know you're trying to be helpful and all, but I really don't want to think about that right now. I'm sorry," She added with a pleading look.

"Alright," Aluna relented and joined her on the bed. "It'll go raster if we both work on it."

Chapter 19

Throughout dinner Chris kept trying to catch her eye, but Charlotte resolutely ignored him in favour of joining Aluna in laying out their plan to infiltrate Warren's computer system and get the documents they needed. It was fairly simple, provided no-one recognised them. Warren Pittman was in charge of welcoming interns at a nearby facility. Jaylen, Akari and Aluna would pose as volunteers and find the access code. They would then relay that back to Charlotte, who would use it to bypass the seriously lax security.

Akari agreed it would be nice to have access to all the information and maybe even get a step ahead for once. Chris seemed to agree just to get back into Charlotte's good graces. It didn't work.

"This is going to be a team effort," Aluna said as they finished eating. "Even Chris." Charlotte finally glanced at him, catching the good-natured sneer he threw at Aluna's back. She could practically hear the sarcastic response he no doubt had ready, but he faltered as his eyes caught hers. He turned back to the sink where he'd been banished to washing dishes by the others as a way of punishment for his transgressions. Charlotte marvelled at the other's ability to forgive him so easily.

With clean-up covered and their plan set, Charlotte retired to her room with her laptop. She mentally walked herself through her part of the scheme half a dozen times before she felt confident enough. Over the faint strains of her music, she heard the footsteps of the others as they bedded down for the night. Once she thought she heard someone stop outside her door, but no one knocked, and she shut down her computer and turned out the lights.

Charlotte lay awake listening to the sounds of the house at night. There was susurrus from outside that was present in every city, but Akari's house held a concert all on its own. She could hear the soft snores of Aluna in the next room, and someone was shuffling near the bathroom in the hall. Her bed creaked slightly as she shifted, and the ceiling fan wobbled now and then before smoothing out. These sounds combined to lull her into a restful sleep, and she was lucky enough not to dream. She woke to the soft murmur of voices that meant her friends were already up and dressed quickly in the clothes Akari had let her borrow.

Just a little under two hours later, Charlotte was sitting on a bench across the street across from the building, slightly obscured by a small coffee stand. She'd placed an order, rehearsing a few times to ensure she used her new moniker. Out of the corner of her eye she saw Jaylen, Aluna and Akari queuing outside with the others.

"You alright?" Chris's voice in her ear startled her, but she stifled it.

"Yes," she whispered.

"Don't whisper," Chris warned, "people will think you're up to something."

"I am up to something," she replied dryly, earning her a soft chuckle from the man on the other end. They'd reached a sort of reconciliation that morning over breakfast, but despite his attempt to charm her, she remained resolutely sullen. He seemed to accept her quiet anger and stopped trying to make small talk. When he'd left to return to the crows in the lab, he'd wished them all luck, but his eyes had never left her.

She heard the barista called her name and retrieved her coffee and moved back to her computer.

"Okay, just launch the program you got from Arianna and wait for the code."

Her heart was pounding as she disconnected her call with Chris to call Akari. With their plan underway, Charlotte forced herself to focus on her part and push aside any thoughts about Chris or her now extremely confusing feelings for him.

Forty-five minutes later they were slipping into their Corolla with matching grins. Jaylen pulled them away from the building as Charlotte turned around in her seat to make sure they weren't being followed.

They all jumped as her phone rang shrilly in the silence of the car, and she fumbled for it with shaky hands. It was Chris.

"Hello?"

"The crows are awake," he said in lieu of a proper greeting.

"What?" Charlotte toned alerted the other three and Akari turned in the passenger seat curiously. "What happened?"

"I don't know," Chris told her. "One of them made a noise and the next thing I knew they were all perched on the edge of the table."

"Are you okay?" By now Charlotte could practically feel the others staring at her intently, but all she could think about was Chris being attacked by the potentially murderous crows currently staring at him.

"Three of them dived at me, but I pulled the screen down." He hissed in pain and mumbled something she couldn't quite make out. The words replayed in her head, and she imagined him sitting on the floor of the lab bleeding from a severe head wound or holding a blood-soaked bandage against his side.

Charlotte angled the phone down and directed her next words to Jaylen. "Take me to the lab." She ignored Chris's protest and relayed the rest of the information as quickly as possible. Jaylen detoured towards the building as he began trying to shoot questions at Chris through Charlotte's phone. After the third exchange, she hung up bitterly, her worry for Chris manifesting as irritation at Jaylen's incessant inquisition. By the time they pulled up outside, Akari had called Chris back and had got the entire story over speakerphone.

Charlotte jumped out and waved a hasty goodbye as Jaylen sped away to help with the egg hunt. She raced through the halls of the building, images of Chris hurt and bleeding spurring her on. The anger and hurt from the day before evaporated as she barrelled through the door to the lab and let out a quiet sigh of relief. There was a visible gash on the left side of his forehead, but someone had taken care of it and he didn't even seem fazed by it.

"What are you doing here? I told you I was fine?" He probably meant his tone to be cool and aloof, but Charlotte recognised the doubt swirling deep behind his eyes. She supposed it was fair; when they'd parted that morning, Charlotte had barely said two words to him.

She tried to match his detached tone, but she didn't quite disguise the worry that was slowly dissipating at seeing him whole and healthy. "Well, I came to make sure you were as fine as you said you were." She closed the distance between them hesitantly, unsure how he would react to her sudden change in mood.

"Well, you missed quite a party," he admitted. The apprehension she'd seen in his gaze just a few seconds ago was gone. Charlotte looked around, finally seeing the wreckage of the room. The crows had not woken up in a good mood. It was a miracle Chris hadn't been more seriously injured.

"I can see that." When she was finally next to him, she didn't resist the urge to reach out and caress the red skin above the cut. "That's a nice little scratch." His skin was warm beneath her fingers, and she smiled a little as he turned into her touch.

 "I know, it's hot, right?" And just like that, they were back. She let her fingers fall away from his face, but she couldn't quite let him go. Her hand settled on his shoulder, returning his teasing smile with one of her own as Jaylen's voice floated through the phone on the desk. Charlotte flushed with embarrassment as she realised the others had heard the entire exchange.

"Okay," he said, all business. "We've got to the forest Chris, where are the team gathering the eggs?"

"Somewhere in that forest," Chris answered, "should be about 500 yards in but keep a lookout."

Charlotte jumped as the faint sounds of gunshots echoed over the line. The call was disconnected abruptly, and Chris tried calling them back three times before giving up.

"I'm sure they're fine," he told her, swivelling in the chair to face her. "Charlotte, look…"

"I'm sorry," she blurted out before he could stumble over an apology that he didn't really owe her. "I just…" She stepped back to put some space between them to think. When his expression fell, she realised he'd misinterpreted the move and rushed on quickly to fix it. "I'm not always the most rational person when it comes to everything that's happened with the dextro-rinoifane. It took a lot of guts to…" She was going to say confess, but that sounded a little too accusatory in her head. "… tell me what you did." That sounded less hostile, but she still winced anyway. "And if you think your plan of feeding Warren some data will work, then we should try it. For your daughter."

His face transformed instantly, and Charlotte marvelled at the depth of emotion this man could elicit in her. His eyes, which had shifted away from her face when she'd began her small speech, snapped back to her. To Charlotte's surprise, they were bright with just the hint of unshed tears. The muscles around his face and neck relaxed, making him look so much younger. He opened his arms a fraction, reaching only a bit to let her know what he wanted. Charlotte didn't hesitate.

He was warm and solid against her, and his breath in her ear as he thanked her made her grip him tighter. She was standing between his knees with her arms over his shoulders, and he shifted slightly to snake his arms completely around her waist. He laid his forehead on her shoulder, clinging tightly as Charlotte felt the ripples of tension leaving his body.

"Thank you," he repeated quietly, and this time she heard the tears he was fighting. Charlotte might never understand the limitless love a parent has for their child, but she understood Chris.

She loved him.

The realisation didn't startle her as much as she thought it would; she'd already half-admitted to herself the night before. She knew now wasn't the time for that revelation, but that was alright. Instead, she let her actions speak for her as she rubbed his back and help on to him as he collected himself. When he pulled away, his eyes were dry and bright.

"So," she smoothed her hands over his shoulders and let them fall away, but she made no move to step away from him. "How is this going to work?" You said you already contacted someone?"

"Yeah," he turned the chair slightly toward the computer but kept one arm around her waist to keep her close. He switched over to the webpage that he'd pulled up earlier and tapped on a face. The name underneath read Reese Sosa, and he looked every inch the rich executive in his expensive suit and fake smile. "This guy is on the board of directors of the division Kelsey Shelton ran surveillance on were running the mind-control experiments. I'm supposed to get in contact with him and tell him when and where to meet to discuss terms."

"He's in New Zealand?" Charlotte asked. At Chris's nod, she sighed. "Then it needs to be soon. Chances are Zofia will send us somewhere else as soon as this thing with the crows is over. Tomorrow morning?"

Chris did some quick mental calculations, then nodded in agreement. "Yeah, okay." He excused himself to make the call, leaving Charlotte standing next to the desk. When he returned, she moved on to the next part of the plan.

"Okay, so we need to edit this data?"

"Yeah," Chris reached around her and picked up his messenger bag. Charlotte watched as he pulled the envelope from its depth and gestured for her to precede out into a nearby office. He scanned the data list into the computer and altered and deleted numerous fields. The printout looked official, and had she not seen the original, Charlotte would have had no idea that it wasn't real.

"Here," she held out the original for him to stow in his bag with the edited documents, but Chris shook his head.

"You hang on to it," he told her. "If something happens, I want to make sure you still have something to work with."

She frowned but kept the container in her hands. "Nothing's going to happen, Chris. Everything is going to be fine."

"Provided the others don't get attacked by murderous crows," Chris added helpfully.

"We should probably check in, shouldn't we?" Charlotte pulled out her phone and dialled Akari's number. She picked up on the third ring, and Charlotte switched on speakerphone as the MI6 agent explained their current situation. The three of them had met up with the government officials and gathered twelve eggs for examination.

"Hey, you should all come back to the lab," Chris said when she was done. "I've got something to show everyone."

"We're on our way." Akari confirmed, disconnecting without a goodbye.

"What is it?" Charlotte stowed her phone in her back pocked and followed Chris back to the computer.

"The DNA results," he told her. "They're strange."

"Strange how?"

"It'll be best if we wait," he shook his head. "I need a few minutes to make sure I'm really seeing what I think I'm seeing."

"Okay," Charlotte looked around. "Is there anything I can do in the meantime? Clean up?"

Chris shrugged one shoulder but didn't take his eyes off the screen. "Suit yourself," he told her. I was going to leave it for the locals."

Charlotte rolled her eyes and started picking up the chaos that had settled over the lab during the crow attack. By the time all these instruments and trays had been rescued and stowed properly, the others had arrived and were bickering among themselves over who was the better driver. Akari managed to get Aluna and Jaylen to focus as Chris turned the workstation so they could see. He'd gathered all the relevant information, though Chris could tell he was still unsure what it meant exactly.

"This," he brought up a panel, "is the DNA profile from one of those crows from the first series of blood tests they did before we arrived." He tapped a few keys and overlaid it with another. "And this is the DNA profile from the same crow when I took a second set of blood tests."

"But they're different." Even Charlotte, with her limited knowledge regarding anything remotely science related, could see the differences.

"Yup,"

"Because of the dextro-rinoifane solution?" she added.

"Essentially, yes."

"And what does that mean?" Akari was growing impatient.

"If we can identify the other substance in the solution, then it might be possible to neutralise it, stopping the DNA changes."

"You can make a cure?" Charlotte abridged, ignoring the affronted glare he threw at her oversimplification. "How?"

"That doesn't matter," Akari cut him off before he could launch into another long-winded explanation chock full of words none of them would understand. "All that matters is that it will work. Are you sure it will?"

"Reasonable sure," Chris shrugged. "Nothing is absolute, but I'm fairly confident I can concoct a… cure." Charlotte stifled a grin at the exasperated look he tossed her as he used her word.

"Zofia needs to be informed," Akari pulled out her phone. "I need to meet with her. Here," she dug in her bag for her apartment key. She handed it to Jaylen, then scribbled her address on a scrap of paper on the desk. "I'll meet you back at my apartment."

Chapter 20

During the drive, Charlotte told Aluna and Jaylen about Chris's meeting. Aluna caught her eye in the rear-view mirror as she navigated through the streets of Tokyo while Jaylen turned to ask Chris for details. She answered with a smile, just a small twitch of her lips, to let her know everything was fine.

"But is it a good idea to take it with you?" Jaylen was saying.

"I don't know," Chris shrugged. "I've never actually bribed a member of the US government before."

"All I'm saying is," Jaylen ignored Chris's sarcasm, "you might not want to take the doctored data with you yet. Make sure he's ready to give you what you want first."

"Look at you, Jason Bourne," Charlotte reached up and slapped him playfully on the shoulder.

"Who?" Chris's face wrinkled in that adorable way that meant there was something he didn't understand, and he didn't like it.

"Never mind," Charlotte waved him off, "Jaylen is right. You should probably leave it at Akari's. That way Reese can't take it by force."

Chris looked like he wanted to protest, but he was outnumbered and relented with another shrug. The conversation turned to the adventures in the forest as Aluna parked the Corolla in front of Akari's apartment building. Charlotte was laughing at Jaylen's re-enactment of Aluna walking into a tree as they entered.

"I'll get started on dinner," Aluna offered.

"I need a shower," Jaylen excused himself and disappeared into the guest bathroom with his bag, leaving Charlotte and Chris standing in the living room. She glanced around for something to occupy their time until dinner was ready, finally settling on a small bookshelf that held an assortment of novels or a few board games.

"Wanna play scrabble?" she moved over and slid the game box from underneath two others as Chris laughed.

"I'm actually wondering how intoxicated I would have to be to play Scrabble with someone who studies law at Oxford," he shot back. "I'm gonna grab some wine and find out. Want some?"

"Sure." She set the board up on the dining room table anyway, and when he returned with two glasses, she gave him her best pleading stare.

"Fine," he chuckled.

Jaylen emerged before Chris could play his first word, and Charlotte talked him into playing with them. He drew a set of tiles reluctantly but perked up when Aluna brought him a glass of wine.

Predictably Charlotte won the first game, though Chris had kept up well in the early rounds using scientific terms. The first time he'd played one – borealis – it had netted him quite a few points for nabbing two triple word score tiles. Charlotte had immediately challenged the word, claiming it was a Latin term and not a real word. Chris came back with several examples of the use of it in everyday language, and Jaylen had ended the argument with a quick internet search. Charlotte begrudgingly accepted her defeat; and Chris grinned as Jaylen added his ninety points. Charlotte had fired back in the next rounds with woolly and quick, earning her 65 and 64 points respectively, and kept a commanding lead for the rest of the game.

Aluna joined them for the second round as his casserole baked in the oven and surprised them all by giving Charlotte a run for her money. He held the lead for most of the game, but Charlotte had dug deep into her extensive vocabulary and managed a bingo on her last seven tiles, earning her an extra fifty points plus everyone else's remaining tiles.

"That's it," Chris held up his hands in surrender, "there's only so much humiliation I'm willing to stand." He stood and collected his empty wine glass. "Refill anyone?"

"Just bring the bottle," Jaylen was already bagging the tiles for a third game. "I'll go again."

They were halfway through a third game – with Chris sitting resignedly in his seat once more – when Akari came home. She paused in the doorway, and Charlotte looked up with an inquisitive smile.

"Everything okay?"

"Yes," Akari looked around the room at her friends, relaxed and happy in her home. "Everything is perfect."

"You want in on this massacre?" Chris offered his own seat with a flourish. "Charlotte's won the last two games and is now over a hundred points ahead of the next closest competitor."

"Sure." She took Chris's place as he went to refill his glass. "Is there more of that?"

Chris jiggled the bottle and grimaced. "No, but I can open another."

"Please." Chris disappeared into the kitchen as the game resumed. Akari played 'grain', which earned her a hefty score but not nearly enough to bridge the gap. Charlotte added a B, L, and Y to Aluna's right and connected two triple word scores. He added 207 to her already ridiculous lead and Jaylen shook his head.

"Okay, from now on you're restricted to five tiles instead of seven."

Charlotte smirked and finished her glass of wine. "If you think that'll help," she teased.

"What happened?" Chris returned with a fresh bottle and topped off everyone's glasses. He glanced at the score sheet over Aluna's shoulder and scoffed. "Did you make a sacrifice to the gods of Scrabble in your youth?"

"Nope," Charlotte's tone was just this side of smug, "but my aunt and I played almost every night. And I was in a club in college."

"A Scrabble club?" Chris raised an eyebrow. "And they called me a nerd."

Charlotte gasped and tossed a P at his face, but he dodged it and grabbed one of Aluna's letters for a return volley. It hit her shoulder and bounced noisily onto the table. Akari held up her hands to stop Charlotte before she could retaliate as Jaylen and Aluna tried to muffle their laughter. A bell went off in the kitchen and Aluna stood.

"That will be dinner." He escaped as Akari picked up her wine and pointed at Chris and Charlotte.

"You two clean this up."

"But we didn't finish the game," Charlotte protested.

Jaylen stood and followed Akari into the living room. "We surrender, you win," he tossed over his shoulder. Charlotte frowned and Chris laughed, earning him a sharp glare from the journalist.

"What?" she snapped.

"Nothing," he was still smiling despite her tone as he scooped the tiles into the bag, "I just had no idea you were such a board game fanatic."

She shrugged and folded the board into a smaller square. "I know it's hard to believe, but there's not a lot to do where I grew up." Aluna came back with her casserole in hand, and Charlotte cleared the game box from the table as he set it down. Akari and Jaylen came back chatting about her meeting with Zofia.

"You gave him an ultimatum?" Jaylen sounded impressed.

"Not really," Akari shook her head as she sat down. "I just told her if she was unhappy with the way I'm directing this team, then she could feel free to replace me."

"Sounds like an ultimatum to me," Charlotte laughed. "What did she say to that?"

"Nothing. We parted ways and I came back here."

Jaylen frowned as he reclaimed his seat. "You don't think he'll actually replace you, do you?"

"No, I don't think so," Akari reassured them. "When she came round asking for volunteers there were only three of us willing. Virginia and Heather were sent on other missions so there isn't anyone else."

Conversation turned as they ate dinner, and Akari fielded questions about her life growing up in Tokyo and moving to London at seventeen. In no time at all the casserole was gone and an air of contentedness settled over them.

"Thank you for dinner, Aluna," Akari toasted her with a near-empty glass and the others followed suit.

Jaylen stood and collected everyone's plates. "I'll clean up."

IMPULSUM

The group dispersed then, retreating to their own corners of the apartment to get ready for bed. Charlotte found Chris fluffing a small pillow on the chaise lounge in the front sitting room.

"That looks uncomfortable."

Chris grunted noncommittally and grabbed the ends of the quilt Akari had found for him. "I've slept on worse." Charlotte watched him continue to prepare his sleeping space, silently debating with herself about her next move. Finally, she decided to go with her gut. No, she amended. With her heart. Just as Chris was turning down the corner of the quilt, she reached around him and gathering it all up in her arms.

"Charlotte, what -?"

"Come on, Dr. Pearson," she turned and made way down the small corridor with Chris at her heels. She pushed through the door that led to her guest room and dumped the bedding on the floor by the dresser.

Chris was hovering by the door when she turned around, his face a mixture of hesitation and confusion. "Is more of my punishment for the Warren thing? I have to sleep on the floor?"

"No," she laughed and beckoned him over. "I think you need a good night's sleep in a real bed. You've got a cure to make, after all. We can't have our scientist falling out from exhaustion."

"Okay, so you're sleeping on the floor?"

Sometimes his awkward cluelessness in social situations was just a little more adorable than Charlotte could handle. She raised herself up on her toes to kiss him, encouraged when he responded quickly. It lasted longer than Charlotte had planned but she wasn't complaining.

"Bedtime," she directed him, turning him around and giving him a slight shove. "Go change into whatever it is you normally sleep in and come back."

"I normally sleep nude," he tossed over his shoulder, but went to do as she asked. Charlotte changes into her own pyjamas while he was gone, a comfortable tank and soft flannel pants. When Chris returned in a t-shirt and boxers she was already under the covers. With the light off, Charlotte felt more than saw his hesitation.

"Stop thinking so much and get in here." It took some adjustments, but eventually they both found a position that was comfortable. Charlotte suppressed a shiver as his fingertips traced over her bare shoulder in a light caress. He was already half asleep, she mused, as she pushed herself up far enough to kiss his cheek. "Goodnight."

"Night," he mumbled. "And I apologise in advance for anything my body does without my knowledge while I'm asleep."

She huffed in amusement but kept quiet as the sound of their breathing filled the room. Charlotte stayed awake for a while longer, her mind refusing to wind down even after all of the wine. Even with the data safely at Akari's, Chris was walking into a dangerous situation tomorrow morning. Reese Sosa could have bribed any number of law enforcement agencies or government entities, making sure Chris would disappear and they'd never see him again.

"Now who's thinking too much?" Chris rasped quietly. "Go to sleep Charlotte." She sighed and forced herself to close her eyes and concentrated on her breathing like her Uncle had taught her to. After her father's death, sleep had been an elusive creature. And when it did come, she was plagued by nightmares. Her Uncle had sat with her one night and taught her the trick, and ever since Charlotte used it when she had trouble sleeping. She felt the rise and fall of Chris's chest beneath her and matched him as her thoughts quieted and she dozed off.

Charlotte felt the bed shift, and when her eyes opened, she was surprised to see the early hint of daylight sifting through the blinds. Chris was trying to get out of the bed without disturbing her, but as she moved and stretched languidly, he gave up with an apologetic smile.

"Good morning," he said, swiping their glasses from the bedside table.

"Morning," she kept her face half-turned into the pillow, groaning the word more than saying it.

Chris chuckled and sat on the edge of the mattress. "Not a morning person?"

She made an indistinguishable sound of displeasure.

"Me either. But I have that meeting in little over an hour."

She was awake then, pushing herself into a sitting position. "Be careful."

"I will," he promised. "You lay back down. No sense in both of use getting up this early. He left the room, presumably to get changed, and Charlotte drifted off into a light doze. When the bed sank again, Chris was dressed and staring down at her. "I'll be back soon." He stood up, pausing when Charlotte's hand shot from beneath the covers to grip his sleeves. She hauled herself up and kissed him quickly, her eyes still half-closed in sleep.

"Good luck."

She watched him go, waiting until he'd closed the door behind him before turning over and going back to sleep.

Chapter 21

"We're getting on boat to the island," Jaylen told them as they deplaned at Alexandra Aerodrome. "Chris, you sure you'll be alright on your own?"

"Yeah," the scientist shouldered his bag and adjusted his glasses. Charlotte had talked him into taking the day away from their madness and spending time with his daughter. He'd resisted at first, citing their newest mission. Zofia's latest assignment was cats raiding a casino. They might need him, he'd argued. Akari had actually jumped in, telling him they were going to capture two specimens anyway and he'd have a chance to examine the cats before sending them to Zofia. Charlotte had grinned triumphantly and prodded him until he'd called Gina to set it up. He felt his stomach flip nervously at the thought of seeing his daughter again. A million different emotions coursed through him, all warring for dominance. He finally settled on hesitant optimism, but the doubt and far he'd been feeling at her possible rejection were lurking just beneath the surface.

"Besides," Akari went on, "it would be harder to explain our presence to Reese if he had anyone shadowing you."

"There's a fun thought," Chris mumbled.

Aluna chuckled and began leading them toward the large glass doors that led to the causeway. "I, for one, will be happy for a mode of transportation that's not airborne. I've had enough of planes for a while, thank you."

The others had to agree. In the past few weeks, they'd never stayed in one place longer than a few days at a time.

"We can take a taxi to the docks," Jaylen said, but Chris shook his head.

"It's on the way to Elliana's," he told her. "I can drop you."

He ended up parking and walking with them to where the boat was waiting to ferry them across the water. Charlotte was the last out of the car, and when Chris turned back, she had a pinched look on her face.

"You alright?"

"Yeah," she shook her head and pushed her hair back away from her face. The breeze from the bay danced through it again and she huffed in annoyance. "I'm just not the biggest fan of boats."

"You get seasick?"

"I've only ever been on a boat once," she admitted as they followed the others toward the dock. My uncle took me out once when I was eight. I threw up over the side and my cousins laughed at me."

"You never went again?"

"Nope," Charlotte shook her head. "And I don't have to go now."

"Charlotte…" It wasn't that he didn't want her with him, but Akari was right. He couldn't meet Reece with someone else in tow and there was no way in hell he was leaving her at Gina's. Besides, he told himself, it was probably a little too early in the relationship to introduce her to his daughter. And there was that pesky matter of Dustin Proctor's death that still hung over their heads.

"I'm just saying all four of us don't need to go," she was beginning to sound a little desperate. "I could stay in a motel and go through the data and stuff while you meet with Reece."

"I think you should stay with the others," he told her. Her hopeful face fell, and he reached out to take her hand. "A day away from here is a good way to stay under the radar. And" he added, "if anyone is looking into Dustin Proctor's death, the more people you have watching your back the better."

"Careful," she said as her lips quirked into a smile, "you keep saying things like that people are gonna start to think you care."

"Well," he adjusted his hold on her hand so he could slip his fingers between hers, "as long as those people are you, that's fine. Just don't spread it around." He tugged her to him and kissed her quickly.

She pulled away but kept a hold of his hand. "Enjoy the say with your daughter. And don't overthink stuff. "Just... be you." He winced and she laughed. "It'll be fine, Chris." She paused then, and Chris knew she was debating on voicing her thoughts. He squeezed her hand to let her know he was listening, and she took a breath. "After my mum left, I spent so many nights wishing he'd come back."

"Charlotte," he swallowed heavily and shook his head.

"No, let me say it. Because I need to, and you need to hear it. She's gonna be angry, it's normal. But she's also going to be so happy to have her dad back. So, focus on that second part and don't be discouraged by the first."

He smiled and nodded, pulling her close for another kiss. "Be careful."

"You, too." She glanced over her shoulder at the boat that would take them off the coast. "Man, I really don't like boats."

"Here," he lifted her hand and turned it over, palm up. He let his fingers dance over the delicate skin on the inside of her wrist, tracing the veins and tendons there. He heard her take in a sharp breath, but she didn't say anything. "If you're feeling sick," he told her, "Find this point." He let his thumb sit just between the two tendons about two inches from her wrist. "Push deep and hold it until the nausea passes."

"I thought acupressure wasn't scientifically proven," she quipped, and he tried not to notice how her voice had dropped to a near whisper.

"Well," he cleared his throat, "there isn't any verifiable proof that the points exist. But my mum swears by them." He let his thumb caress her skin for a few seconds. "Time to go."

She groaned and dropped her head in defeat. Chris laughed and released her, waving at the others who had gathered at a discreet distance away to wait for Charlotte. None of them had mentioned anything about him and Charlotte, but ever since they'd shared Akari's guest room Chris had caught Jaylen giving him sly glances. Even Akari and Aluna seemed not to care, though more than once Chris had caught Charlotte and the two other girls whispering frantically, whenever they had a moment away from the guys.

He waited until the boat was underway before pulling out his phone and texting Gina to let her know he was on his way. She responded with a thumbs up, and Chris could almost feel her antagonism through the phone. She hadn't been happy when Chris had requested to spend a day with Kendall, but Gina was at her core a glass half full sort of person. As long as she felt Chris was being sincere, she wouldn't deny him the opportunity to reconnect with Kendall no matter how she felt about it personally.

The drive to the quaint suburban neighbourhood took a little longer than Chris liked, though he chalked most of his irritation up to nerves. He pulled up to the two-story house and sat in the car for a full five minutes before he was able to talk himself into ringing the bell.

Fifteen minutes later Kendall was buckling herself into the passenger seat of his rented car as Chris settled her guide dog Spartan into the back. It hadn't been quite as bad as he'd thought it would be, though Kendall had apparently inherited his snide aloofness. The ride to the café was silent except for her quiet reading of the directions Gina had embossed onto a sheet of paper, and the sounds of Spartan in the backseat. When they pulled up Chris grabbed his bag and Kendall's rucksack and locked the doors as the girl walked towards what appeared to be her usual table.

At Kendall's request he ordered both of them a cheeseburger and they sat in awkward silence until it arrived.

"Is it good?" Chris asked in an attempt to start a conversation.

"I've had better. The cheese isn't really melted." There was a pause again, slightly less awkward but still relatively uncomfortable.

"Do you have a wife? Or a girlfriend?" Kendall's question caught him off-guard, and he choked slightly on his half-chewed bite. He swallowed and tried to figure out how to answer her question.

"Uh," he glanced down at his food as though it held an answer that would be satisfactory. He decided on the truth. "Sort of. Charlotte and I have been seeing each other for a few weeks now."

"What's she like?" Kendall's open honesty and child-like naivety was refreshing, and Chris found himself willing to share in a way that only Charlotte had ever elicited from him.

"She's tenacious, and smart. She's a law student at Oxford." Chris left out the part where she'd been suspended and was currently part of a super-secret team with him trying to find the cure for a mysterious drug solution that was part of mind control trials and causing animals to try and murder people.

"Is she pretty?"

"Yeah," Chris smiled.

"Can I meet her?"

"Maybe next time."

They ate for a few minutes before Kendall began talking again. He guessed silences weren't really her forte. "You haven't met Wade, right?"

"No," he shook his head. "Just on the phone. You like him?"

"I do," Kendall nodded. "A lot." Chris felt a small pang of jealousy but squashed it immediately. Gina and Kendall were lucky enough to have found someone to love them; Chris certainly wasn't going to begrudge them that. "He's awesome," Kendall continued. Then, because she must have sensed some tension, she added, "I don't call him Dad or anything, in case you were wondering."

There was nothing to say to that that didn't make him sound like an ass, so he settled for, "Okay." Honestly, he hadn't ever thought about it – figuring it wasn't his business after deciding to remove himself from their lives. But, if he was being honest about it, it made him feel better. When Kendall shifted a little in her seat, he searched for another topic.

"What else do you do for fun?"

"Mum and Wade take me to the farm or the science museum. Sometimes we go shopping or they find a cinema that has audio description." Based on what they'd seen, he would probably never take Kendall anywhere near a farm and was seriously considering just getting another job away from the crocodiles. Spartan worried him a little, but unless he showed any signs of aggression Chris wouldn't deprive Kendall of the support he provided.

"Well then, let's go shopping. Anything you want?"

"This isn't one of those guilt things where you over-do it on the gifts and special trips to make up for leaving, is it?"

"Kendall, there is nothing I can do that can make up for not being around. And I'm not going to suddenly start sending you enormous gifts to buy your love or anything like that. But I want to spend time with you, get to know you."

"What changed?" she asked after a while.

"I met Charlotte," Chris smiled wryly. "She lost her father when she was about your age, and it shouldn't have happened. He got sick and the people who caused it didn't take responsibility. And instead of burying her father and moving on, she devotes every day of her life getting justice. She reminds herself of that pain every day, instead of running from it."

"She sounds… pretty cool."

Chris nodded and turned his head to wipe his eyes dry. "She is."

"Does she know about me?" Kendall had relaxed in her seat and her question was curious rather than accusatory.

"Yeah," Chris nodded. "I told her a couple of weeks ago. She's the one who suggested I come over today. And she even gave me a pep talk before I came over."

"What did she say?"

"She said you would be angry," he told her honestly. "Her mum left after her dad got sick. She hasn't seen her for a long time, so she knows what it's like." He cleared his throat quietly. "She, uh, also said that even though you'd be angry, you'd be happy to meet me?"

She gave a small smile. "Yeah, I am."

They were okay again, and Chris relaxed in his seat. "So, where do you usually go shopping?"

Chapter 22

The shopping trip had been about as much fun as Chris had predicted, but it now left him with nothing to think about except his looming meeting with Reese. He pulled out his phone to call the man and noticed that Kendall had managed to get onto her text messages. He knew she could text thanks to modern day technology but seeing as he still struggled to download apps without help it was a surprise. Somehow, she'd found Charlotte's name and had an entire conversation with the woman without his knowledge. It started with a voice recording.

'Thank you"

You're welcome. Are you having fun?

'Yeah. We went to get burgers and went to a movie and he took me shopping.'

Oh? How did that go?

Chris groaned as he imagined the merciless teasing that was in store when he caught back up with the others.

'It was good. I made him get a makeover once he let me get one and then we went to the cinema.'

LOL Get any pics?

'Unfortunately, no, but I might be able to convince him to do it again. I have to go now, Chris's coming back.'

Chris hit the phone icon next to Charlotte's name as he pulled away from Gina's house. She picked up on the second ring and he could hear the smile in her voice.

"Hey."

"Hey yourself," he caught himself smiling. "How was your day?"

"Don't get me started. If I never see another cat again it will be too soon. Yours?"

"Good. It was good. But then," he added slyly, "you already knew that."

"Busted," she laughed. "She seems like a great kid."

"She really is." Chris had never seen himself as the proud parent type. His own experiences with his father had put him off ever having children of his own. When Gina had come to him crying one night, he knew that plan had failed. Now, though, he couldn't imagine a world without Kendall in it. "Listen, I'm on my way to meet with Reese. It shouldn't take me more than an hour, but I don't know."

"We're staying here overnight and catching a plane back in the morning." Charlotte told him. "Will you text me when you're done? You know, so I know everything went well."

"Yeah, let's think happy thoughts, shall we?" Chris knew very well what could happen at his meeting. He could be arrested on sight, though he doubted Reese would involve any official authorities. It was likely he could disappear down a corporate rabbit hole, never to be seen again. Or he could be killed and dumped in the river.

"Chris Stuart, the optimist?" Charlotte teased.

"No," he shot back, "Chris Stuart, the pragmatist. The easiest solution for Reese is to give me what I want. It's of minimal cost to the company and nets them the greatest gain."

"The data."

"Exactly. So, I'll talk to you later."

He hung and began weaving along the route to corporate headquarters. He parked in the structure and took several calming breaths before getting out. His bag felt heavier as he walked quickly through the empty garage to a lift. Reese had told him there was a bridge on the fifth floor that led right into the company building. Three was a special code to access the door, and Reese had warned Chris that the four-digit number would only work for one hour. It was ten minutes to ten when he keyed it in, watching as the red light flashed green and the door buzzed as it unlocked.

Chris found Reese's office by following the signs for the executive suite. When he arrived, there was a thin man with dark hair and angled features sitting behind a small desk.

"I'm here to see Reese Sosa," Chris stated.

"Your name, sir?"

"Just tell him someone's here to see him, will you? He knows who I am." Chris had been hesitant about giving Reese his name. He didn't want anything to come back on him or the others once they were clear. The assistant stood with a frown but did as Chris asked. After a few moments he returned and ushered Chris forward.

Reece's office was the epitome of executive luxury. Large glass windows displayed the majesty of the city skyline, and a traditional wooden desk sat in front of them. There was very little in the way of personalisation a single photo frame sat next to the computer screen on his desk. Reese himself wasn't there, but his assistant gestured for him to take a seat.

Chris held his messenger bag in his lap, willing his heart to stop pounding so hard. Footsteps startled him but he masked his surprise as Reese entered.

"This would have been much more civilised if you'd just give me your name."

"Can we just get this over with?"

"We have relocated the trials to the opposite coast and this," he handed Chris a small black case, "will protect your daughter in case there were any chemical traces we missed. Do you have out data?"

Movement over Reese's shoulder caught his attention, and Chris realised that he could see into the far corridor through the window behind him. Time seemed to freeze as Chris focused on the familiar face, distant though it was.

Zofia stood conversing with another woman, looking for all the world like he belonged there. Reese didn't seem to notice Chris's revelation and reached his hand across the desk for the container.

"The data."

Chris felt his stomach drop as the truth washed over him. They'd been played from the beginning. Just before he could hand off the envelope and be gone, Zofia looked up. Her eyes locked with Chris's and she froze. She tried to keep her attention on whatever her companion was saying, but her entire body language spoke another story. Chris knew she was already planning how to intercept, how to keep Chris from leaving the building.

He needed to get out. Now.

Chapter 23

Charlotte's phone rang loudly in the small hotel room. Next to her Akari stirred but didn't wake. She grabbed her phone and pressed the green button, stepping outside to keep from disturbing roommate as she brought the device to her ear.

"Chris, where are you?" She had been on edge from the moment they'd disconnected earlier. He had walked into the proverbial lion's den holding a piece of bloody meat, and the fact that the hadn't called yet worried her.

"We have a problem," he rasped, breathing like he'd just run a marathon.

"What?"

"Zofia was at the office. She's working there." She could hear the bustle of traffic around him, like he was still on the move. Charlotte banged on the door next to hers, waking Jaylen and Aluna even as she moved back to her own room. When they stepped out, she gestured frantically for them to follow as she opened her door.

"You're on speaker," she switched over as Akari began to rouse and Jaylen closed the door behind him. "Repeat that."

"Zofia is working with the team testing the dextro-rinoifane solution," Chris said, "she was at the office talking to another woman in a suit and looking very comfortable," Akari sat up and swung her feet to the floor as Charlotte sat down on the edge of the bed. "She's not who we think she is."

Aluna crossed her arms over her chest as he leaned against the small dresser. "How can you be so sure? Maybe she had a good reason to be there."

"I saw her face," Chris snapped back. He sounded very agitated, and Charlotte's worry for him ramped up.

"Are you in a safe place right now?'

"I think so," he told her.

Akari finally woke up enough to join the conversation. "Did Zofia see you?"

There was a beat of silence. "Yeah," Chris sighed. "Listen, we obviously can't go back to the hotel that Zofia set up. Just stay safe and call me when you land tomorrow?"

"Okay, be safe," Charlotte urged. She hung up, casting the room into a heavy silence.

Akari was the first to break it. "This is bad."

Aluna shook his head and pushed off the dresser to stand at her full height. "So, the people that put us together are the same people who we are now trying to take down?"

Charlotte shrugged. "It appears that way."

"But why?" Jaylen spoke up for the first time from his place by the door. "Why would Zofia put us together if there was a chance of us uncovering the truth?"

"I don't know," Akari answered. "But maybe we can get more answers from Chris tomorrow."

Charlotte didn't sleep at all that night. Her thoughts were split between worrying for Chris and trying to figure out the new twist in the mystery they'd been asked to solve. Jaylen's question repeated over and over in her mind until finally she couldn't lie still anymore. Keeping her screen angled away from Akari's bed, she spent the remainder of the night flipping through Kelsey Shelton's documents.

Charlotte was running on adrenaline and caffeine as they arrived at the airport. Chris was leaning against a pillar, his relaxed posture belied by the clench of his jaw and the deep circles under his eyes. Charlotte made a beeline for him, wrapping her arms around him for a brief hug as the others huddled around them.

"You okay?" Akari asked him, and Chris nodded. Her phone rang and she slipped away from the group to answer it.

"So how exactly are we going to make a cure?"

"Theoretically, we can combine the results from the animals we've studied to identify the missing chemical from the dextro-rinoifane solution. Then we have to find an animal to test it on who doesn't already have it in their bloodstream, and hopefully a neutraliser will reverse its effects. One slight problem; however, this solution could be in an animal's blood without any negative side effects. Look at the crocodiles; over a hundred drank the contaminated water, but only two went off the rails."

"How are we supposed to find this animal? This solution is all over the world."

"I know. It's like trying to find a needle in a stack of needles. But without that needle, we don't have our cure." As the enormity of their new task sank in, Akari re-joined them with a panicked look on her face.

"We have to go," she urged.

"What happened?" Jaylen asked.

"That was one of my colleagues at MI6," she told them. "There's been a warrant issued for my arrest, Charlotte's too."

A cold stab of dread shot through Charlotte as she covered her mouth. "Dustin Proctor," she muttered. "Oh my God, Akari. I'm so sorry." She felt Chris's eyes on her, and as she looked up at him, he grasped her hand in his. Dustin's ghost had been haunting her since that fateful day in the hotel spa. She'd managed to make peace with it by remembering that he would have killed her and Jaylen if she hadn't acted. It still didn't make her feel any better about being a fugitive or dragging her friends into the mess with her.

"There's nothing to apologize for," Akari ushered them away from the airport. "But it's only a matter of time before they connect the rest of you. We have to go, guys."

"Hey, hey, hold on," Jaylen held up a hand. "Go where? Zofia is working for the dextro-rinoifane team, there is no one in our corner anymore!"

"Yeah, I don't speak spy," Chris added, "but it pretty much feels like game over." Charlotte felt him squeeze her little tighter as he spoke. She thought briefly again about turning herself in. She might be able to strike a deal and keep her friends out of prison. But she knew even as the thought hit her that the others would never accept it. Chris alone would fight tooth and nail to keep her away from the hands of the government.

"First, we should get out of the open," Aluna marshalled everyone and gestured for them to head to the car. She took the keys from Chris and climbed into the driver's seat as the others piled in. "Akari can you find somewhere nearby for us to get new phones?"

As Aluna, Akari and Jaylen discussed their next moves, Charlotte leaned back in her seat and closed her eyes. The image of Dustin Proctor's surprised face was forever burned in her memory. She knew it was likely she would never forget it. The exhaustion from last night compounded with the weariness she was beginning to feel as their mission grew even more insurmountable, and she sagged under the weight of it.

"You okay?" Chris's voice was pitched low to keep from alerting the others, and he was angled toward her in the back seat with only a few inches between them.

Charlotte didn't open her eyes as she replied in the most sardonic tone she could muster. "Peachy."

"Listen, for what it's worth," he settled a warm hand on her leg, letting his thumb stroke the outer edge of her knee, "I'm sorry. If I had known Zofia was there…"

"No," Charlotte raised her head and opened her eyes. "It's not your fault. No one could have known." Her attention turned briefly to the plans hatching in the front of the car and she grimaced. "If anyone should be apologising, it's me. Akari's right – it's only a matter of time before they connect all of you to me, and to Dustin Proctor's death. What will your daughter think when she hears that her dad is wanted for murder?"

"It wasn't murder," Chris insisted firmly. "It was self-defence. But there's little chance of the truth being told as long as this department hold the cards. We need to get the cure, and then expose them and all of their corruption. Then we can clear your name."

She had nothing to say to that, so she let her head fall back against the headrest and stifled a yawn. She could practically feel his concern for her coming off of him in waves.

"Did you get any sleep last night?"

"No." Exhaustion made her honest; she couldn't even utter a white lie to ease his worry. "I was up all night going through Kelsey's documents."

"You didn't really sleep on the plane, either" he pointed out. "You need to rest, Charlotte."

"I can rest when I'm not on the FBI's most wanted list," she shot back. He seemed to sense her snappish attitude stemmed from her lack of sleep rather than irritation with him, so he fell silent and let her be.

Aluna pulled up a few blocks from a small phone store tucked into a string of shops next to an alley. They all piled out to go inside, but Aluna stopped them before they reached the door.

"Maybe I should go alone," he held out his hand for the cash Akari still had, and she pulled out a few bills. They posted up just outside the door, leaning against the storefront and trying to look as casual as possible.

Charlotte was the one to point out they were probably failing. "Maybe we should not be standing around in a clump like this."

Before anyone could agree, the door opened, and Aluna walked out with a large bag. They followed her into a side street as she handed out the phones. "From now on, we pay cash for everything. And no more contact with friends or family."

"Yeah, I can't do that," Chris argued. "This has to get to Kendall." He held up the black case Reese had presented in their meeting.

Behind them, a siren whooped, and Charlotte's heart seized with fear. Had someone spotted them? Recognised them? Would her friends now face accomplice charges? Panic gripped her as she tried not to stare at the police car that was cruising down the street. It didn't seem to be slowing down, and so she kept cool. It passed them, and they collectively breathed a sigh of relief as it turned a corner out of sight.

"Guys, look, we need to actually make a plan. Lurking around looking suspicious on the street is not the best way of avoiding suspicion" Akari pointed out.

Jaylen seemed surprised that they were all suddenly looking at him, but he took it in stride and nodded. "Alright, first off we need to get this information out there. The more people who know about it the harder it will be to sweep it under the rug. Do any of you know someone we can talk to?"

"One of Arianna's contacts lives around here; she works at a radio news station." Charlotte quickly pinged a message to Kayleigh Camacho hoping that the girl would be able to help.

"Okay," he turned to his oldest friend. "Aluna, take Chris and the car to get that to Kendall."

"What about us?" Akari asked.

"I've got that covered," Jaylen said cryptically.

"We need somewhere to meet up," Charlotte realised.

"How about there?" Chris pointed across the street to a local bar. "It's close and has the added benefit of adult beverages to top off our very wacky day."

A response from Kaleigh came quickly, "Guys Kaleigh can meet us in the cemetery just across town."

"A cemetery?" Jaylen questioned.

"She lives next to it, cheap places to live aren't that easy to find around here."

"Okay then. Everyone be careful." Jaylen and Akari moved off to hail a taxi, heads bent discussing whatever plan Jaylen had come up with. Aluna moved to the car, mumbling something about changing the plates as Chris turned to Charlotte.

"You going to be okay on your own?' His forehead was wrinkled with worry, and Charlotte mustered her most confident smile.

"Yeah, Kayleigh and I have met up before. I trust her."

"Here," he rifled through his bag and pulled out a hat and sunglasses. "I grabbed these after my meeting. If they've released your picture to the public then this will keep you safe."

She chuckled as she took the proffered items. "I think maybe you've seen one too many spy movies." He returned her smile with one of his own, but she could see the agitation that tightened his shoulders. She slipped the hat on, tucking her hair behind her ears before adding the sunglasses. Chris nodded in approval and reached out to adjust the hat.

"Very spy chic," he joked, though she could see the hesitation lurking in his eyes.

'I'll be fine," she told him. "You get that to Kendall. See you back here in a few hours."

She could feel his eyes on her as she turned the corner and pulled out her phone. She had spent the drive copying down every number of importance from her phone before she shut it off. She was glad for it now; she didn't want to risk anyone tracking her movements and finding her before she could get her story out.

They decided to wait in the bar until it was time to leave for the meeting. They had commandeered a table at the back while Jaylen bought a round of drinks and Charlotte took off her hat and glasses, leaning her head against the wall, feeling the effects of the alcohol and exhaustion taking over. She closed her eyes briefly only to snap them open again when someone sat down across from her. She stiffened for a second, ready to bolt, then recognised Akari's worried frown.

'You didn't sleep last night, did you?" she asked.

'Nope," Charlotte took a long sip of her drink, hoping the caffeine would stimulate her enough to get through the rest of the day. Of course, they had no idea where they were even going to sleep, so Charlotte wasn't banking on a terribly restful night. "Guys, Zofia's about to pay a lot of money for someone to make us disappear."

'How the hell are we at a point where that doesn't even sound insane to me?" Jaylen responded.

"Okay, let's not get carried away. We're going to leave now, see Kayleigh and meet up with the others. Then we can worry about what happens next."

Chapter 24

Kayleigh was waiting next to the gate when they arrived. There was no one around, and Charlotte's greeting was brief as they stepped inside.

"Who are these guys?" Kayleigh indicated the two people behind Charlotte.

"They're friends of mine. Listen, what we've found is…"

"Huge," Kayleigh cut her off, "yeah, you said that. What is this all about?"

And so, she told him. Kayleigh was one of the few people who knew what had happened in her hometown and her crusade against the government and didn't think she was crazy.

"So, the US decided to experiment with mind controlling drugs and now those same drugs are causing animals across the world to kill people?"

"Basically, yeah."

"And you can prove it?"

"We have pages and pages of original data."

Kayleigh looked taken aback. "Damn."

"I told you this was huge," Charlotte said.

"Can you help us?" Akari asked.

"Yeah," Kayleigh answered firmly. "Yeah, I can help."

Charlotte sighed in relief.

"POLICE! STAY WHERE YOU ARE!" Charlotte's heart stopped for a brief moment as the shout echoed in the open space. They all turned, and out of the corner of here eye Charlotte saw Akari reach for her gun. One of the officers saw it too. "Don't," he warned. "Lay your weapon on the ground."

Akari dropped the gun. "I'm Akari Powell, MI6."

"Not anymore you're not." Charlotte's hopes of getting away were dashed but she still jumped when the officer turned to her. "Annabelle Summers?"

"Yes," she hated that her voice trembled on the word, but the prospect that she and her friends were likely headed for prison did not sit well.

The officers stepped towards them, and Jaylen suddenly noticed the trailer parked next to them. In one swift motion he knocked the safety catch and the bales it was carrying fell in front of the officers.

"Run!" shouted Akari.

They weaved through the cemetery, slipping down an alleyway and turning right sharply through a gate. Charlotte was right behind Akari as she darted through it. Jaylen was the last one out, ducking as a gunshot pinged off the scaffolding next to him. He'd managed to shut the game, and Akari took aim firing several shots through the gap.

Kayleigh was white as a sheet as they bolted for safety. "My God! You didn't tell me about that!"

"Sorry!"

They slowed to a brisk walk to avoid many odd glances, but they didn't stop until they'd put several streets between them and the cometary. Kayleigh bent over to catch her breath as Akari pulled out her phone.

"Who are you calling?" Charlotte asked.

"Aluna," she said. "We need to get out of the city as fast as possible."

"I need to get back to my place," Kayleigh said finally.

"I'll follow up with you later," Charlotte told her. "Thanks again,"

"Yeah," she waved and disappeared around a corner without another word. Charlotte guessed she was probably still in shock at the fact she'd been shot at not five minutes ago. Her own adrenaline was still pumping, and her hands shook as she fought to regain control of her heart rate.

Akari shut her phone and nodded her head toward a side street. "They're on their way to Chris's ex-girlfriend's house. I have the address."

They flagged a taxi and piled in the back as Akari gave the driver the address. Charlotte was sitting on driver's side, squished between Akari and the door. She could feel her muscles cramping as her adrenaline wore off, and the nausea hit her hard as the driver took a turn a little too fast. She quickly sought the pressure point on her wrist that Chris had shown her, and she pressed down hard right up until they stopped in front of a quaint two-story home. Chris's rented car was parked on the road. Akari paid the driver and Aluna quickly ushered them inside.

Charlotte sought out Chris immediately, finding him at the dining room table swabbing at a cut on his hand. He looked up at her when she arrived, and she watched a myriad of emotions play across his face. He stood without a word and gathered in her arms; Charlotte couldn't tell who was more relieved.

"What happened to your hand?" she asked.

"Squirrel attack at the café," he said. "Gina and Kendall were out in it." Charlotte closed her eyes, for a moment fearing the worst. "They're okay," he told her. "But three people were killed."

"I'm glad your daughter's okay," Charlotte whispered.

"You're shaking," he said, pushing her back gently do he could look for any injuries.

"I'm fine," she told him. "Just… being shot at tends to send my adrenaline into overdrive."

His grip on her shoulders tightened as he panicked for a moment. "You were shot at? By who?"

She almost didn't want to meet his eyes. "The police."

"Jesus," he tugged her against him again. "I can't leave you alone for even a few hours, can I?" She chucked into his shirt and held on for several long minutes, soaking in the warmth and safety he offered. It was weird, she mused silently, that someone she'd known for less than three months could suddenly become the most important person in her life. She felt the hum of rightness settle in her bones as his hand rubbed up and down her back, and she was reminded once again that she loved him.

It felt like the right moment, and Charlotte steeled herself for the admission. She tried saying the words over and over again, hoping that eventually they would spill out onto her tongue. She had just sucked in a breath to speak when someone cleared their throat behind them. They both turned to find Aluna hovering in the doorway.

"I am sorry to interrupt," he said, looking completely unapologetic and just a little amused, "but we need to discuss what to do next."

"I need to call Kayleigh," Charlotte stepped back and smoothed her hair away from her face, hoping her own erratic throughs weren't too obvious. "Is there a phone I can use?"

"Yeah," Chris gestured toward the kitchen, seemingly oblivious to her inner panic. When Charlotte looked a little hesitant, he added, "Gina and Kendall are upstairs packing. It's probably best if we don't linger for long. It won't take the police too long to find us here."

"Right." She moved to the phone and pulled out her small notebook of numbers as Chris joined the others in the living room. She dialled her friend's number and tried to think about their next steps.

"Kayleigh," she answered as she always did.

"Kayleigh, it's Charlotte."

"Charlotte." She sounded not at all like the all-in reporter they'd left just a short while ago. Now she just sounded scared.

"That's not a good tone," she tried to joke, but it fell flat.

"It's not," he agreed. "Listen, something's changed."

Charlotte slammed the phone down a few minutes later and cursed under her breath. She could hear the others talking in the other room and took a few steadying breaths before joining them.

"More bad news," she began. "Kayleigh's out. It turns out you can't exactly go on national radio and attack the American Government."

Discussion turned to their next course of action. They couldn't talk to the press, and there was no way any of them would even see a fair trial if their turned themselves in. That left one option.

"The only people that can help us now are in this room," Jaylen declared.

"Hey guys," Aluna unmuted the television as repots of the bird attacks came flooding in. Chris moved past her to the stairs, but Charlotte couldn't tear her eyes from the screen.

"It's getting bigger," she said. "The animals are getting more aggressive."

From his seat by the window, Jaylen came to a decision. "If it keeps progressing like this, it won't matter what we decide to do. Because then it will be too late." He looked up with a determination Charlotte hadn't seen in him before. "We have to do something now."

"I agree," Aluna said. "But what?"

"I don't know," Jaylen stood up and began pacing. "We need to get out ahead of this thing. We need to find out what makes up the rest of the solution and then find an animal that hasn't been contaminated."

"That will take time," Charlotte shook her head. "We don't have that right now."

"We need to get somewhere safe," Akari agreed.

"I know," Jaylen stopped by the stairs and turned. "I'm open to suggestions."

Before any of them could say anything, Chris came barrelling down the stairs. "Jaylen, do you remember when you showed those notes your Uncle made?"

Charlotte recognised a Stuart epiphany when she saw one, and so did Jaylen. "Yeah, of course."

Chris came to rest in the middle of the living room as he turned to face the group. His hands were moving erratically as his brain worked faster than the rest of him could keep up with. "There was a page dedicated to polar bears."

"I remember," Aluna's words were more of a question, one they were all thinking. What did it mean?

"There has to be a reason for that," Chris answered. He turned to Jaylen, "What if your Uncle was searching for the same thing we're searching for?"

"Polar Bears?" Akari asked, but Charlotte was already on the move. A laptop was open on the kitchen table – probably Gina's – and Charlotte sat down to search the web.

"There have been attacks in Alaska, Russia, Greenland and Norway. None in Canada."

"I think we just found our needle," Chris said. They all sat in silent celebration for a moment, soaking in their first real victory in what felt like forever.

It was Aluna who finally stated the obvious. "We cannot stay here much longer."

"Agreed. Alright, Chris go get Gina and Kendall. They need to get out of here as soon as possible."

"What about us?" Akari asked.

"We need to get to Canada."

"There's no way we can just go to the airport," Charlotte pointed out. "Not with my picture plastered all over the news."

"So, we drive North," Chris said. "We get as far from here as we can and figure it out."

"Then let's go." Charlotte grabbed her bag and made a beeline for the door with the others as Chris got Gina and Kendall loaded into their car with Spartan. Jaylen started the car as Aluna jumped into the passenger seat. Charlotte scooted to the middle seat as Chris squeezed into the back with her and Akari, and Jaylen took off down the street.

"Hey," Chris brushed her wrist with his thumb, "you alright?"

"Just tired," she admitted. Truthfully, she was a hair's breadth away from losing it, but she managed to send him a convincing enough smile that he took her words at face value.

"Then get some rest," he offered. "Come here." He let her hand go and raised his arm as he angled his body against the door to give her room. She leaned against him gratefully, laying her ear against his chest as his arm settled around her. She vaguely heard him conversing quietly with Akari and even heard her name, but she was too tired to pay attention. The steady rise and fall of Chris's chest as he breathed combined with the heat of his body to send her into a restful sleep.

Chapter 25

They were five hours into the trip when Jaylen announced they needed fuel. Chris looked down at Charlotte sleeping against him and frowned. She looked completely wiped. Still, he thought, she might like to grab a bite to eat before they got on the road to… well, none of them knew exactly where they were going. They just knew that they needed to get out of New Zealand and find a way to Canada without Akari and Charlotte getting arrested at an airport.

They ended up at a small petrol station with a burger restaurant next to it. There were picnic tables outside and the only security cameras Aluna could see were the ones on the pumps themselves. Jaylen pulled up and let them out as Chris nudged Charlotte awake.

"Hmm?" she mumbled groggily and sat up, pushing her hair back from her face as she blinked blearily.

"We're filling up with petrol and getting food," he told her. "You hungry?"

"Yeah," she turned her head back and forth to stretch her neck out. He'd tried to make her as comfortable as possible, but there was very little room with three of them crammed into the backseat.

Aluna volunteered to look after the car while Jaylen and Akari got them all food. Their cash stores were running dangerously low, and none of them knew how much longer they would need to worry about fuel. They agreed to fill up here and keep their food purchases small until they could find another money source. Akari had already contacted a friend from M16, though she still had no idea if he could help them or not.

Chris and Charlotte camped at a picnic table as the other two went inside to place their order. They emerged a few minutes later but stayed near the door talking in low tones; Chris wondered if they were planning their next move. Charlotte was still a little out of it, and Chris's frown deepened at the dark circles under eyes. She needed a good night's sleep in a real bed, but it looked like none of them were getting that any time soon.

Chris pulled out his tablet and perused a few local news sites, wincing as he stumbled on two large pictures of Charlotte and Akari above the words 'Manhunt Underway for Suspects in the Death of Police Officer'. He saw Charlotte tense next to him, and unconsciously he reached out to lay a hand on her back. He knew Dustin Proctor's death still plagued her and being the subject of a manhunt was likely not doing anything good for her stress levels. He clicked away from the site, settling on perusing the growing reports that were creeping up all over the country.

"Do we have a plan?" Charlotte asked after a few minutes.

"That depends on what you call a plan," Chris quipped. "As of now, I think it's something along the lines of get away from Invercargill, then figure out how to get to Canada."

Charlotte looked at him with a hint of a smile. "That's sort of vague."

"Not sort of," Chris shot back. "And that's not even the whole of our dilemma. I've been thinking about this missing chemical and we're going to have to get a hold of it." He tapped his screen to bring up a page of notes. "I've narrowed it down to two substances and I'll need to test both of them. Phropenesomna and Felcatril."

"And they probably won't be so easy to find when we're illegally sneaking into Canada."

"No," Chris agreed. He moved to stand up, closing his tablet cover as Jaylen gathered their food.

"So, we're going to have to take them with us," the younger man said.

"And it's not like we can just swing by a convenience store and pick one up," Chris continued as they made their way to the car.

"Where do we find them?" Akari asked.

Chris squinted against the sun emerging from behind the clouds and thought about her question. "Research facilities mainly, some cosmetics labs. "Aluna had finished filling the spare tire with air and was standing at the open driver's side door as they arrived. "So, we can add that to our list of impossible stuff to do." He couldn't help it – blunt pragmatism had always been his modus operandi. Sugar coating things simply wasn't in his nature.

"Well, no one said saving the world is gonna be easy." And as always, Charlotte was there to keep that little spark of hope alive. Chris followed her around to the opposite side of the car, bypassing her to lean against the open passenger door.

"So, I have a question," Chris leaned back and crossed his arms. No one else seemed to want to ask it, so he would. "If we keep driving north, we are eventually going to end up on the bottom of the ocean."

"I actually think I might have a solution there?" Jaylen had perked up.

"What?" Akari sounded confused.

"Let's go to Waipu," Jaylen explained unhelpfully.

"Why?" Chris asked.

"I think there is a way to get from Waipu to Canada." Jaylen was adamant.

Charlotte looked to Chris for help, but he had no idea what Jaylen was on about. She leaned into the car to address Jaylen directly. "Well, what's in Waipu?"

"Oh no," Aluna groaned. "You're thinking of Giselle, aren't you?"

"Yes, I am," Jaylen affirmed.

Aluna shook her head, meeting Jaylen's muted excitement with a firm refusal. "No, not that, Not Giselle."

Charlotte had finally had enough of their ambiguity. "Who is Giselle?" she snapped.

"She's a nightmare," Aluna sounded resigned and, judging by the satisfied smirk on Jaylen's face, Chris guessed it didn't matter now bad this Gisselle was. If she could get them to Canada, it was really their only option.

"Okay," Akari sensed the tension between the two friends and intervened. "Look, we might as well start driving that direction. We can meet Giselle and see if she can help us. In the meantime, I'll keep pressing my contacts in Tokyo and try and get us a plan out of the country."

It was a plan of sorts, and it was more than they had five minutes ago so they all piled into the car for the long drive to Takaka. Aluna drove while Jaylen divvied up the food from the backseat. They ate in relative silence, the drone of the news station buzzing just shy of discernible. Aluna pointed them in north as Chris rummaged through his bag for his charging cable. He plugged his tablet in and began perusing all of the news channels looking for any indication that people had a clue what was happening.

"Anything interesting?" Charlotte's voice over his shoulder startled him, though thankfully he managed to repress the urge to jump in his seat.

"Not really," he sighed. "No one seems to have a clue what's going on."

"Except us," she finished. "It's not surprising, though. If Kayleigh wasn't allowed to make a radio statement, I can imagine what's happened to anyone actively looking into this."

For a moment she sounded like that headstrong law student that had tracked him down in the crocodile sanctuary and peppered him with questions. She had been so sure then, so driven. The past months had tossed her about pretty handily, and her fire had been dimmed with each subsequent setback. But here she was, once again railing against injustice with an assuredness that bordered on obsessive. Her resilience astounded him.

"You should get some more rest," he told her.

"I'm alright," she told him, but the yawn that punctuated her declaration betrayed her. "Okay," she relented under his pointed stare. "We all need rest. Aluna, you okay for a while?"

"Yes," the woman kept her eyes on the road. "I will be fine for some time. Chris is right; you should rest."

"Here," Chris reached into his bag and pulled out his flannel shirt. He'd taken it off at the café in a rush as he'd tried to find his family, and it had been hastily stuffed in his bag on their way out of Elliana's. He handed it back to Charlotte to use as a pillow or a blanket. Jaylen was already passed out against the door, Akari leaning against his arm as she slept.

"Thanks," Charlotte traded his shirt for her phone. "Can you charge this?"

"Sure," he tucked it into his bag where his tablet normally sat so he would remember later. He heard her shuffling around behind him, adjusting to find a comfortable position in the cramped space. It took a few moments, but finally there was nothing but silence from the back seat. Chris glanced in the sideview mirror, angling his head just enough to make out Charlotte's profile against the window. Out of the corner of his eye Chris thought he saw Aluna smirking, but when he turned his head the woman's face was devoid of emotion.

After a few more minutes of surfing the internet, Chris gave up on learning anything helpful. He shut off his tablet and let it charge, turning his attention to the radio. "What kind of music do you listen to, Aluna?'

"Anything is fine," she said. "Just keep it low."

Chris found a classic rock station that seemed to play more music than commercials, and he let himself drift off into a light doze.

Chapter 26

It was almost dark when they stopped again, pulling in to fill up. Chris rubbed his eyes as he checked the time to find that over six hours had passed. Aluna glanced over at him hopefully.

"How are you on cash?"

Chris dug into his bag, taking a moment to trade out his tablet for Charlotte's phone. He plugged it in and made sure it was charging before counting what little money remained in his bag.

"We've got enough to fill the tank." He handed it to Aluna before twisting in his seat to pop his back. His muscles protested the confined space, but he stretched as much as he could. Charlotte hadn't stirred, which spoke more about her exhaustion than anything. Akari and Jaylen were still out as well, which meant Chris was probably next on the driver's list. He got out and walked a bit to relieve the ache in his legs and back, and when Aluna had paid they switched seats.

"How much further?" Aluna asked

"If we don't stop and there isn't traffic it's about 13 hours until we reach Waipu." It took a moment, but Chris finally figured out the on-board navigation system. He'd been off on his estimate by only a little bit, and the map showed it would be 13 and a half hours.

Aluna settled into the passenger seat and passed Chris a water from the pack of twelve she'd bought. "Well, let's get going then."

They traded off drivers three more times in the next thirteen hours, and it was Akari who pulled them into the car park of a motel. Chris had managed a few hours of sleep in the back, but he was still stiff and cranky when they all piled out into the thick, humid air.

"Wonderful," he grumbled as they surveyed the two story, green building. All of the doors were weather-beaten and faded by the sun, and through the windows Chris could see the thick woollen curtains that seemed to be a stable of every roadside motel. "I'm guessing room service is out of the question."

Charlotte came up beside him shielding her eyes against the midday sun. "Maybe it's cleaner on the inside."

He didn't even grace her statement with a response, instead choosing to shoot her a withering glare. She just smiled back and patted his arm sympathetically. Akari came around the car and handed Charlotte a wad of cash.

"Just get one room," she said.

"Uh," Charlotte took the money but didn't move. "Shouldn't someone else book the room? Someone who isn't wanted for murder?"

"You're the only one of us with a working alias right now," Akari countered. "There might be police on our trail. They're looking for Annabelle Summers and not Charlotte Roberson."

Charlotte accepted the explanation and moved in the direction of the office – a small, windowed room tacked on the end of the row of rooms. The others milled around the car and discussed just how they would go about tracking down Giselle."

"She will be in whatever place allows her to cause the most chaos," Aluna pointed out.

"She sounds like a charmer," Chris leaned back against the bumper. "Are we sure we want to get involved with someone causing trouble?"

"Yes," Jaylen said just as Aluna said no, and he glared at his friends. "Giselle might be a bit unconventional, but she's our girl for getting to Canada under the radar. We don't have a lot of time and out options are limited."

Aluna grumbled but didn't reply. Chris was beginning to feel a twinge of unease in his gut. He usually ignored it – preferring hard facts and logical reasoning – but for some reason he couldn't push it aside like he usually could.

"We got two adjoining rooms," Charlotte came back with two keys – real ones, not the magnetic cards of modern hotels. They were each attached by a single ring to large plastic numbers, six and seven. She handed Akari one of the keys and the leftover money.

"How?" Akari looked down at the change and the key incredulously.

Charlotte just shrugged. "It's not tourist season," she said.

Chris rubbed the back of his neck where sweat had soaked through his collar. "I wonder why."

They unloaded their bags as Charlotte opened the door to room six, and Chris prepared himself for a very dismal scene. He was not disappointed.

"I think my room at university was bigger than this," he remarked. The square room was maybe ten feet on each side, with a tiny dressing table on the back wall and a door that no doubt led to an equally tiny bathroom. The adjoining door was closed, but Chris unlocked it as he heard Aluna speaking in the next room. Akari opened the door and peeked in.

"Cosy," she joked. "This one's the same. But at least we've got four beds." Chris glanced at Charlotte out of the corner of his eye, suddenly very self-conscious. Akari had no doubt assumed – as Chris had – that he and Charlotte would be sharing a bed like they had at Akari's apartment. Of course, he hadn't actually discussed it Charlotte, and felt like an ass.

Hoping to divert the topic until he could speak with her in private, Chris jumped to their entire reason for being in Waipu in the first place. "Any idea how to find this Giselle?"

Akari shook her head. "I was actually hoping Charlotte might have some ideas."

"Me?" Charlotte reeled back slightly.

"Yes?" Akari nodded briskly. "Jaylen said it only took you a matter of hours to find Kelsey Shelton. A woman like Giselle should be no problem at all."

"Okay," Charlotte unzipped her bag and pulled her computer from its sleeve. "So, who's this friend of yours?"

"She's not her friend," Aluna insisted as she and Jaylen came from the next room.

"She's an animal rights activist and spends a lot of time protesting at animal testing facilities."

They spent the next few minutes offering up a few suggestions on where she might be, but none of the numbers Charlotte found led to Giselle. After almost half an hour of surfing, Charlotte stilled in her seat. At first Chris though something had popped up on her screen to elicit the reaction, but closer inspection told him otherwise. She had a look on her face he'd only seen only a few times, often followed by one of her unorthodox but brilliant ideas.

"We're looking at this wrong," she shook her head and began typing faster than any of them could keep up with. A few pages flashed on her screen as she clicked on links and paged back at nearly inhuman speed. Finally, she clicked one final link and sat back triumphantly. "Found her."

"Where?" Jaylen leaned in to peer over her shoulder.

"With everything you and Aluna were saying about Giselle I guessed she probably didn't need me creating enemies for her – she probably has enough on her own. And I was right." Chris couldn't help but smile at the pride in her voice. It was nice to hear her spirits lifting, even if it was a small thing in the grand scheme.

"*Eco-Terrorists Behind Bombing of Cosmetics Factory,*" Jaylen read aloud." Oh yeah, this has Giselle written all over it." He stood up and turned to Aluna. "Looks like we're headed to the river."

"I'll go with you." Akari insisted. Neither Aluna nor Jaylen had any protests, and they all promised to call Chris or Charlotte if and when they found Giselle. They were talking and planning even as they walked out, and as the door closed behind them it left a silence in the room that was almost deafening. Charlotte closed her laptop and stood, stretching as a yawn escaped.

"I'm gonna grab a shower," she announced, moving to her bag to grab a cleaner set of clothes.

Chris suddenly felt the grime of the last few days on his body and nodded. "I think I'll join you." The words were out before he had a chance to think about them, and both of them froze at the implication. Mortified horror gripped him, and he began to stumble through him and be began to stumble through an apologetic explanation, but Charlotte just laughed. She padded over to him and stopped his rambling with a kiss.

It was extremely effective.

When the kiss ended Chris opened his eyes, surprised and wondering when he'd closed them. Charlotte stayed close, laying her palms flat on his chest and looking up at him through fluttering lashes. "I know what you meant," she let him off the hook. "But," she added after a few seconds, "when all of this is over, and the world is back to normal and I don't have a warrant out for my arrest…" She raised her chin to look at him squarely, and he saw even in the dim yellow light of the hotel lamps how the black of her pupils seemed to swallow the grey of her eyes. "We will definitely revisit that topic."

She kissed him once more and left him standing in the canter of the room as she moved to the small bathroom. The door clicked shut behind her, and Chris finally figured out how to move again. Aluna had left the adjoining door opened, so Chris took advantage of the second bathroom to take a shower of his own.

When he emerged, he felt cleaner, though he didn't reel as rejuvenated as he usually did after showering. He blamed it on exhaustion and decided to catch a nap before the others called or returned. Charlotte, it seemed, had beat him to it. She was curled up on top of the covers on the bed nearest the bathroom, her hair still wet from her shower. He stood in the doorway for a moment, his eyes darting between the expanse of bed next to her or the empty one nearest the door. After a few seconds of silent deliberation, Charlotte's voice startled him.

"Chris." It held a note of warning, and he smiled as he remembered the last time, he'd heard that tone.

"I know," he chuckled quietly, "stop thinking so much." He turned off the lamp and discarded his damp towel, leaving it in a heap on the floor as he settled onto his side next to her. she manoeuvred enough to get the top blanket over them, and as Chris's head hit the pillow, she slotted herself against his body. He wrapped an arm over her to tug her to more comfortable position. Finally, he gave up and rolled to his back, pulling her to lay halfway on hop of him. She was slight enough that her weight wasn't oppressive, and he felt her breathing deepen and even out in a matter of seconds.

Chapter 27

Hushed voices woke him sometime later, and as he came to, he identified Aluna's first. The others had obviously returned and were discussing something in the other room. Someone had pulled the adjoining door to but hadn't closed it completely, allowing only a soft murmur through. Chris laid in bed for a moment more, soaking in the feeling of Charlotte in his arms. He hadn't been able to properly appreciate it the last time because of his early morning meeting, and the only other time he'd held her like this had been just after Dustin Proctor's death. He'd been so focused on making sure she was alright that he hadn't really paid attention to the way she fit so naturally against him. Her head was pillowed on his shoulder, and he could smell the bland floral fragrance of the hotel shampoo whenever he breathed in deeply. One of her hands was lying simply against his chest, and without thinking he brought his free hand up to grasp it.

It was too dark to make out her face, but Chris had already memorized every detail anyway. It still baffled him that he'd only known her a few months; sometimes it felt as though she'd always been a part of his life. She hadn't of course - he had the proof of that in Kendall. In a rare moment of fancy, Chris wondered what his life might have been like had he met her first. Before Gina, before Nia. He probably would have ruined her. His father had done quite a number on his psyche, and it had taken him a lot of years and half a world of space to get to a place where he was at peace with it.

And that's when Charlotte had come into his life. She'd appeared so suddenly - all business, so focused on her goals and completely unaware of the effect she'd had on him from day one. He let his mind wander back to that morning at the sanctuary, running blood tests on supposedly murderous crocodiles. Then she'd called his name and his entire world had tilted on its axis. The carefully constructed walls he'd built up around himself had been dismantled at the utterance of her name. He still had no idea what had possessed him to call her up and invite her to lunch but looking back he was glad he had. Who knows where they would be if he hadn't?

"You're thinking again, Doctor Stuart." Charlotte shifted against him, raising her head to stare at him with a sleepy smile.

"Busted," he confessed. "The others are back."

She raised her head and paused, and when Akari's soft alto floated through the crack in the door she sagged against him. "I guess that means we have to get up."

"Probably." He made no move to leave the warm nest of blankets. She didn't either. "Do you feel better?"

"Yeah," she finally pushed up to a sitting position and ran her fingers through her hair to comb out any large tangles. "Ugh." No doubt that was meant as some comment on the state of her appearance, but Chris thought she looked beautiful. He told her so. "Thanks," she smiled at the sudden compliment. "But I'm pretty sure your opinion is biased."

"Well sure," he returned just as cheekily. "But mine's the only opinion that matters."

"Is that so?" her smile morphed into a playful smirk. "And why is that?" She was baiting him, and he knew it. She wanted him to take that first step in defining their relationship, to put a name to it. If it had been any other woman, Chris would have shut her down and refused to play her game. But Charlotte wasn't any other woman.

He was pretty sure he was in love with her. And, if he was reading the signs correctly, she was more than a little infatuated with him as well. Despite that, he couldn't force the words past his lips. It didn't matter how many times he reminded himself that Charlotte and Nia were as different as night and day, or that he and Elliana had only kept dating because of some chivalrous notion that he had to stay in a relationship with the mother of his child. Charlotte wasn't any other woman, and she certainly wasn't either of the two who had wrecked his heart and shoved him into this cynical shell. Still, he couldn't say it.

"You guys up?" Jaylen interrupted their non-conversation with a light knock on the door. Chris saw Charlotte's face fall, but only for a second before she schooled her features. He didn't think she knew he'd seen it, and she stood up with a languid stretch.

"Yeah, give me just a sec." She disappeared into the bathroom without looking back. Chris cursed inwardly and resolved to talk to her the next time they were alone. She deserved that, at least, and he could get past his aversion to confronting his emotions if it meant he never had to see that disappointment on her face again.

"Everything okay?" Jaylen asked.

"Yeah," Chris stood and made a half-hearted attempt at making the bed. Akari and Aluna came up behind Jaylen, and when Charlotte came back out all of them were perched in various places around the room discussing what had happened with Giselle.

"She's agreed to help, but we have to help her first. She's taking a group of friends to liberate animals from a local testing facility, and we have to go with her."

"She wants us to what?" Chris had been listening quietly as Jaylen explained how they'd found Giselle Collins, but he balked at the word "liberate." He had no issue saving the animals, but releasing domesticated, poorly socialised creatures into the wild was almost always a death sentence.

"She's crazy," Aluna added, but Jaylen just glared.

"She's not crazy." Then, a little less convincingly, "She's just not uncrazy."

Akari decided to intervene before the two friends could erupt into a full-blown argument. Chris grabbed one of the bottles of water from the 12 pack they'd bought in Picton. "I've dealt with these kinds of people before. They don't know the first thing about animal welfare." His time spent at various sanctuaries and wildlife reserves had exposed him to all sorts of animal rights protesters and activists. While most of them had their hearts in the right place, they had no clue about what conservation and animal protection actually entailed.

"Not to mention some of us are already wanted by the police," Charlotte put in. "Maybe committing another crime doesn't help our case." Chris raised his hand in acknowledgement of another point against this foolish endeavour.

"Well, I agree," Jaylen said, "but we have to get out of here and we have to get out of here fast." No one seemed convinced, and Jaylen sighed. "I admit, okay? Giselle... Giselle can be a bit of a loose cannon." At Aluna's pointed stare he shrugged. "Maybe more than a bit. But everything she has ever done has been for the animals."

"Look," Aluna pushed away from the door, "I know desperate times require desperate measures, but this isn't desperate. It's reckless."

The debate went on and on, with Jaylen and Akari on one side and Aluna, Charlotte and Chris on the other. Ultimately, it was the breaking news on the television that decided things for them. Chris kept his expression neutral as he looked at his picture next to those of his friends in connection with Dustin Proctor's death. Charlotte was across the room, but a brief glance revealed all he needed to know about her state of mind. The guilt was written on her face, and he knew what they had to do.

"Alright, there is also the possibility that whichever cosmetics lab we break into will have stocks of Phropenesomna and Felcatril" he reached down and turned the set off. "Let's go." They packed all of their things back into the car, unsure if they would be able to return to the hotel before they flew out of the country. Charlotte left the keys on the nightstand with a note apologizing for not returning them to the front desk. Chris watched her dig into her pocket for whatever cash she had left to leave for the housekeeping service, marvelling once again at the depth of compassion she held in her heart.

They squeezed in the back with Akari as Jaylen rocketed off toward wherever Giselle and his friends were holed up. Chris felt sick to his stomach at the thought of helping these people. Fanatics like Giselle and the rest of the members of her gang typically held an extremely narrow - and often incorrect - view of anywhere that kept animals. In his experience, they were ignorant and militant - a combination that often led to terrible things. It went against everything he believed in regarding animal conservation and welfare, yet here he was about to help them break into a pet store and remove animals who knew no other life than the one they lived. The odds of them surviving in the wild were almost nil, but Chris knew he couldn't say it. They needed Giselle and his plane to get out of the country.

"You alright?" Charlotte kept her voice low as Jaylen and Aluna continued their good-natured argument about which of them had first befriended Giselle Collins.

Chris guessed she'd seen the pinched look on his face, and he forced himself to relax. "Yeah," he nodded. "I'm just not looking forward to dealing with the level of ignorance these people are likely to display."

"I guess in the animal world, these guys would be like your nemesis." She was trying to lift his spirits with a joke, but she had spoken truth.

"Yeah," he nodded. "A few years back, I was working at a zoo and we rescued a small herd of elephants from Swaziland. They have a managed population there, and their herd was getting too big, encroaching on the habitats of other animals, because of a major drought. The local government wanted to cull the herd, but we said we'd take a few of them instead." Chris shook his head as he remembered the uproar that announcement had caused. "So called animal activists protested almost daily, tried to sneak into the zoo and disrupt operations, stuff like that."

"Wow. Anyone get hurt?"

"No," Chris shook his head. "They're persistent, but mostly harmless. But people like Giselle, like her gang? They're the really dangerous ones."

Charlotte's face morphed from curious to apprehensive. "Dangerous?"

"They're fanatics, and from what Aluna and Jaylen have said they're militant. Add to that the risk that comes with transporting unpredictable animals - and ones that don't know us to boot - let's just say I'm not looking forward to the next 24 hours."

"If we had another option -"

"No, I get why we have to do this." Chris stopped her before she could somehow find a way to add more blame onto her already overburdened shoulders. "I'm just warning you that I may not be my normal charming self for a day or so."

She chuckled and laid her head back against the seat. "Fair enough."

Chris closed his eyes and didn't open them until Jaylen pulled up to an old rundown warehouse at the end of a long road. He was already picturing the para-military scene he was likely walking into as he followed Aluna toward a side door. Jaylen knocked loudly, banging his fist against the metal three times in quick succession. A rusty bolt slid back, and the door cracked open. A woman peeked through, her face a stony mask until he saw Jaylen and Aluna on the other side.

"Friends!" she lit up and opened the door wider to let them in. "Glad you could make it. The gang's through here." She jabbed her thumb over her shoulder as Chris followed his friends into the dimly lit warehouse. Empty shelves and spare sheets of metal had been hastily constructed as some sort of foyer, with only a small gap serving as the entry into the main area. Jaylen took the lead and made the introductions.

"Giselle Collins, these are the other two members of our team, Charlotte Roberson and Chris Stuart."

Charlotte took Giselle's proffered hand quickly but firmly. When the woman turned to him, Chris stuffed his hands in his pockets and nodded quickly. Giselle seemed to sense his hostility, but it didn't faze him. Instead, she turned back to Charlotte with a charming smile.

"Jaylen, you've been holding out on me, man. You didn't tell me you were working with these gorgeous women." There was a beat of silence as Giselle waited for her compliment to be acknowledged. When no one spoke up, Chris decided he should be the one to do it.

Jaylen cut him off before he could potentially damage whatever deal they had struck. "Giselle, we're here. We'll help you, as long as you can promise me that you'll get us to Canada."

Giselle grinned. "Oh, I'll get you to Canada, buddy boy. Got the plane ready to go. All we have to do is go liberate the animals." Chris sneered at Giselle's words but kept silent.

"There is something else," Aluna added. "We will need to get into the storeroom and find samples of Phropenesomna and Felcatril."

Giselle seemed as confused by the request as she was by the chemical names. "What for?"

"It doesn't matter what it's for," Chris finally snapped. "We just need it."

"Okay," Giselle held up her hands and nodded toward the opening. "We're putting the final touches on the plans now. Come on."

They made their way to a larger open area, lit by crudely erected floodlights. A low table sat in the centre with what appeared to be a jumbo-sized map of the testing facility. Two others were hovered over the it, speaking in low tones as they approached. The first was stern looking with a tight bun and angled features. Her hawk-like eyes surveyed the newcomers silently. Chris got the feeling she was as against their involvement as he was.

The third member of the group was a young man with dark skin and bright eyes. He was less apprehensive about Giselle's hired help, but his enthusiasm for their upcoming task was immediately dampened upon their arrival.

Giselle ignored the obvious tension in the room and made introductions like they were meeting for dinner rather than a covert operation. "Cory, Camille, these are my old pals, Aluna and Jaylen. They've brought us some manpower for tonight's liberation."

Cory nodded at them, but Camille wasn't so welcoming. "As long as they do what they're told, fine."

Chris opened his mouth to fire back, but Charlotte nudged him sharply in the ribs and he clamped his mouth shut. Giselle went on like she hadn't noticed. "We found what works best for us is a two-pronged assault, so four of us are gonna go in here, four of us in here."

She indicated two points on the map that corresponded with vehicle loading points. One team was set to breach the cages, the other had the storeroom. Chris guessed he was in that team.

Camille sounded almost boastful when she added, "Toss in a couple of flashbangs and they won't know what hit them."

"Flashbangs?" It was Charlotte who couldn't contain her surprise. "Seriously?"

Chris decided the moratorium on keeping quiet was off. "The term 'gung-ho' comes from the Chinese meaning 'work together,' but I find it can also mean excitable morons groping for a cause.'"

To his surprise, it was Cory who rounded on him. "You're kidding me, man?"

"My friend," Aluna warned, "I wouldn't, if I was you." There was a moment of tense silence as Chris stared down at the man, almost daring him to continue. He weighed his options and decided it wasn't worth it.

Cory had backed down, but Camille had had enough. "Who are these guys again, Giselle?

"These are some old chums of mine," Giselle said evenly, "who are presently of the mind that the animals are uniting against us. Which we deserve, by the way."

"Good for them," Camille was sounding more and more disconnected from reality. "I mean, we have been eating them and keeping them in cages since the dawn of time."

Chris couldn't let that crazy stand. He took a breath to rebuke her fanatical viewpoint, but Jaylen spoke first. "Alright, how about we just focus on what it is we're trying to do here."

Giselle nodded sharply. "Okay, once we're in one of your people can go fetch the drugs."

"Phropenesomna and Felcatril," Chris corrected tersely.

"Sure. That." Giselle matched his tone. "Rest of us are gonna free the animals, load them into the truck. We're in and out in under thirty minutes."

"What if we try a different approach?" Jaylen asked.

Chris had reached the end of his patience with these lunatics. "Yeah, like the one where we don't break in and free the animals."

"What, do you think this is funny?" Cory had apparently overcome whatever hesitation he'd had at their initial confrontation.

Chris rose to the occasion and let go of his own inhibitions. "Oh, there's nothing funnier than adrenaline junkies trying to mask their thrill-seeking in altruism."

Camille was still atop her high horse, preaching her nonsense to the masses. "Animal captivity is an idea whose time has come and gone."

Her blind ignorance was starting to piss him off, and Chris added a bit of bite to his next words. "Tell that to the dozens of species who have benefited from captive breeding programs."

"Alright, relax," Giselle stepped between them. "Relax." She glanced sharply at Camille and she backed off with a sour look. "Camille did a couple of tours in Afghanistan," she explained calmly. "Took some mortar fire. Unfortunately, the doctors couldn't save her sense of humour."

Akari joined Giselle in refocusing the group. "Jaylen, you were saying?"

"I was thinking that maybe we try a stealthier approach," Jaylen said. "One where we get in and out without security even knowing we're there."

Giselle stood up and crossed her arms over her chest. "And how do you propose that?"

Jaylen smiled. "We'll figure something out." Chris didn't like the sound of that at all, but if it meant getting one over on these losers then he was willing to roll with it.

"Oh, you will?"

"We do," Jaylen turned to Chris and pointed. "Chris?"

Camille's disgust was plain. "You've got be kidding me."

Chris recovered from the surprise quickly. "Well as it turns out Miss Jarhead, I know a thing or two about animals." And then, because he had no idea how he was going to do it alone, he turned to Charlotte. "And Charlotte knows a thing or two about getting information from people." She looked up for a moment but schooled her features quickly. Before anyone could argue or offer a counterpoint, Chris went on. "Give us ten minutes."

"Ten -"

"Alright," Giselle interrupted Camille before she could go off on a tear. "Ten minutes. See if you can come up with a plan better than the one we've been using for years." She sounded confident they couldn't, and Chris resisted the urge to snipe back. Instead, he steered Charlotte toward a smaller area separated by more sheet metal.

When they were out of earshot, she predictably rounded on him. "Thanks for volunteering me."

"We were already volunteered," he countered, "I'm just giving us an opportunity to keep aggravated assault off of our rap sheets."

"Okay," she saw the sense in his argument, "so what now?"

"Now," he said, "we figure out how to get into the facility without being seen."

Charlotte thought for a moment, pacing in the small space before turning to him. "Does every area have cameras?"

"Yeah," Chris confirmed. "Security will use them to check in when they're not around."

"They can log in remotely?" Her tone had picked up, now more encouraged than curious.

"Theoretically, yes."

"What if we can have someone monitoring all the cameras at once? That way we know when security is around and when it's clear."

"Okay," Chris could see the benefit of it, but the execution would be difficult. "How do you get the login information? They don't just give that to everyone."

"Getting information from people is what I do, remember?" He smiled at her teasing tone, accepting the shot at his earlier comment with a nod. "Can you send Giselle and his goons on an errand? I need smart phones, like a dozen of them. And they all need internet access so I can set each one to look at a different camera."

"Alright," he was beginning to see her plan. "What about the alarms?" he asked. "We'll need to cut those without messing with the cameras."

"Aluna can do it," she answered assuredly. She sounded like she knew from experience, and he didn't question her. Instead, he went off to relay her instructions to Giselle and the others.

They were understandably sceptical.

"Just do it, Giselle," Jaylen cut off their protests with a sharp rebuke. Giselle glared at them but eventually backed down. Camille and Cody followed her out of the warehouse reluctantly, leaving Chris and the team alone.

"Aluna," Chris turned to her, "Charlotte seems to think you're the one who can cut power to the alarm system without interrupting the camera feed."

Aluna pressed her lips together for a moment, then nodded. "I can do it."

"Fantastic," Chris clapped his hands together. "I need some coffee."

Akari directed him toward the tiny makeshift kitchen that was set up on a balcony in the back of the warehouse. He brewed the instant coffee with a sneer of disgust, grimacing at the bitter taste. He found a smaller version of the map next to the mini-fridge, and he took the time to make sure he knew the fastest route to the storeroom. They would likely split into teams once inside to allow for the greatest chance of success. Chris just hoped he wasn't paired with anyone from Giselle's team.

"What are you thinking about?" Akari's voice startled him, and he half-turned to acknowledge her as she walked up beside him.

"I'm just trying to figure out how I went from working at an animal sanctuary to illegally releasing domestic animals into the wild in the span of three months." He couldn't keep the acid from his tone, and Akari nodded sympathetically.

"This goes against everything you believe in," she said. "I understand this is difficult for you."

Accepting the opening she was giving him; he took the opportunity to vent his frustration. "It's just these animals were more than likely born in a pet store or at this facility. This life is all they know. Taking them to a foreign environment and setting them free is practically a death sentence." He ran his free hand through his hair in a gesture of irritation. "And these so-called activists don't give a damn about the animals. They think they're doing good, and it makes them feel like they're accomplishing something when in reality they're making things so much worse." He paused, working through the last barrier to utter what was really bothering him. "And I'm helping them do it. I'm condemning these animals to death."

"But on the other hand," Akari spoke what he would not, "this is the only way we can get Charlotte out of the country and away from the police. Your head is at war with your heart." He stayed silent, but it was enough of a confirmation for her to continue. "Have you spoken to her about this?"

"No," he shook his head. "And I'm not going to. She's already got enough on her mind without adding my own crap onto the pile."

"Do you love her?" Akari's question caught him off-guard. He glanced at her for a moment in panic, but from her expression he knew she already had the answer. She was just giving him a chance to say it.

"Yeah," he breathed. "Yeah, I do." It felt good to get it out there, even if he was telling the wrong woman.

"Then tell her. Speak to her about your feelings...all of them. She deserves that much." She left him then, giving him space to think about what she'd said. He stared at the map for a few more minutes, but all of his earlier thoughts had been drowned out by Akari's words. She was right - they needed to have a long talk - but now was not the time. Right now, they needed to focus on completing their task and not getting caught by the authorities.

He made his way back down into the main area, listening as Charlotte expertly manipulated whoever was on the other end of her phone call into giving her the login information for the cameras. When she hung up, he saluted her with his half-full mug.

"Nicely done."

"Let's just hope it works." Her computer pinged, alerting her to a new email. She opened it and showed him. "Now all we need is the phones." She moved away, pacing in the small space for a moment before speaking again. "I don't know about this."

"About what?" There was a hesitation in her tone that he wasn't used to hearing from her. Usually when she decided to do something, she was all in.

"This," she gestured vaguely. "The cameras...everything." She was second guessing herself, and he silently cursed Dustin Proctor for the millionth time. She had been the one to give the officer the benefit of the doubt, to trust him when the others were still unsure.

"But this part was your idea."

"I know," she was agitated now, rocking her weight from one foot to the other like she couldn't decide whether to pace or not. "But look, it should work - it should work. But what if it doesn't?"

Empty platitudes were never his thing. "If it doesn't, I'm gonna be breaking into a testing facility with a bunch of nut-job radicals and no one is gonna have my back." He saw her panic for a moment before he went on. "But I'm not worried about that. You know why?"

"Why?"

"Because I have faith in you." He let his words sink in, watched as she let them seep into her bones and settle. She relaxed enough to smile at him, and he nodded.

"Got what you wanted," Cory and Camille came in carrying what looked like a pillowcase.

"Okay," Camille handed Charlotte the sack. "How's this supposed to work?"

Chris listened as she laid out her plan to monitor the cameras and alert them to the presence of security. She sounded so naturally confident in her explanation he almost forgot how uncertain she'd been just moments before. When she was done, Cory shook his head.

"Seems complicated."

"Yeah, it is," Charlotte tried for a positive tone, but missed the mark.

"No, it isn't," Chris pushed. "You got this. She's got this, right?" At his pointed question Charlotte nodded sharply. It wasn't the most convincing, but Cory and Camille seemed to accept it. They glanced once more at the map before disappearing into the depths of the warehouse for the last of the preparations. Once they were gone, Charlotte deflated slightly.

"Chris -"

"No," he set his coffee mug down and moved around the table to stand next to her. "It's not complicated, and it's a brilliant idea. In a few hours this will all be over, and we'll be on our way to Canada." He reached out to rub her shoulder, and when she leaned into him he wrapped both arms around her.

"I miss my bed," she murmured.

Chris's shoulders shook with amusement as he laughed softly. "I think it's safe to say it'll be a while before any of us see a bed again."

"It's time, boys and girls," Giselle snapped her fingers and spun a finger over her head to indicate they should get going.

Chris rolled his eyes and sighed as Charlotte stepped back. "Wish us luck." He turned to walk away, but Charlotte grabbed a hold of his hand to stop him. "She tugged him back and pushed up her toes to kiss him. Chris savoured it, lingering just a little longer than he meant to.

"Be safe," she whispered. She let him go and opened her mouth to say something else, but whatever it was caught in her throat. Finally, she muttered. "I'll be here."

He knew in that moment what she had wanted to say. It was the same thing he'd been trying to tell her for a few days now. Somehow, the thought that she was having just as much trouble saying it gave him enough confidence to overcome his own hang ups.

"Charlotte, I -"

Giselle whistled loudly, making both of them wince. Chris closed his eyes and fought the urge to strangle the woman. Charlotte nudged him out the door with a quick warning not to kill their comrades before they could get to the plane.

"No promises," he grumbled back, but followed the other six to the large truck idling outside. The moment was lost anyway, he told himself. Cory was behind the wheel, with Giselle riding shotgun and Jaylen in between them. Camille was driving her own truck, and as Chris climbed into the backseat, she turned to glare at him over her shoulder.

"Nice of you to join us."

Next to him, Akari shook her head to warn against a reply and Chris clenched his jaw shut. It was almost four in the morning and they were all stressed and exhausted. Adding the vehement protests Chris had against this entire endeavour, and it was a wonder he hadn't completely snapped. It's almost over, he told himself. The words repeated like a mantra in his head as they made their way to the testing facility.

Chapter 28

Camille pulled her truck up behind a service entrance. She'd obtained the security code somehow, and as the large gate rolled back, she led Cory through the back roads of the zoo toward the loading dock. Cory backed up to the ramp as Giselle and Jaylen jumped out. Once everyone was situated for the easiest getaway, Aluna followed Giselle over to a power box as Camille and Cory went over the plan again.

"I'm going to the rabbits first," Camille said. "Once Giselle and Aluna are done, they'll grab the other cage room nearby. You two can go grab whatever you need from the storeroom, but when you're done you need to get back here to help." It was clear from her tone she had expected Chris to be of no help whatsoever. He thought about stalling on purpose to keep them from taking too many animals, but Camille's sharp eyes were levelled on him as she finished her speech. "We need to be out of here in half an hour."

The building was dark and freezing cold. Aluna managed to cut the wires leading to the alarm and on confirmation from Charlotte, didn't take out the cameras. The animals were being held on the basement level, so the rest of the group headed down there while Chris and Cory went to find the drugs. The Phropenesomna was easy to find, located right by the door in a labelled container. Felcatril, being a potentially toxic substance was more difficult but eventually Cory managed to locate it on the top shelf.

They were back to join the others when Charlotte called.

"Chris, I've made a huge mistake. Two of the camera feeds cut out and I was trying to fix them when I accidently cut out the whole east side of the building. I got them working again but there are security vehicles out in the car park you guys need to leave now!"

She hung up and the two men sprinted down to meet the others.

"We need to leave. Now!"

"No way! There are two rooms of cages left!" protested Camille. Giselle, on the other hand, was actually taking Chris's statement seriously.

"Camille we can come back another night! If we get caught here no one is coming back for the animals."

She relented and the group sprinted up the stairs and along the dark hallway. A voice behind them caused Akari to turn around in panic.

The security guard had a gun, and it was pointed straight at them. Camille drew a matching weapon and pointed it back at him.

Two shots were fired, and Cory hit the ground. Giselle clutched at her hip and Jaylen carried her all the way back to the van, stopping the blood flow with Aluna's jacket.

The next half hour turned out to be one of the worst in Chris's life, which was pretty astounding given his life so far. Adrenaline was currently overriding his anger, but he knew the moment things calmed down he was going to erupt. Aluna was currently navigating the semi full of animals as Chris tried to keep Giselle from bleeding out in the back of Camille's truck. She was driving erratically, alternating between asking how he was doing and cursing under her breath. Chris was certain he wouldn't like what she was saying if he could hear her, so he focused instead on keeping Giselle alive.

They screeched to a halt in front of the warehouse, and Aluna drove the truck around to the alley as Camille and Jaylen rushed to find something to help get Giselle out of the truck and into the building. Charlotte was pacing nervously when they burst through the doors, and Chris saw the colour drain from her face as she saw all of the blood.

"What happened?"

Camille rounded on her with fire in her eyes. "Giselle got shot and Cory is dead because we didn't have back up we could count on!"

Aluna beat Chris to an angered reply by a breath. "Back up you could count on? Nobody said anything about guns." Chris had never heard him so much as raise his voice. Now he was livid. "No one said anything about guns!"

"Alright, everybody calm down," Jaylen yelled. "We can point fingers later. Charlotte, help us."

"Why didn't you take her to a hospital?" she asked.

"Because if she goes to the hospital, then she goes to prison," Camille snapped. "Besides, your friend says he can help her."

Charlotte looked at him in surprise. "You can?"

"I hope so," Chris checked the wound and winced. "Otherwise, GI Jane here is gonna put me down."

Camille ignored his comment and handed him a towel to staunch the blood flow. "Okay, what do you need me to do."

Chris replaced his hand with the cloth and glanced around, mentally compiling a list of things he would need. "Just get me whatever first aid supplies you have around here."

Luckily for all of them she was used to taking orders. "Okay, got it!"

"Sharpest knife you can find!" he added. "And a lighter to sterilize it." She nodded and dashed off. "Grab some rope or electrical cord, whatever you got," he added quickly. Charlotte hovered just out of reach, her breathing short and erratic. Chris knew she was still freaking out about Camille's outburst and he needed to refocus her before she hyperventilated.

"Charlotte, I'm going to need you to help me." She didn't respond, and when he looked up her face was still white as a sheet. "Charlotte!" She jumped but he couldn't feel bad about it now. Giselle was bleeding heavily, and he needed to get the bullet out. "I'm going to need your help."

Her eyes snapped back into focus and she took a few deeper breaths, though her face was still very pale. "Okay," she breathed. "Okay."

"I need to get the bullet out of her, but I don't have any anaesthesia. We'll need to hold her down." Under his hand, Giselle bucked twice then stilled. Camille chose that moment to reappear.

"Oh God, is she -?"

"She's passed out," Chris nodded at the bundle of rope in her hands. "Tie her to the table."

"Why?" Camille asked, tethering Giselle's left leg as Aluna, Akari and Jaylen each took one of his other limbs.

"Because this is gonna get rough," Chris said brusquely.

"Giselle's in good hands," Aluna spoke soothingly. "His bedside manner notwithstanding, if Chris says he can help him, he can."

Camille finished tying Giselle's leg down, cinching the knot a little more tightly than necessary. "Look I know where the plane is, but it's not gonna do you any good."

"Why not?" Jaylen asked.

"Because Giselle's your pilot!"

Everyone froze for a moment as the implications of her statement sank in. "Wonderful," Chris mumbled, turning to set Akari to sterilizing the knife and tongs. Camille was hovering very near Giselle's head, and Chris felt the last of his patience snap. "Go somewhere else!" She sneered at him and didn't move from her spot. It was Aluna who finally stepped in.

"Camille, Giselle will be fine. We should prepare the plane for take-off." He reached out to cup her elbow, steering her away from the makeshift surgery table and Chris's acid tongue. She resisted for a moment, but Aluna's gentle coaxing eventually brought her around. She promised to meet him outside in ten minutes and moved off, presumably to wash the blood from her hands. Chris wished he could do the same.

Akari returned with the small instruments and excused herself, leaving Chris alone with Charlotte. He turned and grabbed the bottle of rubbing alcohol.

"Bullet's in a bad place," he told her as he opened the bottle and drenched his hands. "This isn't going to be pretty." He wasn't evenly really sure he could do this, but he couldn't back out now. The others expected him to save Giselle's life, but that wasn't the reason he was working so hard to keep her from bleeding out. If Giselle died, Charlotte would feel responsible. She couldn't have known the guards were there, but she had been the one in charge of the cameras. In her mind, Giselle's death would be her fault, just as Cory's was. Chris would do everything in his power to shield her from any more pain.

"You ready?" She seemed more together, though she still looked a little shaky as she nodded. "Okay, hold her down." Charlotte placed her hands on Giselle's chest, and Chris realized she didn't have the proper leverage to exert any real control over her if she decided to buck. He hoped the ropes held. Using his left hand to pry the wound wider, he leaned over Giselle's hip and slid the tongs into the gaping hole.

Giselle bucked. Her eyes opened, wide and wild from the pain. A strangled cry bubbled from her throat as Charlotte tried to calm him down. "No, you're okay, you're okay," she told her. She couldn't keep her completely on the table, but Chris noted she was surprisingly strong for her size. Giselle didn't lift more than a few inches, and he was able to probe for the bullet. "You're gonna be fine," he urged. "You're gonna be okay."

"What the hell is wrong?" Giselle groaned, turning her head to glance at Chris. Her entire body was tensed in agony, and she grunted several times before going limp. As soon as her muscles relaxed, Chris found the bullet and carefully pulled it from Giselle's flesh. It made a satisfying plink as it hit the bottom of the bowl Charlotte held out for him.

"Now what?"

"Now," he traded the tongs for the needle and thread, "I stitch her closed and get cleaned up."

"Do you need me to help with that?" There was something in her tone that alerted him, and when he looked up, she was once again pale and shaky. She was about to pass out on him, and if she did, he wasn't entirely certain he would give a damn about closing Giselle's bullet wound.

"Go lie down," he directed. "Find something to drink that isn't coffee." She moved off quickly, and Chris split his attention between sewing the hole closed and listening for the sound of her body hitting the floor. When it didn't come, he assumed she'd made it to the cots and focused on his task. The woman was still out when he was done, so Chris cleaned up as much blood as he could and left her to rest.

He found Charlotte lying on a cot upstairs, her arm thrown over her eyes and a half empty water bottle on the floor next to her. She'd taken her shoes off and unbuttoned her jacket, and if Chris didn't know any better, he'd think she was just napping. He sat on the edge, reaching for her wrist to take her pulse. She looked at him sluggishly but didn't move. Her heartrate was normal, but she was still very pale.

"How do you feel?" he asked quietly.

"I'm alright. How's Giselle?" She sat up slowly, and he scooted back to give her room.

"She'll live." There must have been something in his tone, because she gave him a half-hearted glare. "What?"

"You might disagree on some things -" he scoffed, but she ignored it, "- but he's still a human being. You did the right thing by saving his life."

Chris thought that he and Giselle probably disagreed on just about everything, but he didn't say it. Instead, he just shrugged one shoulder and stood. "Yeah, well, she's our pilot. She dies, we don't make it out of the country."

"Chris!"

"The woman nearly got us killed, Charlotte," he countered. "She and her band of wackos opened fire on security guards, and we were caught in the crossfire."

"It's not his fault you didn't know the guards were there," she shouted back. "If I had been paying more attention, if I'd had seen the feeds were crossed -"

"There's no way you could have known," he argued. "And it was their decision to bring guns in the first place!"

"If they hadn't, you'd be in jail right now."

"Don't," he hissed. "Don't you dare try to justify anything they did tonight."

She opened her mouth for a rebuttal, but he was keenly aware of how amped up he was and didn't want to say anything he'd regret. He held up a hand and turned away, retreating to the small area that acted as a kitchen. Someone had made a pot of coffee on a hot plate, and Chris looked for a clean mug as Jaylen and Akari came crashing through the door.

"What's going on?" Chris glanced between them, noting how Akari's hands were shaking.

"Something's wrong with the animals," she said.

"Yeah," Chris snarked. "That's sort of why we're all here right now."

"She means the ones in the trailer," Jaylen explained. "They were all growling at us. First a little black kitten, then the rest."

"And you were expecting them to behave themselves? They're in a place they don't know with people they don't recognize," Chris knew he shouldn't be taking his irritation out on his friends, but Giselle was unconscious, and Camille was taking Aluna to the plane. Unfortunately, they were convenient targets.

'Not to mention whatever the hell the dextro-rinoifane solution has done to their brain chemistry. So, I don't really blame them for being a bit tetchy."

'Look," Akari's tone was sharp as she stalked over, "I understand that you're under a great deal of stress right now. You don't want to be here; you've made that abundantly clear. But we're here now, and we all have to deal with it. Including you."

Chris clenched his teeth together to keep from saying something else he didn't really mean. Instead, he turned his back to them and poured himself a mug of bitter coffee. It was awful, but he choked it down anyway. He had never been great at apologies, so he addressed Jaylen's concerns about the animals instead.

'So, they were all growling at you?"

'Every single one of them," Jaylen confirmed. He seemed to sense Chris's intent and accepted it in stride. "Like they'd all found a common enemy."

'Us," Akari put in. She, like Jaylen, was willing to move past Chris's outburst and forget about it.

'And at first it was just the serval, but then the rest of the animals joined in?" Chris began walking back toward the cots and Charlotte. She would want to know what was going on.

Jaylen and Akari followed him, posting up by the makeshift doorway. Charlotte was cinching the knot on her shoe when they arrived. Chris glanced at her as he walked by to lean back against a rail, but he couldn't tell from her neutral expression if she was mad at him for his earlier behaviour.

'Yes, but not all at once," Jaylen said. "It was more like it was passing from one animal to the next."

Charlotte had turned toward them, placing her feet on the floor but making no motion to stand. "What is it? What's going on?"

'I don't know," Chris told them honestly. Animal behaviour was more Jaylen's expertise. He'd only heard one thing that could explain it. "Maybe it's some kind of emotional contagion?"

Akari crossed her arms across her chest. "What's that mean, 'emotional contagion?'"

"It's a biological phenomenon," Chris fell back on his scientific explanations; they were infinitely easier to understand than human emotions. "Nobody quite understands it, but it's real. Like yawns are contagious," he offered. "You see somebody yawning, you can't help but yawn yourself. Same thing with laughter."

"And you think that's what happening with the animals?"

The scientist balked at the absolute in her statement. "I can't say for sure, but it's a theory."

"But if it's true, that would explain why the abnormal animal behaviours have been increasing so much these past weeks," Jaylen latched onto the theory and ran with it. "Because animals in proximity could be triggering each other."

"Like inside the truck." Akari said. "You're saying one of the animals starts displaying the behaviour, then it spreads from one to the next."

"Like a spark." Jaylen's voice sounded distant, like he was recalling a long past memory. When the others turned to him, he explained. "Something my uncle said - I didn't understand at the time - but he called it 'the spark.'" Chris frowned, still put off at the mention of Kelvin Hudson and his ideas. Jaylen didn't seem to notice his disgust and kept going. "Okay, he said that once the spark was lit, it would spread all over the world from animal to animal, like wildfire. And that once this happened, it would be impossible to put out the flame."

There was a beat of silence as Jaylen's words sunk in. Chris was the one to break it. "Dramatic - and slightly apocalyptic - ramblings aside, we need to get out of here. Fast."

"Aluna said she would call when they reached the airfield." As if on cue, Jaylen's phone rang loudly, echoing in the almost empty warehouse. "That's her now." He answered it, nodding once and promising to be careful after extracting a similar promise from Aluna. He hung up and sighed. "We've got a plane."

"I'll make sure our things are packed in the car," Akari stepped back toward the door. "You three check on Giselle and get whatever we need from here." Chris went straight for the drugs they'd stolen while Jaylen went to look in on Giselle. Charlotte didn't follow either of them, choosing instead to visit the kitchen and pack up any remaining food.

Chris found a spare backpack lying on the floor beneath the table. He tried not to notice the blood that had congealed on the far side of the slab, but it was difficult. Eventually he grabbed Giselle's discarded shirt and tossed it over the mess before unzipping the pack and dumping the contents to make room for the ill-gotten equipment. The screen went in first, padded by one of Chris's own shirts from his bag. The second large piece just barely fit, and Chris silently thanked his antisocial adolescence and his almost cult-like devotion to mastering Tetris.

Jaylen came up beside him as he was packing the power cord into the outer pocket. He quietly began loading all of the leftover first aid supplies into his own pack, offering silent companionship as Chris worked up the nerve to say what he needed to.

"Listen, I'm...sorry. About blowing up before." Chris didn't look at Jaylen, but he could feel the other man's presence. "I just can't believe we let it get this far." Suddenly, everything he couldn't say before came bubbling to the surface. "One minute Charlotte's wanted for killing a police officer, the next minute we're in a gunfight. At the testing lab of a cosmetics business."

Jaylen finally spoke, his tone firm but friendly. "You think I wanted it this way?"

"It was your idea to contact this Giselle character," Chris finally turned to Jaylen. "Doesn't take a fortune teller to figure out that bad things might occur when she's around."

"Yeah, well I didn't hear you come up with any ideas about how to get out of the country undetected."

"Right," Chris conceded the point and countered with one of his own. "But my no ideas beats the hell out of robbing a business to get out of here." He zipped the pack up more forcefully than he intended.

"We had no other options, Chris. None."

The bubbling became a rolling boil. "People got shot, Jaylen!" And, he added silently, it could have any of them that were shot instead. The fact that the security guards hit two members of Giselle's gang instead of one of his friends was sheer luck.

Charlotte had finished with her packing and came downstairs as the two men were talking. Jaylen was apparently done with what he finally realized was a futile argument. "Well, at least you got your drugs."

Charlotte stepped in before Chris could reply. "Giselle still out, huh?"

Chris had finally reached the end of his civility. "Yep. And I say we leave her."

"We're not leaving the girl, okay?" Jaylen protested. "She's hurt."

With a final zip, Chris stood tall and stared Jaylen square in the eye. "I'm a neurobiologist," he said coldly. "I didn't take the Hippocratic Oath." Without another word, he turned and walked away. Akari was waiting with her bag next to the door, and as Chris approached, she opened it. Chris followed her out as Jaylen and Charlotte caught up.

"Are we really just gonna leave him here?" Charlotte asked.

"We could put a bow on him, leave him front of the police station," Chris offered.

"We'll call an ambulance once we get to the airport," Jaylen had at least seen the sense in leaving Giselle behind. "Then we'll call the testing facility, tell them where they can find their animals."

"And to use extreme caution when approaching them," Akari added.

"Hold on, everybody."

Chapter 29

Giselle's voice halted them all in their tracks. Chris bit back a groan and turned with the rest of them to find a very pale but very determined looking woman staring them down. With a gun. Charlotte was standing next to him, and he saw her flinch at the sight of the weapon. Chris shifted ever so slightly to angle his body between her and Giselle.

Jaylen held his hands out but didn't sound at all cowed. "Seriously, Giselle? What is it with your lot and guns?"

"Well, my charm only gets me so far, pal." Giselle was holding his left arm tenderly, no doubt due to the crudely stitched bullet wound in his shoulder. He was clearly in pain, but the gun in his right hand was convincing enough. "Where's Camille?"

"She's with Aluna. They went to the plane."

"Good," Giselle gestured with his gun. "Let's go get 'em. It's my plane, after all."

Chris saw Jaylen debate their options, coming up with the only answer he could while standing at the wrong end of a gun. "Fine. Come on." He turned back toward the car, his intent clear.

"No, the plan abides," Giselle commanded. "We're taking the animals."

"We can't." Akari was just as adamant, but Giselle wasn't swayed.

"Sure, we can." She nodded toward the truck behind him, as though they had forgotten it was even there.

"No, it's impossible," Akari tried to explain rationally. Chris thought she was wasting her time. "Something is wrong with them."

"And we can make it right by setting them free." Giselle gestured again, demonstrating why they couldn't really say no. "So, get in the truck, and let's go to Canada." When no one made a move, his face hardened. "Now!"

A look passed between all four of them, a resignation that said they didn't really have a choice. Almost as one, they began walking slowly toward the truck.

Giselle turned in front of the car and smiled. "So, who's volunteering to ride in the back? Or do you want to draw straws? All five of us can't fit up front."

Chris was willing to go along in the face of a gun, but the thought of any of them having to make the trip locked in the back with already agitated animals didn't sit well. "Look, you're not getting it. The animals, they're not right. It's not safe back there."

"I'll ride in the back," Jaylen offered. Giselle wasn't budging, and the longer they stayed where they were the greater chance they had of being caught. Chris understood, but he didn't like it.

Charlotte didn't either. "Jaylen, no. You cannot do that."

"I'll come with you," Akari followed Jaylen around to the trailer, leaving Chris and Charlotte standing with a half-crazed gunman.

"How sweet is that, huh?" Giselle mocked. "All this saving the world stuff is really working out great for you, Jaylen!" Chris didn't bother hiding his look of disdain as Giselle turned back to them. "Chris, you drive."

Chris had no idea how to operate an eighteen-wheeler, though he assumed it was similar to towing a trailer with a truck. Charlotte climbed in first, situating herself in the middle as Giselle came in behind her. She was panting and sweaty from the effort, her lips white from suppressing her pain. Chris wondered if any of his friends would object to dumping her on the side of the road when she inevitably passed out.

"Let's roll."

It took Chris a few tries, but he'd always been a quick learner. By the time they made it to the highway, he had the hang of it. Charlotte had scooted close enough that she was pressed against him from hip to knee. He knew she was trying to keep from jostling Giselle injured hip, but he took it as a sign that she'd forgiven him for his earlier outburst.

"Appreciate you saving my life, sport," Giselle said as they passed a sign for the airfield. 26 miles seemed like a million.

"You say that now," Chris shot back snidely. "But I might have left a penny in your chest. Shouldn't hurt but getting through airport security might be an adventure." It was petty (and untrue), but he didn't care. Giselle had already been afforded more chances and grace than Chris thought she deserved, and the woman knew that he didn't like her. There was no need for false civility.

They ate up the miles to the airfield in good time, and Chris followed the signs as they neared the entrance. The entire truck gave a sudden shudder, then jerked. A loud bang echoed from the back, and Charlotte reached out to grab his arm.

"What is that?"

"I'm pulling over," Chris announced, fighting to keep the truck steady at fifty.

Giselle adjusted his grip on the gun in his lap pointedly. "Like hell you will. We're almost there." He nodded at the sign welcoming them to the airport. The Cargo Terminal was just past the main gate.

The truck lurched again, and this time Chris wasn't experienced enough to correct it. He slammed the brakes, hoping to keep the thing from jack-knifing or rolling. Charlotte's grip on his arm tightened painfully, but he didn't care. After several terrifying seconds, the truck came to a stop in the middle of the road.

Chris bailed first, jogging to the back to make sure Jaylen and Akari weren't being stampeded by crazed animals. The trailer door had come unlatched, and the animals were escaping out onto the street. Charlotte and Giselle came around the other side just as the peal of sirens began to grow closer.

Jaylen came out of the trailer, followed closely by Akari. "We have to get to the airport," he said. He took off at a run for the airfield just beyond the perimeter wall. The others were right behind him.

Charlotte, at least, had the sense to remember the important things. "Chris, the drugs!"

He was already on his way back to the cab. "Yeah, I got them!" He snatched the strap and hauled the pack from its place in the floorboards. Half a dozen police cars screeched to a halt behind the truck, and Chris wondered how they'd found them so quickly. He caught up to the others easily, and like a flock of birds they moved as a unit toward the open cargo door of Giselle's plane.

Jaylen slowed his pace, letting Chris and Charlotte ahead of him. "Go, go, go!" he yelled as they neared. Aluna was already sitting in the cockpit, and Chris saw the propellers spin up as he began the take-off procedure.

Charlotte made it in first. Chris turned and ushered Akari in ahead of him before boarding in two long strides. The cargo netting on the walls helped steady him as he moved as far in as he could. Jaylen was moving toward the cockpit as Camille reached to help Giselle the last few steps.

"Hey! Go!"

"Hold on!" Aluna yelled, and suddenly the plane lurched forward. Chris reached out to steady Charlotte as she nearly toppled over, and she gripped his hand like a lifeline. They began taxiing down the runway, and Giselle finally made it to the front of the plane.

"Let's get out of here!"

Chris glanced back, surprised to see a car chasing them down. It stopped, and an older man in a black suit got out and started running after them. After a few paces he stopped to aim his pistol at the wide-open bay.

"I've got this." Chris watched in horror as Camille braced a military style rifle against her shoulder.

"No!" Both Jaylen and Akari moved to stop her.

Akari got there first. She tackled the other woman in an effort to keep her from killing the man. The slick surface of the metal ramp caused them both to pitch forward out of the plane and onto the concrete runway.

"Akari!"

"Camille!"

Both Giselle and Jaylen moved toward the door, but they could only watch helplessly as the two women tumbled to the tarmac. The plane was picking up speed now, and soon Aluna would have to close the door to take off.

Jaylen shrugged his rucksack off and sank down onto the small platform under the netting. There was no way they could go back for her now. Chris felt all of his anger and frustration suddenly disappear at the quick, cold fear that shot through him. Akari would be arrested, tried as an accessory for the murder of a police officer, and there was nothing any of them could do.

The bay door began to close slowly, forcing them back into the main cargo area. Aluna glanced over his shoulder quickly, then turned his attention back to the take-off.

"What happened?" he asked.

"We lost Akari," Charlotte told him. Chris could hear the despair in her voice, and he reached out to hug her to him with one arm. She turned her head into his chest and sheltered there, clutching at the side of his shirt with her hands. Chris carefully slid the bag off his shoulder and wrapped both arms around her as she cried silently.

"We're taking off now!" Aluna told them. "Sit down."

Jaylen reached back and threaded his fingers through the netting to stabilize himself as Giselle took the co-pilot's seat. Chris noted his drawn face, and for once he had no snide remark. As Charlotte settled down next to him on the bench and took his hand, he tried to imagine if it had been Charlotte instead of Akari who had tried to stop Camille. The pang of loss hit him hard, and he felt the first bit of sympathy for the woman who had antagonized him for the last twenty-four hours.

The gravity shifted as the ground fell away, and Chris felt his stomach give a little flip. Next to him Charlotte's head lolled back to the mesh net, and he focused on her to keep from raging against the injustice of Akari's capture. Turning her hand over he began massaging just below her pulse point, pressing his thumb into the niche between her bones to stave off the motion sickness she must be feeling now.

Her eyes opened, but she didn't look at him. "I can't believe…"

"I know," he whispered. His fingers kept up their ministrations as he leaned his head toward hers. She met him halfway, resting against him as she forced herself to take even breaths.

It took a few minutes, but the plane eventually levelled out and Aluna turned the controls over to Giselle in order to check on Jaylen. She met Chris's eyes as he passed, and the two shared a nod of solemn acknowledgement. Chris watched as Aluna knelt in front of her old friend. He couldn't make out what they were saying, but Jaylen nodded a few times in response. Aluna patted his shoulder firmly, squeezing it in a sisterly show of comfort before standing and returning to the cockpit.

"We'll have to stop in Brazil," Giselle said finally.

"Not my favourite place ever," Chris frowned.

Giselle looked at him with an expression that spoke volumes. There was no love lost between them. "This plane can't make the trip from here to North America in one go."

Jaylen finally stood. "Canada," he corrected. "We need to get to Canada."

Giselle looked at him, then at Chris. "What's in Canada?"

Chris had nothing else to say to Giselle that wouldn't devolve into one of them ending up on the floor, so he stayed quiet and concentrated on Charlotte's breathing. Her eyes were closed, but he could tell she was still awake and listening.

"We'll explain later," Aluna answered diplomatically. "For now, let's get to Brazil."

By the time they landed in Lucena all of them were ready to get off the plane. Charlotte eyed the small cargo area and wondered for the hundredth time how in the hell Giselle thought she was going to transport all of those animals in such a tight space. There was barely enough room for five adults, let alone the menagerie they'd taken from the testing building.

Giselle stopped the plane smoothly and reached up for the button that would lower the rear cargo door. Charlotte stood and swayed, steadied by her grip on the netting behind her and Chris's hand at her back. Her legs felt like lead as she stumbled down the ramp, her muscles cramping after prolonged confinement on the aircraft. Next to her, Chris was faring little better.

"When this is all over, I am never stepping foot on a plane ever again," he grumbled.

"Amen," Charlotte shook her legs to restore circulation and to allow her muscles to remember how to move properly. Jaylen and Aluna shuffled slowly out of the plane behind them, followed by Giselle.

Chapter 30

"Welcome to Brazil, boys and girls." Her flippant tone irritated Charlotte, who was still reeling from Akari's capture. It had been Charlotte's fault in the first place that she was even wanted by the police; now she would be held accountable for something she had no hand in. Charlotte's guilt gnawed at her, tightening into a tiny aching ball in the pit of her stomach. No matter how many times Chris and the others had told her it wasn't her fault, that she'd had no choice, Charlotte still felt the soul-consuming anguish that came with taking a life.

"How long will refuelling take?" Aluna asked.

"About an hour," Giselle estimated. "The guy who owns this airfield is a friend of ours, and a very influential member of the gang." The sound of a small electric engine grew louder, and the group turned. "There he is now."

A cart with a single rider was puttering toward them, and as it slowed to a stop Charlotte got a look at their benefactor. He was an older man, mid-fifties, with brown skin and bright eyes. His jet-black hair was peppered with grey around his temples, and beneath the rolled sleeves of his shirt she could make out the ends of a faded tattoo on his right arm. As he parked and stepped onto the cement, Giselle grinned widely and held his arms out.

"Adam," he greeted. "Olá amigo!"

"Olá," Adam returned. "I am glad you made it safely, Giselle." The two men embraced warmly, though Giselle was careful to keep her injured hip away from the contact. Adam seemed to notice the empty plane and the strangers all at once, and when he pulled away from Giselle his face was drawn together. "Something is wrong."

It wasn't a question, and Giselle didn't try to deflect or play it off. "Things didn't go as planned, Adam. Cory is dead, Camille been captured. I just barely made it out in time."

"Without the animals." Something in the older man's tone changed, darkened, and Giselle definitely noticed.

"It's not like we didn't try," he explained quickly. "But something's wrong with the animals. They're not right."

"Of course, they aren't." Adam said. "They have been in prisons their whole lives."

Charlotte felt Chris stiffen next to her, and she quickly reached out to take his hand. He squeezed back, and she could feel the tension in his body coming off in waves. Now was not the time for him to go off on a rant.

"And who are they?" Adam turned his piercing stare on the newcomers, surveying them with a critical eye. Jaylen stepped forward first, ready to take the lead now that Akari was gone.

"Jaylen Hudson," he held out his hand to Adam, then turned to introduce the others. "And this is Aluna, Chris, and Charlotte."

"They helped with the operation," Giselle clarified. "Jaylen, Aluna, and I go way back."

Adam stared at them a moment more, then accepted their presence with a small wave. "You must be tired from the journey," he switched from shrewd leader to welcoming host in the blink of an eye. "Come, come. There are showers at my facility, and food as well. Someone will take care of the plane."

Jaylen cleared his throat quietly, and Giselle picked up on the message. "Adam, how soon do you think we can get going? We need to get to Canada."

"For what?" he asked. "You have no animals to deliver."

"There's something we have to do, and Giselle said she could get us to Canada." Jaylen was insistent. Charlotte just wanted that shower.

"Please, Adam," Giselle pushed. "You know I wouldn't ask unless it was important. There is something wrong with the animals, and these guys are trying to help."

"So you have said," Adam began walking back toward the cart. The others followed quickly. "But you have not said what is wrong."

"He can explain it all," Giselle jabbed her thumb over her shoulder at Chris, who glared back. "But not out here."

Adam thought for a moment, then nodded. "I will hear what you have to say," he said. "Then I will decide if it is worth sending an empty plane."

The cart was meant to hold four, but they made it work. Aluna sat in the small cargo area in the back of the cart while Giselle took the front seat with Adam. Charlotte sat on Chris's lap in the back seat with Jaylen. The tiny engine complained about the extra weight as Adam pressed the gas pedal, but once they got moving it smoothed out.

They passed several hangars holding an assortment of different aircraft, from helicopters to small jetliners. Adam's facility was a converted hangar at the end of the row, and as the cart whined to a stop, they all stepped out and peered up.

"Impressive," Aluna mumbled. The hangar's large doors had been made into permanent walls, and a balcony indicated there were multiple levels inside. Adam led them through a small side door, past an armed guard, and into a sitting room. From here there was no indication they were on an airfield; it looked more like an upscale lounge room at a gentleman's club. Charlotte and Chris sat on the sofa as the others sank into armchairs with sighs of relief.

"I will have my children bring food," Adam said. "And then perhaps you can explain to me this problem with the animals." He left through a second door that presumably led into the inner parts of the complex. As soon as the door was closed, Chris rounded on Giselle.

"What in the hell is going on? Who is this guy?"

"Easy, sport," Giselle held up her hands. "Adam is a good person. He's just...careful. But once he hears the truth, he'll help us."

"You said you would get us to Canada, Giselle." Jaylen sounded angry. "You didn't say anything about Adam, or that we would have to convince him to let us take the plane."

"Well, I was expecting to have a plane full of animals to take to Canada," Giselle said. "But that didn't exactly work out, did it?" She glared at Chris, as though it was his fault the animals hadn't made it onto the plane.

Charlotte jumped to his defence. "Hey, don't blame us for your failures," she snapped. "It was your idea to bring guns to the testing facility!"

"And it was your idea that led to my new scar," she shot back, indicating her hip. "If we had stuck to my plan, Cory and Camille would be here now. And Akari."

It was a cheap shot, but it hit the mark. Charlotte fell silent as another wave of guilt washed over her.

"Enough," Aluna's sharp command silenced all of them. "Arguing about who is to blame is pointless; what is done is done. We cannot change it. What we can do is convince Adam that what we are doing is worth his effort."

The argument ended as the door opened. Two teens, a tall boy of about fifteen and a smaller girl, came in with trays of food and deposited them on a side table without saying a word. They left just as silently eyes downcast as they scurried out of the room. Obviously, Adam had told his children not to bother their guests, and they didn't even glance up curiously.

"Friendly bunch." Chris's tone was dry, and Charlotte could hear the frustration and helplessness she felt echoed in its undertones.

Giselle scoffed and moved to the food, peering into the bowls curiously. "You're in luck, friends. This dish is a Brazilian specialty. Vegetarian, of course."

"Of course," Jaylen took the bowl Giselle offered and found a seat. The others followed suit, gulping down their meals in silence. Charlotte picked at her bowl with a spoon, turning over the rice to inspect the other contents. There seemed to be an assortment of red and green bell peppers, squash, onion, tomatoes, and black beans mixed in a garlic sauce.

"It's good," Chris told her. "Rich."

"It's feijoada," Giselle said around a mouthful. "Adam's mother taught him how to make it. He substitutes the traditional meat with something more humane."

Chris swallowed his bite before speaking. "You know, most plant cells are still respiring and functioning normally after being harvested. So your precious vegetables are still alive when you consume them. At least I kill my food before I eat it." It was a comment designed to get under Giselle's skin. From the look on the other man's face, it had worked.

"Friends," Adam came back before Giselle could launch into what had looked like an impressive tirade against all meat-eaters. "I hope the food is to your satisfaction." Behind him, an older woman entered with a tray of glasses. Each one held a translucent liquid with lime wedges nestled beneath the ice. "I have brought some caipirinha for you to try. It is a very popular drink in my country."

"Is it alcoholic?" Chris asked.

Adam nodded. "It is made from cachaça, a drink distilled from sugarcane juice. It is good."

Chris reached for a glass, plucking a second one off the tray to hand to Charlotte. She accepted it and sipped, wincing at the taste. Chris didn't seem fazed, but he did lick his lips and nod appreciatively.

Adam seemed to sense her hesitation. "If it is too strong, we can get something else. Water, or a limonada perhaps?"

"I will take a water, please," Aluna said.

"This is fine," Charlotte kept hers and took another drink. It was better the second time.

Adam gestured at the woman, muttering something in Portuguese. Charlotte recognized the word for water, and she nodded before scurrying away. He settled onto a plush armchair and turned his steady gaze on Chris. "So, tell me about what is happening."

It took Chris nearly an hour and most of the already depleted battery life on his tablet to explain what was happening. By the time he was done, Adam was leaning forward in his seat.

"Incrível," he whispered. "And you want to go to Canada to stop this?"

Charlotte knew what he was thinking. It was the same sentiment Camille had expressed in that warehouse. She scooted to the edge of her seat and caught Adam's intense stare with her own.

"The polar bears are the key," she told him. "They haven't had any exposure to the dextro-rinoifane solution. Chris can use their DNA and the neutraliser to create a cure. We just need a way to get to them."

Adam considered her words for a long moment, and Charlotte feared the worst. If he was anything like Giselle and her associates, the man would be more than happy to let the animals rise up and overtake humanity. It didn't matter that they were artificially damaged; Camille had made their group's views very clear on the subject.

"Look at the news," she pressed. "Nothing about this is natural. Humans have done this. The animals are changing faster than the world can keep up with, and it's our fault. The entire ecosystem is being disrupted. All we want to do is reverse the effects of this drug and get things back to the way they were."

"You mean back to humans exploiting animals for money? Hunting them nearly to extinction to satisfy our own egos? Butchering them?" Adam wasn't as angry as Camille had been, but he was just as passionate.

Charlotte kept his gaze, pushing her own fervour into her tone to get through to him. "I know you probably think that it's better this way, that we're getting what we deserve. Maybe we are." Charlotte could feel the others' eyes on her, but she ignored them and focused on Adam. "But if we don't do something soon, everything we know will be gone. Your friends, family, your children. They will be lost to this if we do nothing."

Adam stood up, glancing from Giselle to the others. After another beat of silence, he held out his hands toward Charlotte. Trusting her friends to have her back, she accepted the gesture and slipped her smaller hands into his. He pulled her to her feet and met her gaze, staring intently as though he could peer past them into her soul. He seemed to be sizing her up and Charlotte fought the urge to squirm. Finally, he smiled and patted her hands affectionately.

"I will have a plane ready in two hours." There was a collective sigh of relief from the group. "There are showers upstairs for you and your friends, as well as a fresh change of clothes."

"Thank you," Charlotte gripped his hands tightly before Adam released her and turned to go. Just as he opened the door, he turned to address them once more.

"The animals are merely following their biological imperatives. It does not matter how they acquired them. I would only ask that you do all in your power not to kill unless you have absolutely no other alternative." He waited for her nod, then left them alone. When the door closed behind him, the others stood up and surrounded Charlotte.

"Well done," Aluna laid her hand on her shoulder and squeezed affectionately.

"Yeah," Jaylen echoed. "Thanks, Charlotte."

"Alright, we have a plane," Giselle clapped her hands together. "Now we need a plan. I've got a guy in Canada. Did some activist work with him last year. He'll have everything we need to hunt down a polar bear."

With a plan in place and their means of transportation secured, the five of them went off in search of the showers. Charlotte followed Chris up a flight of stairs, surprised when the top step deposited her on what looked like a very upscale hotel corridor.

"Weird," Chris had stopped on the landing. "Presumably we are still in an aircraft hangar?"

"I wonder how much it cost to convert this building," Charlotte thought aloud. "Which way?"

"I have no idea," Chris glanced down each side of the hallway. Doors were spaced every thirty feet or so on either side, and they all looked exactly the same. "Looks like some sort of barracks for members of this gang."

"Makes sense," Charlotte agreed. "This guy seems to be pretty high up the chain, if Giselle's attitude toward him is any indication."

"He has been a bit muted since we arrived hasn't, he?" Chris turned toward her fully. "Nice work back there. I knew we brought you along for a reason."

"Hey," Charlotte poked him in the arm, "if it weren't for me, you wouldn't even be on this wild polar bear chase."

"Yeah, thanks for that, by the way," he drawled in reply.

She could tell he was teasing by his tone, but Charlotte was suddenly struck by the revelation of how much he'd sacrificed in the last three months. His job at the crocodile sanctuary, certainly. His flat, probably, unless he'd paid three months of rent in advance. And all because he'd taken a chance on an eighteen-year-old student with a chip on her shoulder and an eight-year grudge. As he began walking away, she grabbed his sleeve and tugged him to a stop.

"Do you regret it? Getting involved in all of this?" She gestured vaguely to the rich wood of the walls around them, but she knew he understood her meaning. He stepped back over to her, keeping her close but not crowding her.

"Sometimes, I almost do," he told her truthfully. "You know, when something is about to kill me I wonder how the hell I ended up here." She laughed mirthlessly with him. "But then I think about you. If it weren't for all of this madness, we probably wouldn't have ever met."

He was right. Their professional circles were vastly different, and if things were normal Charlotte would likely have gone her entire life without crossing paths with Chris Stuart. The thought was a startling one that left her with an ache in her chest that she'd never experienced before. He seemed to be on the same wavelength again, and he reached for her face to cradle her cheek in his palm.

"For what it's worth," he said quietly, "I'm glad I'm here."

She'd said the same thing to him months ago, both of them still adjusting to the whole team dynamic and wondering how their lives had led them to a hotel in Washington chasing snakes. She'd meant it as a thank you, a quiet utterance to reassure him that his presence wasn't just appreciated, it was wanted. Hearing those words parroted back to her now made her smile.

"You should do that more often." His thumb was softly tapping against her cheek, and she felt the tips of his fingers curling at her neck. His touch sent a warmth through her that was new and exciting.

"What?"

"Smile," he told her. "It makes you...I don't know, brighter."

"Brighter?" She straightened and canted her head slightly, her expression falling into one of confusion. "Is that your version of a compliment?"

Chris shrugged a shoulder and slid just a bit closer. "I've never really been good at compliments," he told her truthfully. His tongue darted out to wet his lips and Charlotte's eyes tracked the movement. When she looked back up, his eyes were dancing with amusement. "There is something I am good at, though."

"What's that?"

His lips descended on hers, tasting her like it was the first time. She let him direct the kiss for a moment, resting her hands on his chest as he pressed her back until she hit the wall behind her. His other hand moved to her waist, settling firm around the jut of her hip bone as his body covered hers almost completely. When she gasped for air his lips moved to her neck, and she heard him mumble something against her skin that sounded like her name.

Her thoughts which had been temporarily silenced by his kiss suddenly amped up again. Foremost in her mind was the rather public area they were currently standing in, but a close second was a rather daring disregard for their location. Decency won out, and Charlotte pushed a bit on his chest. She meant to tell him someone could come up the stairs any moment, to stop him from exploring further.

What came spilling out was something quite different.

'I love you."

It was just as effective. His movements stilled, though he didn't pull away from their embrace. Charlotte held her breath as the seconds ticked on. Panic and doubt seized her as he remained silent, and she almost opened her mouth to mitigate whatever damage she'd done. She wanted to tell him that he didn't have to say it back, that it was okay if he didn't feel the same. It sat like lead in her stomach, pulling her under the wave of anguish that was building.

Under her fingertips she felt his body relax, his breath coming out in an almost laugh as he pulled her against him. The hand that had been on her waist moved to the small of her back, and she couldn't help but settle easily into his arms. It didn't feel like a rejection, and Charlotte felt a swell of hope counter the roaring in her mind.

'Breathe, Charlotte," he whispered in her ear. "I feel the same way." Relief coursed through her, and he laughed again. "I didn't realize I was hiding it that well. I thought it was obvious; Aluna's certainly figured it out already. Probably even before I did." He leaned back and kissed her again, this time slowly.

Every nerve ending was on fire, hypersensitive from the adrenaline still coursing through her. She'd finally said it. And better still, he felt the same. The weight lifted instantly, setting her free and allowing her to soar under his ministrations. She pulled him closer, angling her head to allow him better access as she opened herself completely to him. He hummed in approval and pushed her back into the wall, using his body to keep her there as his hands roamed down to her waist. His fingers were warm as they slipped under her shirt, caressing the sensitive skin of her stomach and lower back.

Charlotte was suddenly very aware that she hadn't had a shower in several days. "Chris," she managed to whisper his name as he broke for air. He understood what she meant immediately, and his hands moved from her skin to grasp her arms lightly. She laid her forehead against his collarbone as she fought to control her breathing. His chest rose and fell beneath her head as he did the same, and they stood there for a few seconds in content silence.

"Come on," she pushed his shoulder to get him to move, allowing her to slip by him. He followed close behind, coming to rest only a few inches away as she stopped in front of the first room on the left. "Let's see what's behind door number one." She turned the knob, unsurprised when it twisted easily in her hand. Inside was a dark room, generic and clean. The curtains were drawn over the window, but there was just enough light slipping through that she could make out a twin bed in the corner and a set of drawers on the far wall. A small bathroom sat to the right of the door, and further inspection revealed a second door past the tub that probably led to an adjoining room. Chris had been right; these were dorms for visiting gang members.

Chris hovered in the door, his eyes intense but unsure. Charlotte wanted nothing more than to pull him in and pick up where they'd left off. But they had less than two hours, and Charlotte was fairly certain that if she did that they would miss their plane. Chris seemed to realize the same thing at the same time, and he combed his fingers through his hair as he stepped back from the threshold.

"I'm gonna…" he gestured behind him to another closed door. "I'll be over here."

"Okay." But she didn't want him to go just yet. Her confession had awakened something, and she couldn't resist padding over for another kiss. He obliged willingly, taking his time until it wound down.

"You know," he rasped, "this trip to Brazil is much better than my last one."

She laughed and pushed him away, waiting until he'd opened his opposing door before closing her own. She turned and leaned back against it, closing her eyes as the sensations of the last few minutes washed over her again. She felt like a teenager all over again. Stolen kisses and late nights in the country flooded her mind, but the feelings those memories elicited paled against the all-consuming fire in her now.

"Focus, Charlotte." She pushed away from the door and walked over to the chest of drawers. Clothes of varying sizes and styles were contained within, and she selected an ensemble that seemed appropriate for trekking across Canada in search of a polar bear. New packages of undergarments were stored in the bottom drawer, and she found her size and tore the package open without hesitation.

She found towels in the cabinet beneath the sink, and when she turned the water on she was pleased to find the water pressure was adjustable. Soaps and shampoos were housed on a shelf above the tub, and she grabbed the closest ones as she stepped into the tub.

Charlotte spent a long time under the warm spray. She could feel her muscles relaxing under the jet, and after she'd scrubbed herself clean, she leaned against the cool tile and let the water sluice off her shoulders. She absently wondered how much hot water a place like this stored at any given time. She could probably stay here for hours and never run out, but she didn't want to be separated from the others that long. Reluctantly she twisted the knob to the off position, cutting off the water. Steam had built up in the room, so it was pleasantly warm when she stepped out onto the dark bathmat.

She towelled off quickly, slipping on the new clothes with a sigh of relief. It felt good to be clean again. She dried her hair as much as she could before throwing it up in a hasty ponytail. The towel she draped over the shower curtain, and her old clothes she left in a heap in the corner. She probably wouldn't see them again, but she didn't really care. Everything else she owned had been lost; it was almost as though she was casting off the last of her old life. These last few months had changed her, moulded her into someone that would likely be unrecognizable to anyone she knew in Carterton. She still wasn't sure if that was a good thing or not.

Chapter 31

She found the others sitting in the same room they'd left, though they were all in different clothes and seemed to be in better spirits. They must have found showers of their own. The only one missing was Chris, and her inquisitive glance around the room hadn't gone unnoticed.

"He is with our host," Aluna supplied helpfully. "We received some news and he left rather abruptly."

"What news?" Charlotte feared the worst, hoping that nothing had happened to Kendall or Elliana. Jaylen looked pale sitting in his chair, his eyes unfocused and sad. "What happened?"

"Here," Giselle thrust a tablet at her. A news article was pulled up, and the headline made Charlotte sick to her stomach.

Suspect Apprehended in Federal Murder Case

Charlotte read quickly through the article, trying to ignore the guilt that threatened to ebb. Akari had been captured by the police, and the lead officer she finally knew - was being hailed a hero.

"There's some good news," Giselle reached over and swiped down to the next article. "Cory's not dead after all."

Two Eco-Terrorists in Custody, One Still At Large

Charlotte felt a small part of her guilt abate at the news. It seemed his gunshot wound hadn't been fatal, and he'd been transported to a hospital almost immediately after their escape. She still felt a little responsible for his capture, but it was a hell of a lot better than his death.

"There's more," Aluna said, coming to stand next to her. "Chris left after reading further." Charlotte swiped quickly, moving to the next article on the page.

Northampton Declares State of Emergency After Animal Attacks Rise

The Northampton Area is now under martial law after hundreds die due to animal attacks. Safe zones have been set up across the region. Authorities are

rging citizens to pack one small carry-on sized luggage and report to the
earest evacuation site.

t was getting worse, Charlotte thought. She wondered why Chris would be so
pset; they knew things were going to be bad. She thought for a moment that he
vas worried about his friends, but then remembered the anti-social scientist
he'd met. Then who could he be -

t hit her like a bolt, a long-forgotten conversation coming back to her. I took
he job at the sanctuary to be close to her. She lives in Northampton now.

Oh no," Charlotte shoved the tablet at Aluna hastily and moved toward the
loor, ignoring their confused inquiries behind her. She stepped into the hall and
topped the first person she found.

Do you know where Chris is? The other man who was with us?" The woman
tared at her blankly, and Charlotte sighed in frustration. She didn't know any
'ortuguese, and the woman didn't speak English. "Adam?" she tried, and the
voman finally nodded in understanding. Charlotte followed her through a series
f twisting corridors until she came to a set of double oak doors. She knocked,
nd Charlotte heard Adam's muffled voice answer.

Entre." Charlotte pushed through the doors, and Adam looked up from his desk
n surprise. "Is something wrong?"

No," Charlotte shook her head. "I was just looking for Chris."

Ah, your scientist. Yes, he seemed rather agitated. He came in ten minutes ago
emanding a phone. He is through there." There was another door on the side of
he room, just as ornate as the two that led to the hallway. Charlotte thanked
uca and slipped through, closing it behind her. Chris was hunched over the
ible at the far wall, his hand cradling a phone.

Pick up," he hissed. "Come on, pick up the phone." He hadn't heard her enter,
nd when she came up beside him he jumped. She laid a hand on his back and
ubbed up and down to soothe the tension that had gathered between his
houlders.

Your mum?" she whispered.

Ie nodded but didn't look at her. After a few more seconds he slammed the
eceiver down. "Damn it."

"I'm sure she's fine," Charlotte said.

"You don't know that!" he jerked back but didn't go anywhere. "I've tried calling her house three times, her phone twice. There's been no answer."

"She's probably at one of the safe zones already," Charlotte tried to be optimistic despite the storm brewing in his eyes.

"Or she could have been killed," he countered darkly.

"You need to stay positive," Charlotte told him. "Thinking like that isn't going to help anything." He didn't say anything, but she could see he wanted to. His natural pessimism wasn't helping the situation, and her hesitant hopefulness probably wasn't sitting well. Still, she didn't let up. He could be mad at her if he wanted; she wasn't going to think the worst until she knew for certain. "Where does she live?"

"Town centre, next right near the mini-Tesco."

Charlotte nodded and reached for the phone. She dialled a number, closed her eyes and sent up a silent prayer that the person on the other end was still alive. After four rings, it connected.

"Hello?"

Charlotte let out a breath and opened her eyes. "Madison? It's...it's Annabelle."

"Annabelle? Oh my god, are you okay? I've been trying to reach you. Your flat is empty, and no one knows where the hell you are! The police are looking for you. They say you killed a man!" His voice was getting faster and higher with each sentence, and Charlotte recognized a classic Madison rant.

"Madison, focus, please. I'm alright, I'm fine. I know about the police, but that's not important right now." She turned toward Chris and returned her hand to the warmth of his back. "I need a favour. Are you still in town?"

"For now," Madison said. "As soon as I hang up this phone, I'm on the next bus to a safe zone."

"I need you to go to Northampton. There's someone I need you to check on." Next to her she felt Chris stiffen under her fingertips.

"Are you serious?" Madison laughed. "Annabelle, it's anarchy out there!"

"Her son is with me, and he needs to know she's safe." When Madison didn't answer right away, Charlotte's tone hardened. "You owe me at least this."

"I owe you?" Madison scoffed. "How do you figure?"

"Madison, please, if you ever actually cared about me…I need you to do this for me. Please." She was begging now, but she didn't care. Chris was worth it. She could feel his apprehension as he shifted his weight from one foot to the other. Her fingers curled into the fabric of his shirt, and he slipped an arm around her waist to tug her to him.

On the other end of the phone call, Madison sighed. "I swear to God, Annabelle, if I get killed because of this I'm haunting you forever."

"Fair enough," Charlotte sagged in relief.

"Who am I checking on?"

Charlotte asked and relayed the name and address, then gave him the number on the note Chris had scrawled. "It's this number," Charlotte told Madison. "Call me the minute you know something." The moment she hung up Chris was pulling her against him.

"Thank you," he breathed into her hair. "Thank you."

She could feel his body trembling, so she held onto him until the phone trilled next to her. She picked it up before the first ring was finished.

"Madison?"

But the voice that answered her wasn't her ex. "Where is my son? Is he there?" She sounded just as Charlotte had imagined her - a tough, stern tone good for wrangling unruly students (and one stubborn son) laced with that hint of softness that seemed to come with advanced years.

Charlotte smiled. "Yes ma'am."

She handed the phone to Chris, then raised up to her toes to kiss his cheek before leaving him to speak with his mother. Adam had left, either respecting their privacy or taking care of other business. Charlotte didn't care; she was just grateful not to have to make small talk with their host.

She waited outside the door, listening to the timbre of his voice rise and fall as he reassured the woman on the other end that he was okay. She couldn't hear exactly what he was saying, but his rich laugh floated through the wooden door and surprised her. She'd heard his dry chuckles, his sarcastic huffs, and even a self-deprecating laugh or two. But this was different. It was honest and open, and she hadn't ever heard it before. Suddenly it was all she wanted to hear. She made it her mission to elicit that sound from him herself, to hear its delight directed at her. She imagined the way his face would light up, the way he would tilt his head just so to allow her to appreciate the way his eyes danced when he laughed. She didn't realize she'd closed her eyes until she heard the sound of the phone being set back on its cradle then muffled footsteps getting closer.

The door opened and Charlotte pushed away from the wall. He paused in the open doorway, taking a moment to just stare at her. When the smile broke on his face she couldn't help but mirror the expression, caught up in this rare moment of happiness in the chaotic and violent life they now lived.

"Everything okay?" she asked.

"Yeah," he closed the door behind him. "She's going to pack a bag and go with that Ethan guy to the safe zone." They began walking down the hallway toward the sitting room they'd come from. "Who is she, anyway?"

Charlotte hesitated, then realized she was being silly. "My ex-girlfriend."

Chris's step faltered for a moment. He glanced up in surprise for a moment, then resumed walking. "I just sent my mother with your ex-girlfriend?"

"Yep." It was rather hilarious when she thought about it like that.

He chuckled quietly. It wasn't the deep-throated laugh she'd heard before, but it lifted her spirits anyway. She slipped her hand into the crook of his elbow and leaned on him just a little. He took her weight and accepted the half-hug.

"If I might ask," he said after a few moments, "what happened with you two?" Charlotte winced as she remembered her last few days with Madison. Chris interpreted her silence to mean something else. "That bad?"

"No," she shook her head. "No, Ethan was...well, she was sort of my lecturer."

"Really?" Chris's scandalized tone was forced, and a quick glance told her he was enjoying this a little too much.

"Yeah, well, she decided that she'd rather break the record for the number of students it's possible to sleep with in one term rather than actually remain in some sort of committed relationship. You know, it was her who sent me that message while we were out for lunch.

"Huh," Chris huffed. "You know, I've never believed in fate or destiny before, but I have to say you're making a pretty good case for it right now."

"There you are," Jaylen half-jogged up them as they rounded a corner. "The plane's ready to go."

"Great," Charlotte deadpanned. "I'm really looking forward to another long plane ride."

Jaylen grimaced in sympathy. "Yeah, well, at least it's not a cargo plane this time. Adam's letting us take one of his smaller passenger jets. He's even sending two pilots with us. We should be there in less than eight hours."

"We're adding miracles to the list of things I'm starting to believe in," Chris quipped. "When do we leave?"

"Right now," Giselle came up behind them and clapped Chris on the shoulder. "It's time to go save the world."

Chapter 32

The private jet was everything Charlotte had ever imagined. There were three rows of seats, plush and leather just behind the door to the plane. Two seats on either side of the aisle meant there was a lot of room to stretch out. Behind them, two couches lined each side. Beyond that a curtain separated the main cabin from the rear area, which likely housed the bathroom. It was nicer than some of the hotels they'd stayed at.

"This is what I'm talking about," Giselle flopped down on one of the couches as the pilots performed the pre-flight checks. "I told you I'd get you to Canada, Jaylen. Now we're doing it in style." The tranquilizer gun Adam had lent him was stowed safely against the bulkhead. It was their only weapon against the polar bear's they were hunting.

"Alright," Jaylen took the first row of seats to the right of the aisle, raising the centre armrest to give him more space. "Let's go."

Aluna took the other couch, intent on sleeping the entire trip as Chris and Charlotte commandeered the seats opposite Jaylen. It took only a few more minutes before the pilot came over the intercom and informed them off their imminent departure. The entire plane shook as the engines warmed up, and there was little warning before they began moving forward.

"I hate this part," Charlotte whined as she gripped the armrest. Her stomach rolled as the plane gathered speed, and she fought the urge to groan. Their take-off was fairly smooth, and Charlotte let out a sigh of relief as they finally lifted away from the tarmac. Chris leaned over and pried her hand from the armrest, slipping his fingers between hers.

"Next stop, Canada."

Two hours into their flight one of the pilots came back with a hastily scrawled message. It was from Madison. He and Eden had made it safely to a safe zone and were being issued quarters and rations. On the note was a number where they could be reached, as well as an address and a seven-digit number Charlotte assumed was some sort of code or identification number. Chris thanked the young man and tucked the note into his pocket.

Charlotte looked up from the tablet she had borrowed from Adam. He'd offered them each one, but Charlotte had been the only one to accept. She hated not nowing what was happening in the world. Still, her curiosity about Chris's mother won out. "What's your mum like?"

Chris thought about her question for a moment, then shrugged. "She was a teacher for almost thirty years before she retired and moved out to Northampton. Her brother lived out there with his family, but he passed away a few years ago. Now she spends most of her days gardening and tutoring kids at the village hall."

"She sounds amazing," Charlotte admitted. "So, you have cousins? Family other than Kendall?"

"I do," he said. "But we're not close. I was always the odd one, the one no one wanted to invite to family gatherings."

"Their loss." Charlotte let that sit, returning her focus to the article she'd been reading. She couldn't find anything more on Akari's arrest, but it had only been a day. Charlotte hoped her MI6 contacts could do something for her.

"What about you?" Chris said suddenly, pulling her from her thoughts.

"Hmm?" She kept her eyes on the screen for a moment more, then glanced up.

"What's your family like?"

"I haven't heard from my mum since she left, and I have no idea about his family. My dad's parents died when I was little, so after mom went Uncle Jaden was all I had."

"You have four cousins, right?"

"Yeah," Charlotte turned her tablet off and stowed it away. This sounded like it was going to be a longer conversation. It wasn't that she minded; she relished any opportunity to get to know Chris Stuart better. She hadn't been prepared to do it now, but they might as well. They had the time to kill. "My teenage years were very...loud."

"Are they all around your age?"

"The twins are," she told him. "They're just a year older. Alex graduated high school the year I moved in with them. Evan's younger than me by five years."

"All boys, right?" Chris shook his head. "I can't imagine."

Charlotte smiled fondly as she remembered the years after her mother's death. "It was chaotic, but they were a big help for Uncle Jaden when the farm was struggling. He didn't have to worry about paying workers; the boys worked the farm until they graduated."

"I bet they made all your relationships hell, too," Chris had half-turned in his seat and was leaning against the bulkhead.

"Oh yeah," Charlotte laughed. "Evan wasn't so bad because he was a lot younger, but the twins were always following me around, chasing away boys at school, that sort of thing. I think Uncle Jaden put them up to it, but I could never prove it." She thought about her prom night and debated on telling Chris the rather sordid details of her youthful indiscretions. Surprisingly, she found that she wanted to tell him - wanted him to know everything about her. "I actually had to come up with a pretty elaborate plan to ditch them after my prom."

"Ditch them?" Chris interest was piqued. "And why would you need to do that, Miss Roberson?" His mockingly innocent question made her grin; she didn't have to tell him why. "Who were they?"

"Nico Kerr," she said.

She decided to change the subject. "And you? Any past girlfriends I should worry about popping up unexpectedly?"

He smiled twisted into one far more self-deprecating as he shrugged. "I know this might come as a shock to you, but they weren't exactly lining up around the block." He shot her a sideways glance that screamed indifference, but Charlotte could see beneath that facade now. "I've had one or two serious girlfriends, and you know about Gina...but no one you need to worry about." He added this last bit more jovially, pulling their conversation back into safer territory.

She recognized his attempt to deflect away from himself, and she let it go. There would be time for deeper conversations later. "Right now, all I'm worried about it not dying in the wilds of Canada while we search for polar bears that are potentially murdering people."

"Yeah, well," Chris relaxed back into his seat, "the sooner we find the polar bears, the sooner we can save the world."

Charlotte laughed, and behind her Giselle let out a soft whoop of excitement. "That is the greatest thing I've ever heard in my life," he proclaimed. "I've always wanted to save the world."

Chris ignored Giselle and leaned forward to address Jaylen across the aisle. "Explain to me again why she's here?"

"Because -" Jaylen began, but Giselle cut him off.

"Because you wouldn't even have a plane if it weren't for me, sport. I've got as much right to be here as you do."

Chris opened his mouth to reply, but Charlotte laid a hand on his arm. "Giselle, do you know where the drinks are? I'm getting thirsty."

"Sure do," she winked at her. "There's a fully stocked mini-fridge just through here." She pointed behind her toward the read of the plane. "Can I get you something?"

"I'll get it," Charlotte pushed up and steadied herself against the bulkhead. "You're injured after all. Need to rest." She was probably imagining the sway of the plane as she walked back to the curtain, but she certainly didn't imagine the burning stare that followed her. Giselle watched her like a hawk as she pushed the curtain aside and stepped into the small alcove. The pressure from the place had muffled her hearing, but she thought she heard Chris's sharp tones behind her as she poured both of them a vodka on the rocks.

"Thanks," Chris accepted the drink gratefully as she sat back down next to him. Charlotte thought there was a bit more tension in the room that when she had left, but nothing else seemed amiss. Jaylen was sifting through pages of his Uncle's research while Aluna was crashed out on the sofa and Giselle was flipping through a magazine. Still, she couldn't shake the feeling that something had shifted in the atmosphere.

"Everything alright?" Charlotte asked, watching his face closely for clues. There. His eyes darted over to Giselle for a fraction of a second, then he shook his head and took a sip of his drink. Something had happened during the short time she'd been gone, but Chris wasn't going to tell her. Whatever it was had set Chris's back up, and she was itching to ask the question. She had a feeling she wouldn't like the answer, so she dropped it.

"We should get some rest while we can," Chris said once they had finished their drinks. "Who knows when we'll be able to sleep again."

Charlotte agreed, and after a few months of fiddling with the seat controls they were both stretched out and snoozing.

Chapter 33

"Charlotte, we're landing," Jaylen's voice pulled her from sleep, and she blinked several times to clear the muddled fog from her brain as she woke up. Chris was rousing next to her, having been poked by Aluna from his seat behind them.

"M'kay," Charlotte sat up straight and set her seat back to its original position. "Time is it?"

Jaylen checked his watch. "Uh, east coast time it's about eight in the morning. It's nearly two in the afternoon local time."

"Where are we?"

"About thirty miles from Edmonton," Aluna supplied. "The pilot said it was as close as we could land safely."

"Close to what?" Charlotte wondered.

"My guy has an outpost set up a few miles from Athabasca," Giselle said as she stood and moved to the front of the cabin. "We'll have to get there the old-fashioned way."

"Horseback?" Charlotte asked hopefully. Giselle just smiled and turned the handle on the outer door.

The sun was nearly blinding after being cooped up for so long, and Charlotte shielded her eyes as she squinted against the bright light. My kingdom for some sunglasses, she thought wistfully. Someone had wheeled a set of stairs over so they could descend to the pavement. She hissed and recoiled in pain as her hand hit the ice-cold metal railing.

"Don't grab that," Giselle shot over her shoulder unhelpfully. Charlotte sneered at the back of her head and followed her to the ground. Once they'd all deplaned, Giselle pulled out her map and pointed to a spot on it.

"This is our target. The pilots are leaving two days from now to return to Brazil, with or without us. As long as we keep a good pace, we should be back in a little over twenty-four hours. With any luck, we'll reach the outpost before nightfall." She folded it up and looked around. "Trust me, you do not want to be stuck out in the wilderness after dark."

Aluna shrugged. "Jaylen and I have camped out here before. There are tricks to keep the animals away."

"Glad you're along, then," Giselle stuffed the map back into his bag. "Let's go." He shouldered the dark green military pack and gripped the tranq gun. Each of them had a bag given to them by Adam, though hers was smaller and Chris's held only the drugs. Charlotte felt bad that the others were carrying all of their food and water, but the thought of a ten-mile hike while lugging a heavy pack made her keep her thoughts to herself.

Two miles in they stopped for a break. Jaylen pulled new water bottles out of his pack and handed them out. Charlotte downed half of hers instantly.

"Aren't we above the equator? I thought it was summer here," she said. "How come it's so cold?"

Aluna laughed and shook his head. "Summers here are quite different from summers back home," she said.

"It's colder than usual," Jaylen added. "Normally it doesn't get this bad until November."

Charlotte soaked in the information and filed it away almost automatically. She usually liked learning new things, but she was on edge due to the nature of their mission and couldn't enjoy it as she normally did. She held onto her bottle as they set off again, keeping their pace easy but purposeful.

"We getting close?" Chris asked about an hour later. They'd stopped for another water break and to check the map. Giselle nodded.

"The outpost is less than a mile," she tapped a crossroad on the map. "We're almost there."

"Thank God." Charlotte's feet were beginning to ache; she wasn't built for this sort of long-distance hiking. Next to her, Aluna and Jaylen barely looked winded. "You two seem to be enjoying yourselves." They grinned in response.

Giselle had pulled a radio from her bag and adjusted a few knobs before pressing the call button. "Athabasca Base, this is Giselle. Over." Silence met his all, and he tried again. "Athabasca Base, come in." He looked at the others and shrugged. "He's probably out poaching the poachers. He'll be there."

Right," Chris turned away from Aluna and brought his hand up to shield his eyes as he peered into the distance. "Come on, then. The sooner we find the polar bears, the sooner we save the world."

That's what I'm talking about," Giselle grinned. "I'm so stoked to be a part of the team."

Charlotte caught Chris's gaze and rolled her eyes for dramatic effect. He chuckled slightly and returned her gesture with a nod. Giselle was annoying, but so far, she'd been fairly useful. As long as Jaylen and Aluna could keep a handle on her, she could be tolerated for the sake of the mission.

The next five miles passed quickly as Giselle recounted a few tales of her worldwide adventures, emphasising how reliable she was and how much knowledge she had of the area. It sounded to Charlotte like he was trying to justify this whole endeavour, but she didn't say so. Out of the corner of her eye, Charlotte saw Chris wipe his face and down the rest of his water in two big gulps. It was good they were getting close; their water supply was getting low.

I'm a little envious of Akari right now," Chris said. "Nice, heated cell." Charlotte had to agree, though she felt bad for it.

My man here in Canada is the real deal," Giselle was still gushing. "He'll have the intel on polar bear sightings, and he'll outfit the lot of us. We're going to need a lot more than a tranq gun."

It was the first intelligent thing Charlotte had heard her utter. Their promise to stick to non-lethal means seemed to mean little to Giselle, but none of them were complaining. Facing off against an apex predator like polar bears with a measly tranq gun for defence was very low on Charlotte's to-do list.

Thanks, Giselle," Jaylen said the thing Giselle had been fishing for. He lit up.

You got it," he said. "I'm with you now and I aim to help, alright? Because?" She turned to Chris expectantly. "Come on, say it for me, sport."

Shut up," Chris looked ready to deck Giselle, help or no help.

One more time," Giselle begged lightly. "Honestly, I can't get enough of it."

Chris sighed, his eyes never leaving the horizon. "The sooner we find the leopards, the sooner we save the world."

"Beautiful."

Charlotte ambled sideways to place herself between Giselle and Chris, hoping that would at least discourage them from attacking each other. Chris glanced at her knowingly, nodding his thanks as Giselle turned her attention to Jaylen.

"There it is."

A small hut shimmered in the distance.

"Thank God," Charlotte breathed.

It was quiet as they approached, the only sound coming from the television sitting on a small table. Something about it set Charlotte's back up, and she hovered near the entrance as Aluna, Jaylen and Giselle went first.

"Hello?" Jaylen called. "Hello!" There was debris scattered on the floor, like a struggle had taken place. Cups had been knocked over, papers strewn about, and two plates of food had been upended onto the floor.

Giselle and Aluna moved to the counter and Jaylen righted a chair as Chris examined a large map on the back wall. Charlotte watched Aluna as she came up to the end of the bar. She stopped abruptly, her eyes freezing on something none of them could see.

"Uh, Jaylen?" Her tone was careful, even.

"What is it?" Charlotte's curiosity got the better of her and she walked forward even as Aluna held out a hand.

"You might not want to -"

His warning came too late. Charlotte rounded the corner and saw pools of blood and shredded flesh. "Oh my God!" She shied back and covered her mouth with her hands as she fought the bile rising in her throat.

Charlotte had backed up to the wall, unable to tear her eyes from the gory scene. Chris came over to her and stepped into her line of vision, pulling her gaze up to his eyes.

"Hey," he whispered. "It's okay. Don't look at it." He rubbed her shoulder soothingly. "Breathe." She forced her eyes away from the floor and focused on the drone from the television as she sucked in deep breaths. "Good." He moved away to inspect the bodies, his biology knowledge kicking in.

Jaylen stood from where he'd crouched to check for a pulse. "Well, that explains why they didn't answer our radio call."

"Damn it," Giselle hissed. "This is my guy," she sighed. "The man with the plan. Looks like he put up a good fight though." Charlotte heard the tinkle of metal shell casings as she tossed them away.

"Who would do this?" Charlotte asked. She knew what had happened - it was why they were here after all - but seeing it with her own eyes was something else. She desperately wanted to believe what had killed these men was anything other than what they were seeking.

"Not who," Chris corrected. "What. Those are claw marks."

"Polar Bears." Jaylen confirmed.

"This is a slaughter," Giselle sounded incredulous despite what they'd been telling her the past few days. "I mean, they weren't even feeding. It's just..."

"Strange," Chris turned from Charlotte to finish Giselle's thought, though she noticed he kept his eyes off the floor as well. "Yeah, strange is good," he said. "Strange tells us we're on the right track."

Something on the television caught her attention, and Charlotte leaned in. "You guys," she reached over and turned it up so they could hear what was being said. The chyron at the bottom read The Experts Debate: What's Wrong with the Animals.

"This is happening on every continent, in every major city," the man on the left was saying. "This is not a coincidence."

"What would you have us do?" the second man countered. "Shoot all the zoo animals? What about farm animals? Pets?"

"My point is this is a virus and it's spreading fast."

"There is no evidence of a virus -" he was cut off by Jaylen switching off the television.

"At least they're starting to pay attention." Aluna could see the bright side of any situation.

Chris rubbed his face wearily. "Which means it's getting worse."

"All the more reason to get moving," Jaylen grabbed his duffel bag from where he'd dropped it earlier. He unzipped it and began tossing in water bottles from the supply near the desk. At least they wouldn't go to waste. Chris had gone in search of a bathroom as Giselle searched for any spare ammo or weapons. That left Aluna and Charlotte standing in the centre of the room. The older woman had found a supply of equipment in the back of the building that would serve them well. A tent, first aid kit, emergency rations, it was all there. Aluna lifted it all and then gestured with her head to the area just behind her.

"The car outside," she said, "you might find some keys on those bodies over there."

"Are you serious?" Charlotte balked. She didn't even want to look at them for very long, much less touch them. At Aluna's nod, she groaned and crouched down, very gingerly sticking two fingers into the man's pocket.

Luck was on her side. She found a ring and pulled out a set of keys attached to an old brass keychain. It had been sun-faded and worn smooth by time, but Charlotte appreciated the detail of the embossed moose. It was standing on all fours, facing forward, and Charlotte could even make out the lines of his antlers.

"They used all our ammo in the fight," Giselle's outburst made her jump, and she quickly turned to hand the keys to Aluna. "Now all we got is this tranq gun."

"Alright," Jaylen zipped up his duffel and lifted it with some effort. At least they had a car now; carrying that much water would be nearly impossible for any length of time. "Let's do what we came here to do."

The others agreed and began gathering their things.

Charlotte stopped them. "We can't just leave them like this." She kept her eyes off the bodies directly, but it was clear what she meant. The others exchanged looks.

"Charlotte is right," Aluna nodded. "They deserve to be treated with respect."

"Yeah," Giselle let her bag slide off her shoulder. "No one should die without words being said, at least." She seemed to accept that it was her job, since they'd been friends of some sort, and began walking towards them. He paused for just a second as he passed Chris. "Help me, will you?"

Chris cleared his throat, and for a moment Charlotte expected him to snap at Giselle. Charlotte wasn't sure there was a force in the world that would let these two get along, even for a short time. To her surprise, however, Chris merely nodded and turned to help.

It took almost half an hour out of their already dwindling day, but as they stood over the two newly mounded piles of dirt Charlotte felt better. It had been the right thing to do. Giselle spoke a few words, and Aluna offered a prayer. It wasn't a full service with all the rights and respects they deserved, but it was better than leaving them lying on the floor to rot.

"Time to go," Jaylen said finally. He slid behind the wheel as Aluna took the passenger seat, leaving Charlotte to climb into the back cargo area with Giselle and Chris.

Chapter 34

It was dark by the time they found a suitable place to camp. Jaylen and Aluna both cautioned against sleeping out in the open, so they found a small copse of trees that would serve as shelter. It took them almost half an hour to set up camp, but soon enough they had a fire crackling and the tent erected. Charlotte glanced at the small space inside and wondered not for the first time how they were all going to fit.

The answer was, apparently, they weren't. They set up shifts to keep watch in pairs. Charlotte had initially volunteered to keep watch with Chris, but Jaylen had pointed out it would probably be better if at least one person in each pair knew about life in the Canadian wilderness or at least how to handle the tranq gun. So, Chris and Aluna had volunteered to go first, leaving the other three to try to get some sleep. Charlotte was given one end of the tent, with Chris and Aluna's stuff acting as a sort of barrier between where Jaylen and Giselle slept on the other. Giselle's snoring almost drowned out the sound of the two by the fire, but Charlotte could just about pick out Chris's voice in any situation.

After a rather uneventful trip to the bathroom (which was just a small, secluded area several yards from their camp) and a changing of the guard, Charlotte was now nestled snugly in between the tent wall and Chris's body. Aluna had discreetly rearranged the sleeping packs so that she was on the far end of the tent near the door, though Charlotte thought it was unnecessary. Chris had already bedded down, his face relaxed in sleep as he curled on his side facing her. Even from fifteen feet away there was enough firelight filtering through the tent opening to partially illuminate the small area, but Chris's face was cast in shadow. He'd left his glasses on, his arm bent up under his head to use as a pillow. His mouth was slightly open, and Charlotte could hear every inhale and feel every exhale on her cheek as she lay on her back.

"Hey Aluna?" she whispered.

"Yes?" Her reply was just as soft, but Chris didn't stir. She knew he was a sound sleeper from the few times they'd shared sleeping space; unless he heard his name or something resembling an alarm, he wouldn't budge.

"Do you think Akari is okay?"

"I am sure she is fine," she said. "Certainly, safer than we are right now."

Thanks for the reminder," Charlotte shivered despite having her blanket and aylen's covering her.

When we find the polar bears and Chris makes the cure, we will return to merica and clear her name. And yours. Then we can go home," he added uickly. "Get some sleep. We will need to be sharp tomorrow."

Right," Charlotte took in a deep, cleansing breath. "Wouldn't want to get eaten y polar bears." She listened for a few more moments to the cries and calls round them. It used to be soothing, a reminder that she was a small part of omething greater. Growing up in the country, Charlotte had always loved the ounds of nature. The chirp of a cricket at dusk or the rustling of wind through ne trees had been constant companions in her childhood. She took solace in the act that no matter what else changed in her life, the spirit and life of nature was verlasting and unchanging. Now everything was tinged with a different sort of eeling, an unease that permeated her bones and left her unsettled.

 low growl sounded in the distance and Charlotte jumped, gasping in the ilence of the tent.

It is a cat," Aluna's gentle voice explained. "I don't believe it will come into ne camp."

Not normally," Charlotte said. "Things are far from normal."

Try to sleep." Aluna's breathing evened once more, and this time Charlotte orced herself to close her eyes. It didn't take long for her body to relax enough allow her to drift off.

Wake up!" Charlotte's eyes snapped open, and she was scrambling to her feet ven before she was fully awake. Aluna had already exited the tent and grabbed torch, and as Charlotte rose to stand beside Chris, she noticed Giselle rouched a few yards away.

Saw something zip by," she told them quietly. "Throw me that box of tranq arts, will you?" she held his hand out as she stood, and Aluna tossed the small ox at her. She caught it one-handed and slipped into her pocket. "If it's a polar ear, I can handle it."

he moved to walk into the tree line, but Aluna stopped her. "Giselle, you stay ere. We're safer together."

Giselle looked back confidently. "Guys, I got this." She vanished into the trees, leaving the four of them standing next to the fire unprotected. It was this thought that caused Charlotte to shuffle just a bit closer to Chris, and he seemed sense her unease. He reached back and grasped her hand, squeezing it reassuringly before letting go.

The rustle of leaves drew their attention, and Charlotte stared at the spot for a few long seconds. She expected a polar bear to erupt from the bush at any moment, and the prolonged noise set her on edge even more. Aluna turned with his torch and tried to illuminate the area, but nothing penetrated the thick overgrowth.

The rustling grew louder and so did the pounding of Charlotte's heart. Her fight or flight instincts were on high alert, and she was almost one hundred percent certain which one her body would choose. She glanced behind her, noting the clear path that led to the jeep sitting just off the road less that fifty yards from where they were now. Could she make it? She doubted it. But there was no way in hell she wasn't going to try.

The trees moved again, and Giselle appeared suddenly in the clearing. Charlotte felt all of the adrenaline that had built up in her system disperse at once, washing over her like someone had doused her with a bucket of ice water.

"Nothing there," she said. She stopped a few feet from them and smiled. "Looks like we live to die another day."

And then a large mass slammed into him.

Chapter 35

Chaos erupted as Giselle went down beneath the polar bear. Charlotte screamed as several shapes came out of the tree line, and she felt Chris tug her forward despite her instinct to flee. He pressed his back into her, putting himself squarely in front of the predator. She gripped the back of the shirt fearfully, her eyes wide and frightened as Jaylen and Aluna swung their torches around to keep the bears at bay.

"Hey, man, look out," Jaylen hissed at Chris. He turned, keeping Charlotte behind him with outstretched hands, as another polar bear closed in on the other side. Jaylen passed Chris a torch, and Charlotte stepped back so he could take it. He jabbed it at the nearest bear, sending it a few steps back. Aluna handed her a torch of her own, and she held it in front of her like a sword. If the beats attacked, they would be little more than annoyances, but for now they were still wary of the fire.

"Charlotte," Jaylen glanced at her for a second before turning his eyes back to the polar bear in front of him, "those glow sticks you have…"

"What?" she turned her head just slightly, keeping the bear in her peripheral vision.

"Your glow sticks," he said. "Bring them here."

Keeping the torch aloft, she back pedalled a few and handed them off to Jaylen before turning back to the polar bears. There were four, one on each of them, and Charlotte wondered how long they could hold out.

"Chris, behind you,", Aluna called, and Charlotte turned almost robotically, sure she was about to witness the man she loved being torn to shreds by the polar bears. A fifth bear had snuck behind him, and Chris twisted back and forth sharply to keep both bears back. It didn't work.

"Ha!" Jaylen screamed and thrust his torch forward, causing the bear in front of him to recoil and roar in defiance. That seemed to be a signal of sorts, and the Polar Bear nearest Chris began creeping forward.

A streak zipped by Charlotte's head, followed by the sound of something impacted flesh and a bright flash of light. Charlotte realized Aluna had thrown his torch like a spear, striking the attacking dog and sending him darting into the woods away from Chris.

And then, as though the silent prayers Charlotte had been repeating rapidly in her mind had been heard, the cats began to disappear. Almost silently they slinked back into the woods, swallowed up by the darkness.

"Oh my God," Charlotte breathed.

"Come on." To her astonishment, Jaylen began to follow them. "Let's go."

"Go?" Chris's voice was still trembling with fear and adrenaline. "Go where?"

"I tagged one of the polar bears with a glow stick," Jaylen explained. "We can track it." He walked back over to the fire and knelt down. "Where are the keys?"

"Jaylen," Aluna tried to reason, "Giselle had the tranq gun. We don't have any weapons. We need a plan!"

"We have a plan!" Jaylen stood with the keys to the Jeep. "This is it. We follow the bears; that's our best chance." No one budged, and Jaylen shook his head. "What else do you want to do?" he asked them. "Stay here and wait for them to come back? Come on!"

He grabbed his pack and slung it over his shoulder as he set off for the Jeep, leaving the others no choice but to follow. Charlotte grabbed her own bag, and after a few seconds' deliberating she grabbed Giselle's as well. She wouldn't be needing it anymore. In the end, Aluna convinced Jaylen to take a few minutes to strike camp; they might need the tent for another night of camping. Luckily, it came down easier than it had gone up and Jaylen was very nearly bouncing in agitation as they finally piled into the Jeep.

Charlotte climbed into the back with Chris. On the ride to the campsite, they had each taken an opposite wheel well to sit on as Giselle sat cross-legged in the centre. Now, after Giselle's death and Chris's close encounter, Charlotte didn't want him out of arm's reach. She crouched in the space between his body and the back seat, using the wall of the vehicle to hold her up as she wrapped her arm around his. She laid her forehead against his shoulder as the Jeep bounced along the rough road, and she heard his quiet whispers above the creaking shocks and worn tires. His free hand was sifting through her hair as he reassured her, they were fine. It was hard to believe.

"Up ahead, on the right," Jaylen cried, and Charlotte looked up. "We're on the right track."

After a few more moments, Chris let his hand fall away from her head. "Maybe somebody should say something about her," he said. "Giselle." Then, because the others were looking at him funny, he shrugged. "I mean, nobody should die without words being spoken, right?"

Charlotte's hold on Chris's arm tightened, and when he looked down, she smiled at him. The depth of his compassion often stunned her, especially for someone with whom he so profoundly disagreed.

Aluna seemed to take up the mantle when no one else said anything. "Giselle was obnoxious, loud and stubborn, but she was passionate." His eyes never left the road as he steered them toward the Polar Bears, but his voice was rich and full of sorrow. "And she cared more about animals on this Earth than any man I've ever met." Sadly, that seemed to be all anyone could say about her. Charlotte tried to think of something, but nothing came to her. Giselle had cared about animals more than her own life. In the end, the very animals she had spent her life trying to save had killed her. Charlotte didn't know whether to label it ironic or tragic. Probably both.

"Looks like the trail's run out," Jaylen said. "We lost it."

"Okay, team," Chris tried to inject a bit of reasoning into what was rapidly becoming a foolish chase. "What now?"

"Let's make camp," Jaylen seemed to give up the hunt as he realized tracking the bears in the dark would likely result in all of them being killed. "We can pick up the trail when it gets light out."

"They set off again when the sun rose, stopping every five minutes or so to make sure they were still on the right track. Aluna had dug up some roots that she claimed worked like a chemical suppressant, and Chris set to concocting a dose of what they all hoped was a tranquilizer as Jaylen led them to the Polar Bears.

As Chris stirred the mixture, Charlotte fought the urge to vomit. "That is the most disgusting thing I've ever smelled in my life."

"Okay." Chris pulled a decent amount into the syringe and held it over his mouth as if to test it.

Charlotte resisted the urge to slap it out of his hand. "Whoa, easy! You sure about that?"

"It's for science," he shrugged, and pushed a drop onto his tongue. It must have tasted as good as it smelled, and Charlotte suppressed a smile as Chris gagged. Professional scientist, Chris Stuart everybody. When he righted himself, he smacked his lips together thoughtfully. "It tingles. Let's hope it does more than that to the bears."

"Stop the truck," Jaylen directed suddenly. "Right up there. You see those trees with the rocks? The rocks along the base?"

"Yes," Aluna nodded. "Looks like their den."

Charlotte watched as Jaylen and Aluna geared up to isolate a Polar Bear and drug it enough to get it back to the Jeep. Where they would put it and how to keep it sedated seemed to be questions no one wanted to address just yet. Just getting one might prove to be impossible.

Charlotte let out a breath she didn't know she'd been holding when Jaylen and Aluna reappeared from the brush. "Where's the bear?" she asked as they cleared the rocks and began jogging back to the Jeep. Jaylen was cradling his bag differently, and as they got closer, she realized why.

"Huh," Chris huffed at the sight of the tiny fuzzy head poking out of the bag. "Guess that works, too."

Jaylen and Aluna threw the doors open on either side of the Jeep. Aluna started the engine as Jaylen handed the pack back to Charlotte. A growling sound came from within, and Charlotte shifted the bag to let the cub look around.

"Careful with him," he warned as she reached out to touch him.

"We found him in the den," Jaylen explained. "The mother went out to hunt."

"Can't be more than a couple of weeks, then," Chris said.

"That young?" Charlotte looked down at the little guy and wondered how on earth he would be able to keep up with a fully grown Polar Bear. "What now?"

"Now," Aluna glanced over her shoulder briefly before returning her eyes to the bumpy road, "we find our way home." She seemed to know where he was going because for several minutes they weren't even on a road. When they found one, it was extremely worn and bumpy but familiar. Aluna was leading them back to he airfield. Charlotte split her attention between the cub in her lap and the road, miling as the inquisitive animal began rolling around inside the bag.

Hard to believe he'll grow up to be one of the greatest predators on the planet, uh?" Chris peered over her arm.

He's so tiny." She reached in the bag to pet him again, but the animal was in lay mode. He latched onto her finger and bit. "Ow!"

hris laughed, and she glared at him. She pulled her hand back and passed the ag to him. "Your turn."

Uh oh," Jaylen murmured as they came to a stop, and Charlotte looked up to ee the remnants of what looked like the bridge they'd crossed earlier this norning. Chris zipped the bag and opened the back door. He let Charlotte out irst, holding her arm as she stepped onto the dry road then following her out.

harlotte stopped just behind Aluna who had been kneeling to inspect what was eft of their way across. "What happened to the bridge?"

The rope's been chewed." He held it up for the others to see. "We're going to ave to drive the long way around the river." He looked at Jaylen hesitantly, and harlotte sensed there was something they weren't saying.

he muted sound of a ringing phone cut through the silence, and they all looked round curiously.

What is that?" Jaylen asked.

hris looked around to pinpoint the source of the sound, surprised when he ound it in his own bag. "It's Akari's phone," he held the item up. "Must have eft it in my pack." He handed it up to Jaylen, who opened it and held it to his ar.

Hello?" Charlotte couldn't make out anything the caller was saying. "This is aylen Hudson. I'm a friend of Akari's. Who is this?" There was a beat of ilence as Jaylen listened to the answer, then Charlotte saw his posture deflate lightly. "She's been arrested. She's fine though, she's safe. She's...she's in ustody." Another moment, and he jerked up. "What do you mean? How do you now that?"

harlotte leaned forward, trying to hear more of the conversation. "What's oing on?" she whispered.

Then Jaylen said something that made her blood run cold. "She didn't kill that officer." Jaylen said something else, but Charlotte couldn't hear it over the ringing in her ears. Akari hadn't killed that officer, but Charlotte had. And now her friend was paying the price meant for her.

"What is it?" Charlotte found her voice once Jaylen had hung up.

"That officer, the one who was chasing us, the one who arrested Akari and Camille," he glanced over his shoulder. "He was killed."

"If that's the case," Aluna added, "then where is Akari? Someone has to have her"

No one wanted to speculate on that particular topic. Akari could imagine some pretty horrific things, but the likelihood was they had simply disposed of her. No, Charlotte amended mentally. They would need her to find out where the rest of them had gone. They had killed this officer to get to Akari so she could tell them the plan. Which meant they were employing God knew what kind of tactics to get that information. Charlotte felt sick.

"We have to stay positive," Chris said quietly. Charlotte recognized her own words from earlier and gave him a half-hearted glare.

"The dextro-rinoifane department have Akari," Charlotte said. "And they're using her to find out where we are."

"Akari is strong," Chris sounded like he was trying to convince himself as well as the others. "We have to believe she is doing everything she can to make sure we succeed. So let's get this little guy back to the plane and make that cure."

"Can you do it on the plane?" Aluna asked.

"I think so," Chris patted the bag underneath his legs. "As long as this thing still works after dragging it all over kingdom come."

"Then let's get to that plane. With luck, we will be there before dark."

The sun was still high overhead when their luck ran out. Aluna took a corner and immediately slammed the brakes as a jeep filled to capacity with armed militants bore down on them. Aluna threw their car into reverse, but they were already being boxed in. The second truck held half a dozen men armed with machine guns, and as they forced their prey to stop, they fired their weapons in

he air. Charlotte reacted to the sound violently, throwing herself forward
behind the seat and squeezing her eyes closed. She felt Chris above her, his
body leaning over hers as he kept his head up to see what was happening.

"Oh God," she whispered.

Aluna jumped out and her and the leader spoke back and forth rapidly, Aluna's
body language conciliatory and submissive. The nearest soldier brandished a
machete at Aluna as the man in charge pointed angrily.

"What are they saying?" Charlotte kept her voice low but didn't take her eyes
off what was happening.

"I have no idea," Jaylen admitted. Suddenly, the man with the machete lunged
forward to grab Aluna and Jaylen was out of the car in an instant.

"Jaylen!"

"No, no," he stepped out with his hands up. "Don't hurt him, alright? Take me.
Take me, don't hurt him."

Aluna said something, but it was too quiet for Charlotte to hear from inside the
car. She looked at Chris helplessly. "What do we do?" she asked him. "We have
no guns, we have no money, we have nothing."

"We have him," Chris nodded down towards the cub.

"What are we gonna do," Charlotte scoffed. "Set a cub on them?"

"The needle on Aluna's spear," he whispered. "Hand it to me." She pulled the
syringe off of the pole and passed it to him, moving back a little to give him
room to work. She watched as he quickly stuck the cub, causing it to cry out in
pain. It continued for a few seconds, it's mewl loud in the small space. She
realized immediately what he was doing, and she smiled proudly.

She took a breath to praise his idea, but it was stolen from her lungs as the rear
doors opened and rough arms grabbed her.

"What are you doing?" she heard Chris's voice as she screamed and struggled
against the men pulling her from the truck. "No, no, no, Charlotte!"

White hot terror shot through her as she was dragged away from her friends.
She reached for Chris instinctively as he surged forward to help her. One of the

men turned his weapon around and viciously rammed the butt of it into Chris's stomach, driving him back and causing him to double over in pain. The sight of it made her fight harder, but the man holding her was stronger.

He dumped her unceremoniously on the dirt, but Charlotte scrambled to her feet quickly and held her hands up. Six or seven men surrounded her, all armed and leering at her like a piece of meat. Her entire body was shaking from fear and adrenaline, and though she couldn't understand anything they were saying, their intentions were crystal clear. Memories of the scene in her hotel room with Dustin started to flash in front of her eyes and she realised she was trembling.

Over their shoulders, she saw that Aluna and Jaylen had been herded into the back of the Jeep with Chris. Their heads were bent in conversation, and she prayed they were figuring out how to get out of here. If Chris's plan worked, the polar bears would hear the cub's cries and arrive to find a veritable feast awaiting them. The trick would be getting back to the vehicle without getting killed, but Charlotte preferred those chances to the ones she faced now.

One of the men caressed her arm, and she whirled toward him with a sneer. He just laughed, reaching up to rub the ends of her hair between his fingers. The others joined in his amusement, and Charlotte felt another hand press against her hip. A rough hand reached its way under her shirt and hot tears started to fall from her eyes. Someone gave a signal, and the other men began to get back into their cars. She closed her eyes as helplessness devoured what remained of her hope. Chris's plan had failed.

Chapter 36

A low growl from her left startled her, and she looked over just in time to see a young man go down under the white mass above him. Instantly the atmosphere changed, and the men surrounding her broke apart and began firing at the small group of polar bears that had materialized out of nowhere.

She didn't waste the opportunity. Her feet carried her to their jeep, where Aluna and Jaylen had just burst from the back.

"Charlotte! Come on." Jaylen reached for her as Aluna made for the driver's seat. She felt Jaylen pull her violently toward the car, and her hand was immediately engulfed by Chris's larger one as he hauled her into the cargo area. Screams of pain erupted from all around them, punctuated by gunfire as the armed men tried futilely to fend off the bear attack. Aluna tossed the man from the driver's seat just as Jaylen slammed his door closed. Charlotte's body was still shaking as Chris pulled her against him, wrapping his arms around her tightly.

"It's okay," he whispered into her hair. "You're okay. You're safe. I've got you." Charlotte crawled up into his lap and dug her fingers into his back as Aluna started the engine.

"Go!" Jaylen was in, and Aluna gunned the gas. They were off like a shot, leaving a bloody massacre behind them.

"It worked," Chris said, his tone both surprised and grateful.

Charlotte hugged him harder in thanks. Her breathing evened out as the adrenaline drained from her body, and he pushed her back to roam a critical eye over her. "I'm okay," she affirmed. "They didn't hurt me."

They bounced and swayed as Aluna sped away, heedless of terrain. He wanted to put as much distance between the polar bears and them as possible, and Charlotte didn't mind. She looked back, but the cloud of dust behind them obscured her vision. Chris grabbed her hand, and she could feel the tension in his grip as she looked up at him. In his eyes she read all she needed to know about his mindset; he was blaming himself for not being able to protect her. Regret and contrition warred for dominance and she knew she had to say something.

"That was great what you did back there," she told him.

"What?" He seemed genuinely confused by her praise.

"What you did with the cub," she explained. Had he forgotten already? Or was the guilt overwhelming everything else?

"What are you talking about?" Aluna asked.

"Charlotte stuck the cub with a needle," she said. If he wasn't going to give himself credit for saving their lives, then she'd do it for him. "His pain sent a distress signal."

"Oh, that was you!" Aluna sounded impressed, but Chris just shrugged.

"This little guy saved our lives," Charlotte looked down at the cub as he sniffled pathetically.

"We did it," Aluna glanced over at Jaylen. "Ah, man, you saved my life. I think…" he trailed off suddenly, and Charlotte looked up in time to see Jaylen's head loll to one side. "What...what happened?"

"It's okay," Jaylen said, but it was weak. Aluna asked again as Charlotte scooted up to see over the back of the seat. Jaylen was holding his right hand over his stomach, and as he moved it she saw the sticky red blood that coated his fingers.

"Oh my God! Jaylen you've been shot!" Panic made her voice rise in pitch, and that seemed to be enough to snap Chris out of whatever funk he'd fallen into. He stripped off his outer shirt and moved closer as his training took over.

"Let me see, let me see," he leaned over.

"I'm fine," Jaylen said, though none of them believed it.

"Alright, here," he balled up his shirt and pressed it into the wound, reaching over Jaylen's shoulder to help him. "Keep that over the wound. Press down, press down," he directed. Chris looked at Aluna, who obviously knew the area better than they did. "We have to get him to a hospital."

Aluna nodded and glanced over at her friend, who was looking paler by the second. "Hold on," she said. "Hold on." She pressed down on the accelerator, moving them faster down the dirt road they had found. Charlotte hoped it led omewhere good. "You're going to make it." It sounded urgent, like a prayer, nd he repeated it a few times for good measure.

'harlotte could tell from the look on Chris's face that the bullet was in a bad lace; they needed to find help sooner rather than later. At her feet the cub rowled again, and she reached down to stoke the soft fur behind his head. She losed her eyes and added her prayer to Aluna.

lease don't let him die.

How far is the hospital?" Chris peered worriedly over the front seat at the eeping bullet hole in Jaylen's abdomen.

The nearest one is at least two hours away."

Okay," Chris ran some mental calculations. "He needs to lie down. Pull over nd let's get him into the back. I'll drive."

Is that a good idea?" Charlotte sounded just as worried as Aluna had. "If he eeds medical attention, you should be back here with him."

Aluna can keep him talking," Chris answered. "I can't do anything that would elp him at this point other than lie him down and put pressure on the bleeding."

luna reluctantly slowed to a stop, and Chris jumped out of the back with 'harlotte close behind. It took all three of them to move Jaylen from the assenger seat to the cargo area. When he was finally situated, Chris took over riving as Charlotte grabbed the map from Giselle's bag.

What road are we on, Aluna?" she asked, unfolding the map to get a better iew.

Just keep heading south," Aluna said. "This will take us into the city."

: took a moment to adjust being on the wrong side of the car, but his analytical iind worked through the processes quickly and his body adjusted accordingly. Alright, just keep pressure on that wound." Chris shifted into first gear with his :ft hand and eased them back onto the road.

Ie had never been a devout man, always preferring the tangible, constant ireness that science offered. Things in this world could be measured, touched, een, heard; blind belief in a greater power that controlled all of these things just vasn't something he could get behind. But as they sped along a road simply labelled "A1" on the map toward a city that may or may not offer some sort of respite, Chris found himself pleading with the universe or God or whatever might be listening to let his friend live.

For the next fifty miles, the only sounds in the car were Jaylen's ragged breaths and Aluna's quiet pleas to just hang on a little longer. As it usually did whenever he had time on his hands, Chris's mind began to wander. His life had changed so drastically in just three short months, going from an anti-social biologist and part-time teacher to a man who had friends willing to put their lives in his hands. He'd performed surgery without anaesthetic on a man he really didn't like, blackmailed a global corporation to save his daughter's life, and fallen in love with a crusading student turned federal fugitive. It all sounded like something out a spy novel. Sometimes, when the others weren't looking, he'd pinch himself just to make sure it was all real.

Out of the corner of his eye he caught Charlotte fidgeting with her fingers. Sure, that he wasn't going to downshift any time soon, he reached over with his left hand and covered both of hers. She responded immediately, moving one of her hands to cover his as the other intertwined their fingers. She held on tightly, squeezing every so often as she fought to maintain her composure.

"How's he doing?" Chris asked over his shoulder.

"His breathing is shallow," Aluna said, "but he is not struggling."

"It's probably just the pain. Can you see where the bullet hole is?" There was some shuffling, then a hiss of pain from Jaylen as Aluna replaced Chris's now-ruined shirt to sop up more of the blood.

"It is on his right side, about halfway between his ribs and his hip bone."

"Okay, it probably missed his liver, but his intestine is likely ruptured. How much is it bleeding?"

"Not as much as I thought it would be," Aluna sounded hopeful.

"Sounds like it missed major arteries, too. He might have gotten lucky."

"Lucky would have been not getting shot in the first place," Aluna snapped. Chris didn't take it personally. "Hang on."

They travelled a few more minutes in silence before the universe decided things weren't difficult enough. A loud bang startled all of them, and Charlotte clenched his hand so tightly he winced.

"What was that?" she cried.

Chris checked his mirrors and gritted his teeth. A flock of birds was following them, and from the feather stuck to the outside of his door he guessed one of them had dive bombed the car. When he said as much, the others balked.

"Why would they attack a moving vehicle?" Aluna asked.

The answer came in the form of a quiet growl from the bag at Aluna's feet. Chris had forgotten all about the Polar Bear cub in the aftermath of their brush with death. Clearly, the animals were not happy about its kidnapping.

"You think they're after the cub?" Charlotte whispered, obviously following his thought process despite not having said a word.

"Is that any weirder than anything else we've seen since we started this mission?"

"And, what," Charlotte continued his thought with more than a hint of incredulity in her voice, "the bears sent birds to find their cub to keep us from making the cure that will keep them from taking over the planet?"

"Sounds crazy when you say it like that," Chris drawled. He shot her a sideways smirk that lasted two seconds before he sobered up. "I don't think it has anything to do with the cure. I'm not sure the animals can understand that. But Polar Bears do have strong maternal instincts, and that cub's mom will be looking for it."

"Well, unless Polar Bears have developed super speed or teleportation, we'll get to the hospital before they catch us."

"Don't joke," Chris warned her, only half-teasingly. There was still so much unknown about the contamination and the effect it was having on the animal kingdom. Chris had a feeling they had only seen the tip of the iceberg.

Another half hour passed, and another wave of birds crashed into the vehicle. It was no less jarring the second time, and Chris had to let go of Charlotte's hand before she broke something. She turned halfway in her seat to check on Jaylen.

"He's really pale," she whispered, though everyone could hear her.

"It's the blood loss," Chris tried to sound reassuring. "How far away are we?"

Charlotte turned back and checked the map. "Looks like we're ten miles from the hospital."

"How's he doing?" He glanced in the rear-view mirror at the worried expression on Aluna's face.

"Not so good." she answered without looking up from her friend.

Another bird slammed into car, hitting Charlotte's window. It held, but she jumped. "That's the third one in an hour."

Chris lifted his eyes from the road to the swirling black mass that was gathering in the distance. It ebbed and flowed like it was a living creature itself, rather than a formation of them. His scientific mind supplied the term for it automatically. Murmuration.

"We're close, my friend," Aluna's voice was soft and soothing as she tried to keep her composure. It didn't last long. "The blood," her tone rose slightly in panic. "The blood is coming through the shirt."

"Keep pressure on it," Chris pressed a little harder on the gas pedal as if following his own advice. "Nice and even. Don't let him pass out."

"Maybe we should pull over," Charlotte suggested, but Chris shook his head.

"Lot of things I can handle in a pinch," he told her. "The kind of surgery he needs. Not one of them."

Charlotte's estimate turned out to be a little long. They reached the city limits shortly after the last bird attack, but Chris had to slow down to keep from running over the throng of people fleeing the other direction.

"What's going on?" Charlotte asked. "Where are they going?"

"Everybody's leaving town," Chris edged over as far as he could to let the trucks and carts pass while still maintaining a decent speed. The mass exodus didn't bode well, but Jaylen didn't have a choice. He needed a hospital now.

Chris screeched to a halt just outside the doors. He jumped out and moved to help Aluna with Jaylen as Charlotte cradled the cub.

"Grab the drugs," he tossed over his shoulder as he took Jaylen's weight for a moment. Aluna shifted to support his uninjured side as Charlotte gasped behind them.

"Oh, my God. That's why they're all leaving." Bodies were strewn through the courtyard, and beyond that into the streets. Arctic Foxes were patrolling, their mouths opened menacingly as they stared down the newcomers. A growl above them drew their attention to a roof across the street, and they all looked up at the Lynx prowling back and forth. It was surreal, and suddenly Chris's spy thriller turned into a survival horror.

"We need to get inside now," Chris told them. He dashed to the doors and pulled hard on the handle. Locked. He tried another as Aluna pounded on the glass.

"Open the door! It's an emergency. My friend needs a doctor!"

A man in a white coat saw them, and Chris noticed his hesitation as he neared the door. He held a shotgun in his hand, his eyes darting over their shoulders to the carnage behind them. After a moment, he pushed the door open just enough to warn them.

"The hospital's closed."

But Aluna had had enough. He yanked the door open and dragged Jaylen inside. Chris reached behind him and ushered Charlotte through first before closing the door firmly behind him. Patients and staff alike were running scared, screams and cries echoing through the halls. Aluna laid Jaylen on a nearby gurney as the doctor followed them frantically.

"Did you hear what I said?" he urged. "We are abandoning the hospital. You have to go elsewhere."

"We don't have time," Chris argued, putting an edge into his voice he hadn't used since his time at university. "This man's been shot."

The doctor glanced down at the blood coating Jaylen's shirt, then frowned. "I can't help him." He sounded genuinely sorry for the fact. "I suggest you drive him to the next town over."

"That's two hours at least!" Aluna protested. Chris agreed; Jaylen didn't have that kind of time.

"I have lost a dozen colleagues and more patients than I can count," the doctor told them. "I am sorry, but I cannot help you."

"You will help him!" It was the first time Chris had ever heard Aluna yell, and the ferocity in her eyes was terrifying to behold. "You understand me? You will help!"

The doctor's answer came as he raised his gun and levelled it at Aluna. Chris saw Charlotte flinch and take a step back. He panicked and dove behind the gurney as the doctor squeezed the trigger.

The shot zipped past Aluna and ricocheted off the pillar behind him. Chris turned in time to see a polar bear move away. The doctor lowered his weapon and turned to make sure the patients behind him had made it to safety. He seemed to be debating something internally, and when he turned back to them he'd come to a decision.

"The last ambulance leaves in an hour. I will do the surgery, but beyond that you are on your own."

"Thank you," Aluna breathed. The doctor moved to the rear of the gurney and began pushing him toward a side hallway. The sign above the archway listed the departments beyond it; surgery was fourth on the list. Aluna followed the gurney silently as Chris turned to Charlotte.

"He's gonna be fine," he stepped close, rubbing her shoulder reassuringly. At least he hoped to offer her some comfort. Her eyes were wide with fear, and he could hear how her breaths came in short gasps. "Hey, I need you to breathe. It's gonna be okay. We're going to be fine."

She leaned into his touch and clutched the bag with the cub just a little tighter. "They're inside."

"Charlotte," he ducked his head slightly to catch her eyes, "we need to get moving. The doctor said the last ambulance leaves in an hour. We need to be done by then."

"Okay." She took a deep breath then, squaring her shoulders with a quick nod.

Chris squeezed her arm once more before glancing around. "We need to find a map." He gestured behind her and began running toward a large set of windows. A giant map of the hospital sat just in front of them, complete with the small red dot that read You Are Here. "There are testing labs on the second floor, they should have what we need up there."

"Hurry, Chris," she kept close enough to brush against him as he scanned the map for his target. "He's getting scared."

He's not the only one. Running around the hospital with wild animals lurking outside was worrisome enough. Knowing that some of them were inside with them was downright terrifying. "There," he tapped the plastic sheet with two fingers. "Third floor."

They turned and began running for the elevators. Aluna met them halfway with a question in her eyes and the shotgun in hand. Chris directed her to follow, and they were all on edge as they waited for the car to descend. Once inside, all three of them breathed a sigh of relief.

"How long will it take you?" Aluna asked as she watched the numbers tick up to three.

"I have no idea," Chris answered honestly. "I haven't really ever done anything like this. I have no basis for comparison." The elevator dinged and the doors opened revealing a bloody scene.

Aluna's grip on the shotgun tightened as she moved slowly into the hallway. "Stay behind me."

Chris pushed Charlotte out next, putting her between him and Aluna in case an attack came from the back. They crept down the hall as silently as possible, only stopping when they came upon a body. Charlotte immediately averted her eyes as Chris surveyed the damage. The right hand had been completely taken off and was lying some distance away.

A low growl echoed down the hallway. Chris felt every muscle in body tense in response to the threat of imminent death.

"Which way are the labs?" Charlotte knew the answer, but her tone told Chris she was hoping to be wrong.

He swallowed around the fear in his throat long enough to give her an answering nod. "That way."

Chapter 37

Miraculously, they made it to the lab with no attack. As Chris set the cub working on a chew toy, Aluna volunteered to go find an affected animal to test the cure on, that wasn't likely to kill them.

"What? No, Aluna." Charlotte started forward, then stopped. Chris knew she understood why the woman had to go, but it made it no less difficult to watch her leave. She promised to be back soon and made sure they locked the door behind her. Charlotte stood staring at the closed door for a moment more.

"This is insane," she whispered. Chris racked his brain for a distraction, something to keep her attention off the fact that one of her friends was on a surgery table and another was headed outside alone with only a single shotgun for backup. His eyes fell on the green bag sitting on the table.

"So, we carted these drugs halfway around the world," he grabbed the strap and turned it around as he unzipped it. "About time we used them."

It worked. She turned from the door and moved to stand beside him. "This has to work...for any good to come out of all of this." From the corner of his eye he saw her shake her head and drop her chin slightly. "I know it's selfish, but ever since my father died this has been my life. This is literally my last chance to finally get justice and make the government pay for what they did."

"So, no pressure then." He meant it as a joke, but from the horrified expression on her face he'd failed. "Listen," he swivelled his stool to face her, "there's no reason to think this won't work. The science is sound and we have what we need. But in case it doesn't," he reached out for her hand and held it firmly, "I want you to know that I'm not going anywhere. If this doesn't work, we'll find another way."

He was rewarded with a teary smile, one that seemed to light up her whole face. She gripped his fingers gratefully, her eyes saying everything she couldn't seem to get past her lips.

Finally, she stepped back and wiped her eyes, indicating the spread of scientific equipment in front him. "Let's get to work, then." Chris pulled out the two vials of the drugs out and inserted them into a machine. Charlotte turned it on and went to check on the cub as he was calibrating.

"Is there anything I can do?" she asked as he began boiling the dextro-rinoifane solution. It was crazy to think they'd found the solution in the tiny kitchen of the Salem village hall.

"No," he shook his head. "This process has to be completely sterile for it to be viable. The fewer hands involved the better."

"How long do you think it will take Aluna to find an animal?" Her natural inquisitiveness turned into nervous rambling in times of stress - he knew that - but it didn't make it any less distracting. He pressed his lips together to keep from snapping at her, concentrating on transferring what he needed. He had to identify which of the two drugs they'd stolen from the testing facility he would have to neutralise. He heard her inhale to ask another question, and finally his patience waned.

"Charlotte, I need to concentrate here," he tried to keep his tone as even as possible. "Aluna will be fine. Jaylen will be fine. We will be fine. But if I make a mistake, if one little thing goes wrong, the cure will not work." The pressure of that statement washed over him as he said the words. He'd known there was a lot riding on this plan - she'd all but said as much - but the fact of the matter was it was really all riding on him. He was the only one who could do this; it's why he was on the team in the first place.

"Okay," she whispered.

"Will you hand me one of those cuvettes over there?" he pointed to a tray of empty tubes on the far side of the room.

"Which one?"

"The square tube with the lid on it," he directed, and she plucked one from its place and handed it to him.

He placed his glasses back on his face as he stood to move to the machine. He inserted the cuvette and pressed a few buttons. When he looked back up, she had an odd look on her face. He was terrible with emotions, most especially his own, and he hoped he hadn't said anything wrong. She was shuffling closer but remained silent, her face still unreadable. He began to panic.

"Charlotte, I'm...I'm not really great when it comes to stuff like this. Honestly, it's one of the main reasons things never worked out between me and Elliana. She always wanted me to talk about my feelings, and I always wanted her to stop talking about hers. But there is something I want to say, and I better say it now before it all goes south."

"Shut up," she closed the remaining distance between them quickly, kissing him before he could get another word out. There was something different about this kiss, something primal and deep that made Chris respond immediately. He tugged her forward, settling her between his legs as she very nearly devoured him. Her hands were everywhere, traveling the expanse between his shoulders, then around to his chest before sliding up through his hair. He kept pace with her but didn't press further, letting her maintain control.

When he'd been thoroughly kissed, she pulled away a few inches and sucked in a deep breath. "Thank you," she whispered against his lips. Her forehead rested against his, and he could feel every rough exhale puff against his cheek.

He forced his eyes open but hers were still closed. "I was going to say that."

That opened them, and she put a little more distance between them but didn't release the hold she had of his shoulders. "Why?"

"For dragging me into this insanity," he told her half-jokingly. Then, a bit more seriously, "For giving me the courage to save my daughter. And for reminding me that it's okay to feel. And look," he shifted his hands to frame her hips, pushing her just a bit further to look into her eyes, "I know you couldn't save your father, but the truth is...you kind of saved me."

He felt her hand lift from his shoulder and settle against the side of his face. Her thumb traced the curve of his cheek bone and he fought the urge to close his eyes under her ministrations. Her eyes were darting back and forth, like she was trying to memorize his face through the tears that had gathered there. Then she leaned forward and pressed her lips against his forehead tenderly.

"You saved me, too," she said when she moved back. "You were the first person in...in a long, long time to really listen to me. To believe me. All my life people have been telling me how crazy I was, how useless it was to fight something as big as a national government. I'd heard them for so long that I'd started to actually believe them. You gave me the best gift I have ever received: faith in myself."

Chris was speechless. He was sure if he could form a coherent sentence his brain would supply some snarky comment about it being a once in a lifetime moment. Instead, he gaped idiotically as she lifted her other hand to his face and leaned in for another kiss. They were interrupted by the machine next to them, a high-pitched beep alerting them that it had completed its task. Charlotte kissed him once more, a quick promise of more to come, and stepped back.

"Alright," Chris carefully pulled the cuvette from the machine and snapped the lid closed. "Well, here we go. This is it." He held it up to the light, then out for her inspection. "Hope to God we were right."

She smiled, her eyes suddenly alight with excitement. She dashed for the door; her fears of failure forgotten. "I have to find Jaylen."

He realized what she was doing a split second too late. She opened the door eagerly and came face to face with a polar bear. All thoughts of the cure and saving the world vanished as Chris gazed at the distance between him and Charlotte. If his hand hadn't already been clamped around the cure, he'd likely have forgotten it in his scramble to reach for her, to put himself between her and the deadly predator. Thankfully she instinctively leapt towards him, close enough that he could reach out and grab her arm. She'd probably have a bruise later from the force with which he hauled her bodily backward and behind him. The polar bear crept closer, its eyes alert and zeroed in on its prey. Chris slowly backed up, feeling Charlotte at his back as he took one step, then another. The bear kept coming.

Later, Chris would make a mental note to personally thank whoever had designed that lab. With the workstation in the middle, Chris was able to carefully manoeuvre them around the island toward the door. As he moved, he searched desperately for something, anything that could be used as a weapon. Unfortunately, hospital labs were woefully short on anything larger than an aspirating needle.

They were almost to the door. A few more steps and Charlotte would be in the hall. Chris debated shoving her through, taking the attack to give her enough time to get away. He could send the cure with her, give her a chance along with the rest of the world. But even as he worked through it, he knew it wouldn't work. The bears weren't attacking to eat; they were attacking to kill. It would likely just take him down then go after her. He needed a distraction, something to stop the attack before it happened.

His eyes fell on the fire alarm just to his right. The Polar Bear gathered itself up, the muscles in its hind legs coiling to pounce. They were out of time. Chris reached out blindly, ripping the plastic cover off. He pulled the handle, hoping this hospital had the same fire countermeasures as other hospitals he'd been in. The shrill bell was deafening as white fog came pouring from the ceiling. Chris turned and pushed Charlotte, who had at least had the sense to grab the pack with the cub as she passed. He could hear the leopard on their heels, but the fire alarm had given them just enough of a head start. Chris slammed the door closed behind them as Aluna came running up the corridor.

"What's happened?"

"The bears, they came after the cub," Chris told him. "And call me crazy," he shot a look at Charlotte, "but that has to be what the birds were doing, too."

"And the cure?" Aluna glanced down at the small container in Chris's hand. He'd managed to slip the cuvette into a hard-shell case not much bigger than the one he had back home for his glasses.

"This is it," Chris held it up. "It's all we got. One shot, maybe two."

"I found a goose," he told them. "I put him one of the patient rooms."

"If this doesn't work…" Charlotte trailed off.

Aluna shrugged one shoulder. "Only one way to find out."

But it did work. No one was more surprised than Chris when the goose stopped charging at them and calmed down.

"You better find Jaylen," he glanced back at Aluna. "We have to get this stuff home."

The cure worked. It was the best news Chris had gotten in a long time, trailed in a very close second by the call they'd gotten from Akari. She was safe in Washington. Charlotte hadn't elaborated much on her phone call past that, but Chris didn't care. Things were finally working out, and there was a light at the end of the tunnel.

"I will go get Jaylen," Aluna said. "You two find us a way out of this hospital."

Charlotte stood with a smile. "Well, I'm glad this story has a happy ending."

Chris tucked what was left of the cure back into the case. "We need to go." Charlotte moved to grab the cub again, but Chris stopped her. "I'll get him. You've been carrying him the whole time." He offered her the small case and gathered the duffel in his arms. Charlotte led the way through the corridors to the elevators as Aluna veered off the other direction in search of Jaylen.

With the ambulances already gone, their best bet for leaving the hospital was the way they had come in. Chris guessed their jeep was probably still sitting right where he'd parked it. Next to him, Charlotte was very nearly vibrating with pent up energy - no doubt a combination of excitement over the cure and fear for their lives. The moment the doors slid open on the ground floor they were out like a shot.

"We need to get out of here," Chris followed her down the hall, his strides only slightly hindered by the bundle in his arms.

"The lobby's this way," she directed, falling slightly behind him as they rounded the last corner.

He saw it first, and instinct caused him to freeze in his tracks. Charlotte's momentum carried her a step past him, but the loud growl from the bear at the front door made her jump back. Chris turned, silently indicating they should go back the other way. A second bear stepped out from the hallway they'd just come from, trapping them and causing them to huddle together in the centre of the hall.

"Oh my God," Charlotte breathed.

Chris stepped closer, staying sideways to keep both animals in his peripheral without staring at them directly. He saw Charlotte shift her weight back and forth, and he pitched his voice low in warning. "Don't move."

"Do we run?" she asked, glancing back and forth. The leopards were creeping closer, closing off any avenue of escape.

"No," he closed his eyes briefly, frantically trying to come up with a way out. "If we do, they'll take us down."

The truth was, there was no way out. Chris thought about letting the cub go; it might be enough of a distraction that he could at least get Charlotte to the elevators. But there wasn't enough time.

Not enough time. It was a cruel truth that had a far deeper meaning than their impending deaths. He'd only known Charlotte for three months, loved her for less than that. It wasn't enough. If he'd lived a hundred years, he still would feel the same, but for fate to throw them together and have it end like this was just cruel. He forced himself to ignore the threats surrounding them, to make himself look at her. If they died, he wanted her face to be the last thing he saw.

never told her I love her. The thought flashed viciously through his mind and or a moment he thought the leopards had finally pounced. But the pain in his chest came from within, his regret multiplying tenfold as he realized he'd never said the words. Chris remembered her confession, replayed that moment over and over in head a million times a day. His answer had been cowardly, a simple one, too when she'd bravely laid her heart bare. He tried to force the words out now, to utter them in the silence that seemed to stretch on. But they wouldn't come. She knows, he told himself. It was a hollow consolation.

Her soft touch was like a whisper on his skin. Her fingers curled into his and he held on, trying to tell her through their connection what he couldn't seem to say out loud. Her grip was like a vice but he didn't care. His last moments in this life would be with her, and anything he could do to lessen the terror in her eyes would be worth breaking every bone in his body.

Suddenly the tension snapped, but it didn't come in the form of a leaping predator. Glass shattered and instinct made him duck, taking her with him and covering her smaller body with his own. He expected an angry roar but heard only a faint hiss, then the sound of boots.

"Tranq em!" Another hiss, then a soft thud as the dart hit its mark. "Secure!"

Chris dared a glance up, not quite sure he was really seeing what was going on. A dozen or so men decked in full military garb were moving purposefully toward them. One stopped and crouched next to them, laying a hand on Charlotte's back.

"Unit two secure!"

Another voice answered from the door. "Extract! Lock it down!"

Charlotte looked up, her eyes still wide and fearful. "What's happening?"

"Looks like the cavalry's here," Chris said. The man who'd come to them began ushering them up and out. Chris kept hold of Charlotte's hand as they were escorted out the front doors and into the streets. The courtyard had been cleared of bodies, and Chris couldn't see any animals around. Large military vehicles dotted the area, accompanied by what was left of the local police force and almost thirty men dashing off in various directions.

Chris's brain asked a dozen questions at once. He settled on the most pressing. "Not that we're not incredibly grateful," he followed their rescuer to a set of trucks sitting near the door, "but where did you guys come from?"

"We're the 74th Special Tactics Squadron," the man answered tersely. The stripes on his sleeve probably signified his rank, but Chris was clueless when it came to anything military related. He settled mentally on sergeant. "Our orders are to get you out of here."

"Okay, listen, there were two others with us," he adjusted the bundle in his arms as they walked away from the hospital toward safety. "They're still -"

"Look, Jaylen!" Charlotte interrupted, pointing to a spot a little further up. Chris followed her finger and found Aluna and Jaylen walking toward them.

Chris was overcome with the urge to hug both of them. The feeling startled him and he settled for a relieved smile. "You look like hell."

Jaylen laughed slightly, still clutching his right side. "Thanks." He looked past his friends to the man escorting them. "Listen, up there with me there were three kids."

"Already on their way to another hospital," he answered. "We'll track down their parents."

"How'd you know we were here?" Jaylen asked.

"All I'm authorized to say is your location was provided by a member of national security." Akari. She'd saved them. Chris shared a knowing smile with his friends, noting how Jaylen's pain seemed to disappear for a moment. "We're gonna get you to Orlando and from there on a flight to London."

"Let's move." They followed the man to a pair of trucks already running. Each had a driver and a passenger armed with a rather large rifle, both sporting full body armour and dour expressions.

"Lends new meaning to the word 'shotgun,'" Chris joked.

"It's the original meaning, actually," Charlotte corrected. At Chris's look, she just shrugged and pulled open the back door. "I got into Oxford; I know weird stuff."

Chris made to follow her, but was stopped by two men. For a moment he feared they were being split up, separated to be debriefed or whatever the hell it was that the military did after something horrific happened. He squared his shoulders, ready to resist tooth and nail. There was no way in hell he was leaving his friends alone.

"Sir, we need that bag," one of them said.

Chris shook his head once and lifted his chin. "No, this stays with me. You have no idea how important this little guy is."

"We have our orders, sir," the other said. Chris guessed he wasn't a day over twenty. "He's to be put in a secure crate and escorted back to the states by…" He trailed off, digging into a small pocket on his vest for the notepad there. He consulted a page and nodded. "Doctor Christopher Stuart?"

"That's me," Chris used his free hand to wave. Akari must have pulled some major strings.

The soldier nodded and stuffed the notepad back into its pocket. "We have the crate ready." He turned slightly to reveal a small brown crate behind him. It was small enough to still be carried, but it was definitely more secure than the bag he was currently living in.

"Alright." Chris walked away from the car. "I'll do it." He took a moment to check the cub's vitals and give him some water. "He'll need food soon."

"We'll make sure you get something on the plane," the young man said. Charlotte had come out of the car to help, and she held the empty bag as Chris lifted the crate. She got in first and reached out, settling it between them on the seat as Chris climbed in. Aluna and Jaylen had already been loaded into the other truck, and once Chris's door was closed the caravan sped away.

The trucks were apparently a means to get to the helicopter sitting half a mile away. Chris had never been in one and judging from his friends' expressions they hadn't either. Aluna and Chris helped Jaylen up into the aircraft and settled him into a seat as the crate was placed in the centre and strapped down with a large net. Chris buckled himself into the seat next to Charlotte then took her hand. He knew she hated boats and the moments of take-off and landing on plane rides. He imagined a helicopter ride was on her list of things to avoid at all costs.

"We're almost home," she whispered so quietly, Chris thought she might have just been reassuring herself. But when he glanced over she was beaming at him, and he couldn't help but smile back.

"We're just one more really long plane ride away." She laughed and squeezed his hand as the helicopter lifted suddenly from the field. "Breathe."

She glared at him half-heartedly before turning her attention to her two friends across from them.

"You must remember to take these on time, Jaylen," mentioned Aluna as she handed him a bottle of pills.

"Thanks." He asked one of their escorts for water, and they were all given bottles. Chris was grateful but it did little for the pang in his stomach. It had been a long time since their last meal.

"I hope that plane has good food," he said. "I'm starving."

Chapter 38

Their landing was just as sudden as their take-off. Chris guessed military pilots didn't really have time for gentle when a mission was in full swing, but the jarring stop made Jaylen wince. They'd landed on an airfield about a hundred yards from a large airliner. Someone had cast a giant net over the whole terminal, tethered to the buildings around it. It was an impressive feat of engineering improvisation, and closer inspection proved that they had strung several nets together to achieve it.

"Birds kept dive bombing passengers as they were loading," one of the men explained. "This was the solution we came up with."

Charlotte stopped next to him and peered up. "How many people died getting it up there?"

"No deaths, ma'am," the soldier responded. "A few nasty cuts and bruises. One of my buddies lost part of his ear."

Chris glanced over in time to see two new soldiers lifting the crate from the helicopter. One of them stumbled and nearly dropped it onto the tarmac.

"Careful with that!" Chris barked, leaving Charlotte's side to oversee the transport.

The young man looked startled at the sight of a dishevelled civilian barrelling toward him with all the bluster and authority of a three-star general, but he recovered quickly. "Sir, we've got it handled."

"Obviously not, or I wouldn't have yelled," Chris shot back. "I'll take that." He reached for the container, only a little surprised when they didn't stop him. He hoisted it up against his chest and walked back over to his friends. "Let's get out of here."

Chapter 39

They managed to snag two whole sides for themselves only a row apart. Aluna and Jaylen took one as Chris put the cub in the window seat of the other. Charlotte took the middle seat and buckled in, and Chris spared only a glance at the back of the cabin before settling in beside her. Her hands were fidgeting in her lap as her eyes danced around. He guessed the shock of their near-death experience was finally hitting her and he racked his brain for a solution.

"If you want," he leaned over, "I can go see about pilfering some of those little bottles. Might calm your nerves."

"I'm okay." She didn't look at him, and for a moment he thought about doing it anyway. God knew he could use a drink right now. Then she turned her head and smiled, a warm curve of her lips that reached all the way to her eyes, and his worry vanished. "Really," she gestured to his own still-unbuckled belt, "I'm okay."

He buckled it and tightened the strap before slipping his fingers between hers. "Listen," he stared at their joined hands, trying to summon the courage he needed to say what was on his mind. "I just…" The engines began to rumble as the plane backed away from the terminal. Chris took several deep breaths as he felt the vibrations through his body. He told himself it was the plane and not his nerves making him shake so roughly, but he imagined his own system was beginning to feel the effects of their adventures.

"Chris?" Charlotte's tone was part curious, part concern. Before her brilliant mind could veer off on a completely incorrect course, he lifted his head and stared directly into her eyes.

"I love you." She took a breath - no doubt to return the sentiment - but Chris rushed forward before his bravery fled. "I realized earlier that I never told you, never actually said the words. And then, the leopards showed up and the only thing I could think about was how we were going to die, and you'd never hear me say them. So I wanted to tell you." It sounded extremely lame in his head, and he cringed mentally as the words replayed. But it was out there now, and judging from the smile that was slowly stretching her face he hadn't completely screwed the whole thing up.

"I knew," she assured him. "You never said it, but you told me anyway. The way you held me after the whole Dustin fiasco, when you told me the truth about your deal with Reese even knowing how much it would hurt me, how you protected me in Canada and at the hospital...you may not have said the actual words, but you let me know every day that you love me."

Chris stared at her in wonder. Forget fate and miracles, he mused, this woman is a gift from God.

"Still," she continued with a wry smile, "it's nice to hear."

He smiled with her, erasing the last of the tension that had gathered in his chest. Chris brought their joined hands up to brush a kiss on her fingers as the plane lifted away from the earth. Finally, they were on their way home.

"So what are you going to do when we get home?" he asked her. "After the cure is disseminated, I mean."

"I don't know," she shrugged her far shoulder. She turned her head to look at the crate next to her. The cub had been unusually quiet. "I haven't really thought that far ahead."

"I know what you mean," he smiled. Been doing that a lot, Christopher. It feels good.

"We should probably find your mum." Her words surprised him, and she squeezed his hand where it rested in hers. "Then I'd like to visit my aunt and uncle - make sure they're okay."

"I'm sure they're fine." They were survivors, and Chris had no doubt they were holding their own in Derby. "But we'll find a way to check on them." Chris marvelled at the ease with which I and you had become we. He liked it.

"Do you think you'll get your sanctuary job back?"

"I don't even know if the sanctuary will still be operational," Chris answered. "According to the news reports, most of the animals broke out of their enclosures. It's going to take some time for things to settle back down."

"You should come to Derby," she stated firmly. "You and your mom. We can stay at my uncle's house until we sort everything out."

Chris had no doubt Jaden Townsend would honour his niece's invitation. He thought about that for a moment, tried to picture what it would be like. He could wake up every morning with her next to him, far away from the craziness this world had become. He had to admit, it had appeal.

"That sounds like a great idea."

She nodded in agreement and laid her head on his shoulder. He turned slightly and kissed the crown of her head before laying his cheek against it. They stayed that way until the seatbelt sign dimmed and attendants came by with bright smiles to take drink and dinner orders. Charlotte ordered the veggie plate. Chris ordered something alcoholic. The attendant returned with their drinks first, depositing two cups, a can of soda and two small bottles of whiskey on Chris's tray table.

"They're holding out on me," Chris grumbled. "I know they've got vodka stashed back there somewhere."

Charlotte pushed up and craned her head to peer over the back of her chair. "No one's back there now. I can distract them."

"Don't tempt me," he pulled the tab on the soda and divided it up between the two cups as Charlotte opened the tiny whiskey bottles. "Should we toast our success?" he asked once the whiskey had been added.

"No," Charlotte shook her head. "Let's not jinx it. We still have to get back and mass produce it. Not to mention the tiny dilemma of distribution."

"Okay," he cut her off before she could work herself up. "Then what should we toast?"

She didn't answer at first, but Chris didn't worry. He knew her well enough now to recognize her thinking face. When she smiled, he knew she'd found something.

"To baby Timmy."

He couldn't help it. The laugh bubbled up before he could stop it, and it filled the space between them as it erupted from his throat. He tried to bite down on it, to at least stop it short. But her declaration had been so deliberate and so unexpected that it was too late. He opened his mouth to apologize, to tell her that her toast was perfect and please don't be mad at him...only she didn't look angry. If he had to put a name to it, he'd called it proud delight.

"Sorry," he said anyway. "That was just...not what I was expecting."

"It's okay," she was grinning ear to ear now, and Chris wondered what was going on in her head. "I'm glad you're enjoying yourself."

He had a million things to say to that, but none of them seemed right for the light, easy tone she had struck. So he tapped the rim of his plastic cup against hers and returned her smile. "To baby Timmy."

Dinner came, and with it two more drinks for each of them. Chris ordered a small steak (raw, of course) which he promptly let Charlotte feed to the cub. She cooed at the little guy like a puppy, and Chris had to remind her that he was probably headed for a zoo or a sanctuary just as soon as they had what they needed from him.

"Can we not return him to the wild?" Charlotte asked.

"Maybe," Chris didn't want to say no outright. "Remember, we took him from his mother before he could learn how to hunt properly. It's likely if we release him, he won't know enough to survive on his own." He downed the last of his drink and waved off the attendant's silent offer of another. He noticed Charlotte had barely touched hers, and after a quick question and her answering gesture he finished that one, too.

Alcohol had always had an odd effect on him. He never got angry or goofy or stupid like some of his college acquaintances. No, Chris Stuart was a philosophical drunk. All the thoughts that swirled in his head with no evidence or hard facts to support them came tumbling out. Thankfully, his tolerance was sufficiently high that the few shots of whiskey he'd had were just enough to alleviate the ache in his limbs that had settled in after their near-death experience and not quite enough for his innermost thoughts to come spilling out.

Charlotte, it seemed, was a sleepy drunk.

She wriggled in her seat, obviously searching for a comfortable position, before her head once again found a place on his shoulder and she nodded off without so much as a mumbled goodnight. He chuckled and turned off their overhead light, leaning his head back against his seat to follow her.

"Ladies and gentlemen, this is your captain." An announcement woke Chris from his light doze. Next to him, Charlotte was struggling to sit up straighter in her chair as the pilot continued. "We've been informed that due to extremely high windspeeds, this air space has been closed."

"What's going on?" Charlotte asked sleepily.

"We've been diverted to -" But the captain never finished his sentence. A horrible rending tore through the fuselage, and the entire top of the plane was suddenly ripped away. Chris's breath stole from his lungs as he was very violently tossed about in his seat. If he hadn't been strapped in, he probably would have been killed instantly. He heard Charlotte scream, and even though she was right next to him she sounded so far away. He tried to turn his head to look at her, but the rest of the jet was in a free fall spin and the force kept his head pinned to his seat.

Chris slammed his eyes closed and reached blindly for the woman next to him. Her fingers clamped on his arm and held on as the pilots somehow regained control. They weren't spinning any longer, but they were still going down. Chris guessed from the vast expanse of black beneath them that they were over the ocean. He spared a thought for Aluna and Jaylen, a row ahead and an eternity away. The cries of terror from the other passengers seemed to echo around him, but he couldn't take a breath to speak.

At least I told her, he tried to ease the despair that was consuming him. She knows.

He tried to say it again, to shout the words into the chaotic tempest around them. His mouth moved to form the words, but his voice wouldn't cooperate. Over and over he mouthed those three words, repeated them like a silent prayer. Finally, in what Chris believed were his final seconds on this earth, his lungs took in a gulp of air and his last breath was spent on her name.

Printed in Great Britain
by Amazon